A drawer in the desk opened; something was coming out of it. A tiny hand found purchase on the edge of the desk top, then another. It—she—pulled herself up. She was only a mechanical doll but she could have been alive, a miniature golden girl, perfect in every detail from her long, yellow hair to the toes of her golden feet. She pirouetted and as she did so she sang wordlessly. High and thin was the music but with an insidious rhythm. She was joined by two more dolls, both female, one white-skinned and black-haired, the other whose body was a lustrous black and whose hair shone like silver. They carried instruments—the white girl a syrinx, the black girl a little drum. They sat cross-legged, piping and drumming, while the golden doll danced and sang.

"These come life-size, too," said the robot maker to Grimes. "Special orders. Very special orders. . . ."

★ ★ ★
STAR
LOOT
★ ★ ★

A. Bertram Chandler

DAW Books, Inc.
Donald A. Wollheim, Publisher

1633 Broadway, New York, N.Y. 10019

PUBLISHED BY
THE NEW AMERICAN LIBRARY
OF CANADA LIMITED

FIRST PRINTING, SEPTEMBER 1980

1 2 3 4 5 6 7 8 9

 DAW TRADEMARK REGISTERED
U.S. PAT. OFF. MARCA
REGISTRADA. HECHO EN U.S.A.

PRINTED IN CANADA
COVER PRINTED IN U.S.A.

Chapter 1

For the first time in his life Grimes was rich.

But money, he was coming to realize, does not buy happiness. Furthermore it is, far too often, a very expensive commodity. It has to be paid for and the price can be high. The cost of his newly acquired wealth was *Little Sister*, the beautiful, golden, deep-space pinnace that had been given him by the Baroness Michelle d'Estang. He had hated parting with his tiny ship but financial circumstances had been such that there was almost no option. The fortunes of Far Traveler Couriers were at an extremely low ebb and Grimes, long notorious for his hearty appetite, wanted to go on eating.

At first the courier business had been moderately successful. There seemed to be no shortage of small parcels of special cargo to be carted, at high freight rates, hither and yon across the known galaxy. Then the commercial climate deteriorated and Grimes gained the impression that nobody at all wanted anything taken anywhere in a hurry and at a price. His last employment had been the carriage of a small shipment of memory-and-motivation units from Electra to Austral, the consignee being Yosarian Robotics. There was absolutely no suitable outward cargo for *Little Sister* available on Austral—and the First Galactic Bank was getting restive about Far Traveler Couriers' considerable overdraught.

Grimes went to see Mr. Yosarian. He knew that the fantastically wealthy roboteer often manufactured very special models for very special customers, some of whom must surely wish delivery in a hurry. He was admitted into an outer office on the very top floor of the towering Kapek Komplex, an assemblage of three glittering tetrahedra of steel and plastic with a fourth tetrahedron mounted on this spectacular foundation.

He sat waiting in a deep, comfortable chair, watching the blonde secretary or receptionist or whatever she was doing something at her desk, languidly prodding a keyboard with scarlet-nailed fingers, watching some sort of read-out on a screen that presented a featureless back to the visitor. She was not at all inclined to make conversation. Grimes wondered idly if she was one of Yosarian's special robots, decided that she probably wasn't. She was too plump, too soft looking and there had been nothing metallic in her voice when she condescended to speak to him. He tried to interest himself in the magazines on a low table by his seat but all of them were trade journals. An engineer would have found them fascinating—but Grimes was not an engineer. From his cadet days onward he had displayed little mechanical aptitude and, quite naturally, had entered the spaceman branch of the Survey Service.

He filled and lit his vile pipe, got up from his chair and strolled to one of the wide windows overlooking the city of Port Southern. The tall, elongated pyramid was a feature of local architecture. Between these towers and groupings of towers were green parks, every one of which seemed to have its own fountain, each a wavering plume of iridescent spray. In the distance was the spaceport, looking like a minor city itself. But those gleaming spires were the hulls of ships great and small, passenger liners and freighters.

Grimes could just see the golden spark that was the sunlight reflected from the shell plating of a ship by no means great—*Little Sister*. She had brought him here, to this world. Would she take him away from it? She wouldn't, he thought bitterly, unless there were some cargo to make it worth her while, some paid employment that would enable him to settle his outstanding bills.

The blonde's voice broke into his glum thoughts. "Mr. Yosarian will see you now, sir. Go straight through."

"Thank you," said Grimes.

He looked around for an ashtray, found one, knocked out his pipe into it.

"That," said the girl coldly, "happens to be a flower bowl."

"But there aren't any flowers in it," he said defensively.

"A ship is still a ship even when there's no cargo in her holds," she told him nastily.

That hurt. She must know how things were with him. Probably everybody in Port Southern, on the whole damned planet, knew. With his prominent ears flushing angrily he went through into the inner office.

Like a statue of some corpulent Oriental deity Yosarian sat behind his huge desk, the vast, shining expanse of which was bare save for two read-out screens. He did not rise as Grimes entered, just regarded him through black eyes that were like little lumps of coal representing the visual organs in the white

6

face of a snowman. His too full red lips were curved in a complacent smile.

He said, "Be seated, Captain." His voice was just too pleasant to be classed as oleaginous, but only just.

Grimes started to turn. The nearest chair had been against the wall, near the door by which he had entered. But it was no longer there. Walking rapidly but silently on its four legs, it had positioned itself behind him. The edge of its padded seat nudged Grimes just below the backs of his knees.

He sat rather more heavily than had been his intention.

Yosarian laughed.

Grimes said, "Quite a trick."

"But little more, Captain. You should see—and use—some of the robot furniture that I design and manufacture. Such as the beds. Custom made." He leered. "And what do you think of *these?*"

A drawer in the desk must have opened—by itself, as both Yosarian's fat hands were sprawled on the polished surface. Something was coming out of it. A tiny hand found purchase on the edge of the desk top, then another. It—*she*—pulled herself up. She was only a mechanical doll but she could have been alive, a miniature golden girl, perfect in every detail from her long, yellow hair to the toes of her golden feet. She pirouetted and as she did so she sang wordlessly. High and thin was the music but with an insidious rhythm. She was joined by two more dolls, both female, one white-skinned and black-haired, the other whose body was a lustrous black and whose hair shone like silver. They carried instruments— the white girl a syrinx, the black girl a little drum. They sat cross-legged, piping and drumming, while the golden doll danced and sang.

"These come life-size, too," said Yosarian. "Special orders. Very special orders. . . ."

"Mphm," grunted Grimes thoughtfully and disapprovingly.

"And you wouldn't believe that they're made of metal, would you?" He raised his hands, clapped them sharply, then with his right index finger pointed at Grimes. The musicians stopped playing, the dancer halted in mid-step. Then all three of them ran gracefully to the edge of the desk, jumped down to the thick carpet. Before Grimes realized what was happening they were swarming up his legs, on to his lap. His ears flamed with embarrassment.

"Go on, touch them. They aren't programed to bite, Captain."

Gingerly, with the tip of a forefinger, Grimes stroked the

7

back of the golden dancer. It could almost have been real skin under his touch—almost, but not quite.

Yosarian clapped again. The dolls jumped down from Grimes' lap, ran around to Yosarian's side of the desk, vanished.

"You must often, Mr. Yosarian, get special orders for these ... toys," said Grimes.

"*Toys?* You offend me, Captain. But there are special orders. Only a short while ago the Grand Duke Oblimov on El Dorado wanted a pair of dancing boys, life-size. Do you know El Dorado, Captain? I have thought, now and again, of retiring there. I've more than enough money to be accepted as a citizen, but I'd be expected to buy a title of some kind—and that I would regard as a sinful waste of hard-earned credits! As a matter of fact it was an El Doradan ship that carried the small shipment to the Grand Duke. She was here on a cruise and all the passengers were Lord this and Lady that. The master of her called himself Commodore, not Captain, and *he* was a Baron. The funny part of it all was that I used to know him slightly, years ago, when he was skipper of a scruffy little star tramp running out of Port Southern. . . ."

"Commodore Baron Kane," said Grimes sourly.

"You know him? It's a small universe, isn't it? But what can I do for you, Captain Grimes? I'm sure that you didn't come all the way from the spaceport just to talk to me and watch my pretty mini-robots perform."

"You have mentioned special orders, Mr. Yosarian. I'll be frank; I need employment for my ship and myself very badly. I was wondering if. . . ."

"I am sorry, Captain. The last special order was the one to El Dorado; the next one will be—" he shrugged and spread his hands—"who knows when? But perhaps you have not wasted your time after all. . . ."

"Then you do have something?"

"You have something, Captain Grimes. Something that I want, for which I am prepared to pay. I will tell you a secret. When I was very young I wanted to become a spaceman. As you know, your Antarctic Space Academy on Earth accepts entrants from all the Federated Planets—as long as they can pass the preliminary examinations. I almost passed—but *almost* isn't good enough. So I had to go into my father's business—robotics. He wasn't exactly poor—but I am rich. I have been thinking for some time of purchasing a little ship of my own, a spaceyacht, something so small that I am not required by law to carry a qualified master. I have the know-how—or my people have the know-how—to make a computer pilot capable of navigating and handling life-support systems and all the rest of it. I may have to import a special m-and-m unit from Electra, but that is no problem. They can send it with the next big shipment that I have on order."

"You mean . . ." began Grimes.

"I mean that I want your ship, your *Little Sister*. I know how things are with you. There is word of a forced sale, engineered by the First Galactic Bank. So I'm doing you a favor. I will pay a good price. And you will know that your ship will not be broken up just for the precious metal that went into her building. She will survive as a functioning vessel."

"As a rich man's toy," said Grimes.

Yosarian chuckled. "There are worse fates, much worse fates, for ships, just as there are for women. And a ship such as yours, constructed from an isotope of gold, will keep her looks. I shall cherish her."

"How much?" asked Grimes bluntly.

Yosarian told him.

With an effort Grimes kept his face expressionless. The sum named was far in excess of what he had expected. With such money in his bank account he would be able to retire, a young man, and live anywhere in the galaxy—with the exception of El Dorado—that he wished. But was it enough? Would it ever be enough?

"I think, Captain," said Yosarian gently, "that mine is a fair offer. Very fair."

"Yes," admitted Grimes.

"And yet you are still reluctant. If I wait until your many creditors force a sale I may be able to buy your ship at a mere fraction of this offer."

"Then why aren't you willing to wait, Mr. Yosarian?" asked Grimes.

The fat man looked at him shrewdly, then laughed. "All right, Captain. It's cards on the table. I happen to know that Austral Metals wants your ship. It is quite possible that they would outbid even me—and that, I freely admit, would mean more money in your pocket after all the legal technicalities have been sorted out. But do you know what they would do with her if they got her? They would regard her as no more than scrap metal—precious scrap, but scrap nonetheless. They would break her up, melt her down. Only the Electrans know the secret of producing the isotope of gold of which

9

your *Little Sister* is constructed. Austral Metals use that very isotope in some of their projects—and have to pay very heavily for what they import from Electra. Your ship, her hull and her fittings, would be relatively cheap.

"If I have read you aright, Captain Grimes, you are a sentimentalist. Although your ship is only a machine you feel toward her almost as you would toward a woman—and could you bear to see the body of a woman you loved cut up and the parts deposited in an organ bank?" He shuddered theatrically. "If *I* get *Little Sister* I'll look after her, pamper her, even. If Austral Metals gets her they'll hack her and burn her into pieces."

And I can't afford to keep her, thought Grimes. Always in the past something had turned up to rescue him from utter insolvency—but this time nothing would. Or something had. If he accepted Yosarian's offer it would save *Little Sister* from the breakers as well as putting him back in the black.

"You really want her as a ship?" asked Grimes. "You don't intend to turn out a line of indestructible golden robots?"

"I give you my word, Captain."

Grimes believed him.

"All right," he said. "I'll take your price—on condition that you clear my overdraught and all my other debts."

Had he overplayed his hand? For long moments he feared that he had. Then Yosarian laughed.

"You drive a hard bargain, Captain Grimes. Once I would have haggled. Now I will not. At least twice—the first time many years ago, the second time recently—I have tried to get the price down on something I really wanted. Each time I failed—and failed, in consequence, to attain my heart's desire."

Grimes wondered what it was that Yosarian had been wanting to buy, decided that it might not be politic to ask. He felt an odd twinge of sympathy.

"My lawyers," said the fat man, "will call on board your ship tomorrow morning to arrange the details. Please have a detailed statement of your liabilities prepared for them."

"I shall do that," said Grimes. "And . . . thank you."

He got up from his chair, turned to leave the office. A slight noise behind him made him stop, turn again to see what was making it. Another mechanical toy had emerged from one of the drawers of Yosarian's big desk. This one was a miniature spaceship, perfect in every detail, a replica of an Alpha Class liner only about fifteen centimeters in length. The roboticist gestured with his fat right hand and, with its inertial drive tinkling rather than clattering, it rose into the air and began to circle the opalescent light globe that hung from the ceiling. It could have been a real space vessel, viewed from a distance, in orbit about some planetoid.

So, thought Grimes, he was letting *Little Sister* go to somebody who would regard her as no more than an ingenious toy.

But in a harshly commercial universe that was all that she was anyhow.

Chapter 2

Much to Grimes' surprise the formalities of the sale were concluded late the following morning. (When Yosarian wanted something he wanted it *now*.) It was early afternoon when *Little Sister* was handed over to her new owner. Grimes was both hurt and relieved to discover that Yosarian did not expect him to stay around to show the new owner where everything lived and what everything did; in fact the roboticist made it quite plain that he wished to be left alone to gloat over his new possession.

"If that is all, Mr. Yosarian. . . ." said Grimes.

"Yes, that is all, Captain. I've made a study of ships, as you know. And, in any case, much of the equipment here is of my own design. The autochef, the waste processor. . . . There seems to be nothing here that is a departure from normal practice."

"Look after her," said Grimes.

"You need have no worries on that score, Captain. When something has cost me as much as this vessel I look after it."

He extended a fat hand for Grimes to shake. Grimes shook it, then went out through his—no, *the*—airlock for the last time. Yosarian's ground car was waiting to carry him to his hotel, his baggage already stowed in the rear compartment. There were two large suitcases and a mattress cover that had been pressed into service as a kitbag. (When one is in a ship for any length of time personal possessions tend to accumulate.) Before boarding the vehicle Grimes paused to pat the gleaming surface of the golden hull.

At least, he thought, *you aren't being broken up. . . .*

11

The chauffeur, a little, wizened monkey of a man in severe, steel-gray livery, watched him dourly. He said, "Old Yosie won't like it if you put greasy pawmarks all over that finish."

"She's had worse on her," said Grimes. "Like blood."

"You don't say, Captain?" The man looked at Grimes with a new respect. Then, "Where to, sir?"

"The Centaurian," said Grimes, taking his seat beside the driver.

The car sped smoothly and silently toward the spaceport gate. It did not reduce speed for challenge and inspection by the duty customs officer; the flag flying from the short mast on the bonnet, black with a golden Y set in a golden cogwheel, was pass enough.

"That *blood*, Captain. . . ." hinted the chauffeur.

"Not human blood," Grimes told him. "Shaara blood. Or ichor. A couple of drones were trying to burn their way in with hand lasers. So I went upstairs in a hurry, out of a dense atmosphere into near vacuum. They . . . burst."

"Messy," muttered the driver.

"Yes," agreed Grimes.

And where was Tamara, who had shared that adventure with him, he wondered. Probably back on Tiralbin, once again the desk-borne Postmistress General, no longer directly involved in getting the mail through come hell or high water. And where were Shirl and Darleen, also one-time passengers aboard *Little Sister*? And the obnoxious Fenella Pruin. . . . And Susie. . . . Susie had never set foot aboard the golden pinnace herself but she belonged to the *Little Sister* period of his life.

He may have lost his ship but he would keep the memories.

The driver was saying something.

"Mphm?" grunted Grimes.

"We're here, Captain. The Centaurian."

The hotel was the usual elongated pyramid. A porter, who could have been a Survey Service High Admiral making an honest living for a change, was lifting Grimes' baggage out of the back of the car, sneering visibly at the bulging mattress cover.

"Thank you," said Grimes to the chauffeur. He supposed that he should have tipped the man but, although he had a fortune in his bank account, he had almost nothing in his pockets. He disembarked, followed the porter into the lobby to the desk. The receptionists, he could not help noticing,

12

were staring at the mattress cover and giggling. But the girl whom he approached was polite enough.

"Captain Grimes? Yes, we have your reservation. Room number 5063. And for how long will you be staying, sir?"

"Probably until *Alpha Sextans* comes in. She's the next direct ship for Earth."

"Have a happy stay with us, sir."

"Thank you," said Grimes.

He accompanied the porter in the lift up to the fiftieth floor, was ushered into a room from the wide windows of which he could enjoy a view of the city and the distant spaceport. *Little Sister* was there among the gray towers that were the big ships, no more than a tiny, aureate mote. He turned away from the window to the resplendently uniformed porter who was waiting expectantly.

He said, "I'm sorry. I'm out of cash until I get to the bank."

"That's all right, sir," said the man, conveying by the tone of his voice that it was not.

He left Grimes to his own devices.

Grimes explored his accommodation.

He treated himself to a cup of coffee from the tap so labeled over the bar. He lowered himself into one of the deep armchairs, filled and lit his pipe. Suddenly he was feeling very lonely in this comfortable but utterly characterless sitting room. He wondered how he would pass the days until he could board that Earthbound passenger liner. He would not, he told himself firmly, go near the spaceport before then. He had made his clean break with *Little Sister*; he would do his best to keep it that way.

The telephone buzzed.

He reached out, touched the acceptance button. The screen came alive, displayed the pretty face of one of the hotel's receptionists.

"Captain Grimes, a lady and a gentleman are here to see you."

"Who are they?" Grimes asked.

"A Ms. Granadu, sir. A Mr. Williams."

The names rang no bells in Grimes' memory and it must have shown in his expression.

"Spacepersons, sir," said the girl.

"Send them up," said Grimes.

He had just finished his coffee when the door chimes tinkled. He had not yet recorded his voice in the opener so had to get up from his chair to let the visitors in. Yes, he thought, the receptionist had been right. These were certainly spacers; the way in which they carried themselves made this obvious. And he, a spacefarer himself, could do better than merely generalize. One spaceman branch officer, he thought, fairly senior but never in actual command. One catering officer.

The spaceman was not very tall but he was big. He had a fleshy nose, a broad, rather thick-lipped mouth, very short hair the color of dirty straw, pale gray eyes. He was plainly dressed in a white shirt and dark gray kilt with matching long socks, black, blunt-toed, highly polished shoes. The woman was flamboyant. She was short, chunky, red-haired, black-eyed and beaky-nosed. Her mouth was a wide, scarlet slash. In contrast to her companion's sober attire she was colorfully, almost garishly clad. Her orange blouse was all ruffles, her full skirt was bright emerald. Below its hem were stiletto-heeled, pointed-toed knee boots, scarlet with gold trimmings. Jewels scintillated at the lobes of her ears and on her fingers. It looked, at first glance, as though she had a ring on every one of them.

"Williams," said the big man in a deep voice.

"Magda Granadu," said the woman in a sultry contralto.

"Grimes," said Grimes unnecessarily.

There was handshaking. There was the arranging of seats around the coffee table. Makda Granadu, without being asked, drew cups of coffee for Williams and herself, replenished Grimes' cup. Grimes had the uneasy feeling that he was being taken charge of.

"And what can I do for you, gentlepersons?" he asked.

"You can help us, Captain," said Williams. "*And* yourself."

"Indeed?" Grimes was intrigued but trying not to show it. These were not the sort of people who, hearing somehow of his sudden acquisition of wealth, would come to ask him for a large, never-to-be-repaid loan. "Indeed?"

"That ship in parking orbit—*Epsilon Scorpii*. You must have seen her when you came in."

"I did."

"She's up for sale. It hasn't been advertised yet but it soon will be."

Grimes laughed. "And so what? The Interstellar Transport Commission is always flogging its obsolescent tonnage."

"Too right, Captain. But why shouldn't you be the next owner of that hunk of still spaceworthy obsolescence?"

14

"Why should I?" countered Grimes. "I've just sold one ship. I'm in no hurry to buy another."

"You would not be happy away from ships," said the woman, staring at him intently. "As well you know."

She's right, thought Grimes.

He said, "All right. Just suppose that I'm mad enough to buy this Epsilon Class rustbucket. What is *your* interest?"

"We want to get back into space," said Williams.

"And what makes you think that I'd help you?" Grimes demanded.

"The *I Ching* told us," said the woman.

Grimes regarded her curiously. With her features, her flamboyant clothing, her garish jewelry, she could well have passed for a Romany fortune teller, one of those who plied their trade in tea rooms and other restaurants. But such women usually practiced palmistry or worked with cards, either of the ordinary variety or the Tarot pack. To find one who consulted the *Book of Changes* was . . . weird. And what was a spacewoman doing as a soothsayer anyhow?

She went on, "We're old shipmates, Billy—Mr. Williams—and I. In the Dog Star Line. Billy was second mate, waiting for his promotion to mate. I was catering officer and purser. Billy was married to a girl on this planet who did not like having a husband who was always away on long voyages. So, just to please her, he resigned and found a shore job. A little while later I resigned too. I had a bachelor uncle on this world whom I used to look up every time that the ship came here. He was an importer in a small way but big enough to have amassed a neat little fortune. He . . . died. When his will was read it was discovered that he'd left everything to me. So, having said my fond farewells to the Dog Star Line, I thought I'd start a restaurant. I'm still running it although I had some very bad patches; now the bank owns most of it. I've come to realize that I was far happier as a spacewoman.

"Billy's of the same way of thinking. He's very much at loose ends since his wife left him."

"You can say that again!" growled Williams.

"It was all for the best," Magda Granadu told him. "Well, Captain, Billy often comes around to my place just about closing time. We have a few drinks and talk about old times. You know. Anyhow, a few nights back we were crying into each other's beer and telling each other how we'd sell our souls to get back into deep space, then Billy suggested that I tell our fortunes, his and mine. No, don't laugh. Quite a few of my customers come to the Tzigane as much for my for-

15

tune-telling as the food. I've made some lucky guesses. Up to now I've always used the cards and it's only recently that I've gotten interested in the Oracle of Change. So I got the book out and threw three coins—I don't use yarrow sticks—and constructed a hexagram. *Ta Ch'u*, it was. It told us to place ourselves in the service of the king and that it would benefit us to cross the great water. The great water is, of course, deep space. And the king—*you*."

"Me, a king?" demanded Grimes incredulously.

"You were a sort of god-king once, weren't you? The story got around. And, in any case, who more kingly than a ship-master who owns his own ship? The local media gave you a good coverage when you brought *Little Sister* in."

"I no longer own her," said Grimes.

"We are well aware of that, Captain, but you were still owner-master when I consulted the oracle. It puzzled us; surely you would not require a crew in such a small ship. Yet yours was the name that came to mind. Too, there was the business of the coins that I used. . . ."

"The coins?" asked Grimes bewilderedly.

"Yes. I used these." She fished in one of the capacious pockets at the front of her skirt, brought out three discs of some silvery alloy. Grimes stared at them. He had seen similar coins in his father's collection. They had been minted on Earth as long ago as the twentieth century, old style. One side bore the head of a woman, Queen Elizabeth, in profile. On the other was a stylized bird with a tail like an ancient lyre, and the number 10. An Australian ten-cent piece, very old yet in good condition.

"Where did you get these?" Grimes asked.

"They're Billy's."

"My father gave them to me years ago," said Williams. "They're out of his collection."

"My father has coins like them in his collection," said Grimes.

"And they're *Australian* coins," said Magda. "And you're Australian. There's a tie-in."

"Mphm," grunted Grimes dubiously.

"So the *I Ching* pointed to you," she insisted. "But we couldn't see how you could help us. And *then*, a day or so later, we heard that you'd sold *Little Sister* to Yosarian at some fantastic price. And we heard, too, that *Epsilon, Scorpii* was coming up for sale. My restaurant is a popular place for business lunches and I often overhear conversations at table. Pinnett—he's Planetary Manager for the Interstellar Transport Commission—was entertaining a couple of ITC masters. They were talking about the *Epileptic Scorpion*. Pinnett was saying that he wished that there was somebody on Austral who'd buy her. He'd get a nice commission on the deal."

"Mphm," grunted Grimes again.

"You're the king the *I Ching* told us of, Captain. At the moment you're a king without a kingdom. But you could buy one."

Why not? Grimes asked himself. *Why not?* A sizeable tramp, carrying sizeable cargoes, might make a living. But he would be obliged by law to carry at least a minimal crew in such a vessel.

"What about crew?" he said. "All right, I seem to have two volunteers. One control room officer. I suppose that you hold a Master Astronaut's Certificate, Mr. Williams? One catering officer cum purser. But I shall require two more control room officers. And engineers, both Mannschenn Drive and inertial drive. And a Sparks. Where do I get them from? More important—where would I get cargoes from? *Little Sister* couldn't make one man a living. Could this Epsilon Class rustbucket make a living for a crew of at least a dozen?"

"To answer your first question, Captain," said Williams, "there are quite a few retired spacers on Austral, many of whom would love to make just one more voyage, and one more after that. . . . To answer the second one—a tramp can always make money if her owner isn't too fussy, if he's willing to carry cargoes that the major shipping lines wouldn't touch, to go to places where the big shipping companies wouldn't risk their precious ships. . . ."

"Take a gamble, Captain," cajoled Magda Granadu. "Ride your famous luck."

"My luck?"

She smiled and said," You're famous for it, aren't you?"

"Let the *I Ching* decide for him," said Williams.

Magda handed him the three antique coins, then from her capacious pocket produced a book bound in black silk. Grimes recalled past encounters with fortune tellers. There had been that drunken Psionic Communications Officer aboard *Discovery* who had read the cards for him with uncanny accuracy, and the old Duchess of Leckhampton on El Dorado who had also read the cards, although she had favored the Tarot pack.

"Shake and throw," ordered the woman. "Shake and throw."

He rattled the coins in his cupped hands, let them fall to

17

the carpet. Two heads and a tail. "Yang," he heard the woman whisper as she drew a line on a piece of scrap paper. "Eight." He picked up the coins, shook them, threw again. Two tails and a head. "Yin," he heard. "Seven." Then there was another yin, another seven. And another. Then three heads—yang, nine. And finally two heads and a tail—yang, eight.

"That will do," she said.

"Well?" he asked. "What's the verdict?"

"Wait," she told him.

She opened the book, studied the chart. She turned the pages.

"Upper trigram Sun," she murmured. "Lower trigram Chen. Increase. There will be advantage in every undertaking. It will be advantageous even to cross the great water. . . ." She looked up at Grimes. "Yes. You are destined to make a voyage."

"That is my intention in any case," he said. "But as a passenger."

"I haven't finished yet," she told him sharply. "It goes on like this. If the ruler strives to dispense benefits to his people and to increase the general level of prosperity he will be given loyalty in return. Thus he will be able to do great things."

Hogwash, Grimes almost said, would have said if he had not felt that in some weird way he was standing at the focus of cosmic lines of force. *Hogwash*, he thought again—but he knew that he was standing at the crossroads.

And he must make his own decision.

He put a hand down to the floor, picked up one coin.

"Heads I buy the ship," he said. "Tails I don't."

He sent the little disc spinning into the air.

It came up heads.

Chapter 3

The next morning, bright and early, Magda Granadu and Billy Williams joined Grimes as he was finishing his breakfast in the hotel's coffee shop. The previous evening they had stayed with Grimes to discuss with him the problem of manning; they, as merchant officers, knew far more about such matters than he did. In the Survey Service his crews had been found for him and, except for his tour of duty in the couriers, he had always been used to a superfluity of personnel. As master of *Epsilon Scorpii*—or whatever name he would give her once she was his—he would have no Bureau of Appointments to dip its ladle into the barrel to procure for him his entitlements. (There had been times when he had been obliged to cope with what was at the bottom of the barrel.)

Williams looked at his watch. "As soon as you've finished your coffee, Skipper, we'll ring Pinnett. He should be in his office by now."

So it was "Skipper" now, thought Grimes. If—if!—Williams became one of his officers such familiarity would not be tolerated. It might be all right for the Dog Star Line but not for any ship that Grimes might command.

He drained his cup, taking his time about it. He did not like being rushed. Then, with Williams and Magda on either side of him, he took the elevator up to the fiftieth floor. He found that the cleaning robots were in his suite, noisily dusting, polishing, changing towels and bed linen. One of the spider-like things was making a major production of quite unnecessary housekeeping in the telephone alcove, buffing each button on the selector panel with loving care.

Williams put his big hands about its bulbous body, lifted it down to the floor and gave it a gentle shove toward the center of the room. It staggered no farther than a meter on its spindly legs and then turned around, scampering back to its appointed task. Again Williams tried to shoo it away. Again it came back.

"Get rid of that bloody thing!" growled Grimes.

"Aye, aye, Skipper!"

Williams kicked, hard. The little robot flew through the air, crashed against the wall. Its plastic carapace shattered and there was a coruscation of violet sparks and the acridity of ozone. But it still wasn't dead. It began to crawl back toward the telephone, bleeding tendrils of blue smoke from its broken body.

Williams stamped on it, jumped on it with both feet.

Grimes said coldly, "That will do. I suppose you realize that I shall have to pay for this wanton damage."

"You can afford it, Skipper!" Williams told him cheerfully.

Grimes snarled wordlessly, then touched the D button for Directory. He said, speaking slowly and distinctly, "Interstellar Transport Commission." On some worlds he would have

19

been put through automatically, but not here; he would have to do his own button pushing once he got the number. Luminous words and numerals appeared on the screen: INNIS & MCKELLAR, SOUTHPORT COMPREDORES—0220238.

Grimes snarled again, stabbed X for Cancel, prodded D and repeated his order in the kind of voice that he had used in the past for reprimanding junior officers.

The blanked-out screen returned to life. INTRACITY TRANSIT CORPORATION—02325252.

"You're getting closer, Skipper," said Williams encouragingly. "But the number is 023571164."

"Why the hell didn't you tell me before?"

"You never asked."

Grimes touched the buttons as Williams called out the numerals. After what seemed far too long a delay a sour-faced, gray-haired woman looked out at them from the screen, not liking what she was seeing from her end.

"Interstellar," she snapped. "At the service of the universe."

"Mr. Pinnett, please," said Grimes.

"Whom shall I say is calling?"

"Captain Grimes."

The picture of the woman faded, was replaced by a gaudy representation of a spiral nebula. This faded in its turn when the woman came back.

"Mr. Pinnett," she said, "is in conference."

"Have you any idea when he will be free?"

"I am afraid not."

"Perhaps," said Grimes, "somebody else might be able to help me."

"I can tell you now," she said, "that we have no vacancies for space crew. In any case we always endeavor to avoid recruiting on outworlds."

With an effort Grimes kept a hold on his temper. He said, "I understand that your ship, *Epsilon Scorpii*, is up for sale."

"From whom did you obtain that information?"

"It doesn't matter. I'm interested in buying her if the price is right."

She did not say it but she was obviously thinking, *Spacebums can't buy ships*. Grimes' name had meant nothing to her. She said, "Even an obsolescent Epsilon Class tramp is very expensive. I do not think that any offer that you can make will be of interest to Mr. Pinnett. May I suggest that you waste no more of my time?"

The screen went blank.

"Good-bye, prune-puss," muttered Williams.

"Would you know the number of Yosarian Robotics?" Grimes asked him.

"No, Skipper, but I'll get it for you."

Williams punched the D button, said the words. On his first attempt he got YOUR SAURIAN PET SHOP. Grimes said that he was interested in buying a scorpion, not a lizard. Williams kicked the console. Something tinkled inside it. He tried again and this time got YOSARIAN ROBOTICS and the number. He stabbed the keys with a thick forefinger. The face of the plump blonde appeared on the screen. She looked at Williams without recognition and said cheerfully, "Yosarian to save you labor. Can I assist you?"

Grimes moved so that he was within the scope of the scanner.

"Good morning, Captain Grimes," she said.

"Good morning. Can I talk to Mr. Yosarian, please?"

"He is down at the spaceport, aboard your ship. Sorry, Captain—*his* ship. Perhaps if you called him there. . . ."

Grimes did.

After some delay the roboticist appeared. He looked as though he had been working; there was a smudge of oil on his fat face. He snapped, "What is it? Can't you see that I'm busy?" Then, "Oh, it's you, Captain. If you want your *Little Sister* back it's just too bad."

"I do want a ship," said Grimes. "but not *Little Sister*. I've been trying to get through to Mr. Pinnett, the local boss cocky of the ITC, to find out how much he wants for *Epsilon Scorpii*. Some frosty-faced female gave me the brush-off."

Yosarian laughed. "Pinnett's tame dragon. She's quite notorious. But are you really thinking of buying that decrepit bitch? Still, there's an old saying, isn't there, about the dog returning to his vomit. . . ."

"And also there's 'Once bitten, twice shy,'" said Grimes wryly. "But I'm willing to take the risk of getting bitten again."

"It's your money, Captain. But what do you want *me* to do about it?"

"Perhaps if *you* rang Mr. Pinnett and told him that you know of a potential buyer for his superannuated scorpion. . . . You pull heavier Gs on this world than I do."

"All right, Captain. I'll do that. You're staying at the Centaurian, aren't you? I'll tell him to call you back there. Oh, by the way, I'm having trouble getting your autochef—*my*

21

autochef—working properly. You must have abused it considerably when *you* were using it. . . ."

His face faded from the screen.

Grimes and his companions were halfway through their second cups of coffee when the telephone buzzed. He accepted the call. A craggy-faced black-haired man looked out at Grimes suspiciously. "Captain Grimes? I'm Pinnett, Planetary Manager for the Commission. Mr. Yosarian called me and said that you might be interested in buying *Epsilon Scorpii* and assured me that you possess the necessary funds. I cannot understand why you did not approach me directly."

"I did," said Grimes. "Or tried to."

"Oh." Pinnett looked slightly embarrassed. "But how did you know that the ship is up for sale? Head Office, on Earth, has yet to advertise."

"I just heard it somewhere," said Grimes. "And I also gained the impression that it would be to your advantage if you, personally, handled the sale."

"How did you . . . ? Oh, never mind, there's always gossip." His manner brightened. "Suppose we take lunch together to talk things over. 1300 hours. Do you know the Tzigane, on Moberley Square?"

Magda's place, thought Grimes. "I can find it," he said.

"Good. 1300 hours then."

His face vanished.

"I hope that you aren't allergic to sour cream and paprika, Skipper," said Williams.

The Tzigane was the sort of restaurant that Grimes categorized as being ethnic as all hell. Its interior tried to convey the impression of being that of a huge tent; its human waiters and waitresses were attired as romanticized Romanies. Magda was there, of course, generally supervising, but gave no indication of knowing Grimes, although she greeted Pinnett personally. The food was good, rich and highly spiced, and the portions generous. Pinnett did not allow business to interfere with the more serious business of eating and drinking and it was only when large mugs of coffee, laced with some aromatic spirit, were placed before them that he was willing to discuss the possible sale of *Epsilon Scorpii*.

"Well, Captain," he said around a slim, black cigar, "you'll be getting a good ship."

"If I buy her," said Grimes. Then, bluntly, "How much do you want for her?"

"Nine million," said Pinnett. "A bargain."

"She's not an Alpha Class liner, straight from the builder's yard," said Grimes.

"I know she's not. But she's a good, reliable workhorse, even if she's not built of gold. She's not a toy."

"At her age," said Grimes, "she'll need a lot of maintenance."

"Don't you believe it, Captain. We look after our ships in the Interstellar Transport Commission."

"I'd like to inspect her," said Grimes. "As soon as possible."

"I'm afraid that you'll have to wait a few days," Pinnett told him. "Arranging a shuttle at short notice isn't easy. Our own tender, *Austral Meteor,* is being withdrawn from service for annual survey."

"There are tugs," said Grimes. He strongly suspected that Pinnett did not wish to have the ship inspected until some attempt had been made to have her looking her best for a potential purchaser.

Pinnett smiled—regretfully or with relief? "There are space tugs, of course. But they aren't here right now. Hadn't you heard that *Punch* and *Percheron* have both gone out to the Dog Star Line's *Samoyed?* A complete engine-room breakdown, all of a light-year from here."

"What about the met. satellite tenders?"

"You know what bureaucrats are. By the time that the Bureau of Meteorology made its mind up about hiring one to us our own tender would be back in service and the two tugs sitting on their backsides in the spaceport, waiting for the next job."

"I think I can arrange something," said Grimes. "I see a telephone there. . . ."

As he got up from the table he saw that Magda Granadu was bearing down upon it, holding a pack of cards in her hand. No doubt she was about to offer to tell Pinnett's fortune—a prognostication, thought Grimes, that would predispose the ITC manager not to hang out for too high a price for the ship.

"You again, Captain Grimes!" complained Yosarian. "Just when I'm in the middle of getting the innie properly tuned. Did you know that it was delivering only ninety percent of its true capacity?"

"But it's working, isn't it? Mr. Yosarian, I'd like to hire *Little Sister* for a day. There's no shuttle available to take me

23

out to *Epsilon Scorpii*, and I want to make an inspection as soon as possible."

"I'm not hiring her out," said Yosarian. Then he grinned. "But I want to see how she handles. We'll regard this as a sort of trial run. I can be ready for space in thirty minutes. That suit you?"

Chapter 4

Yosarian, as promised, had *Little Sister* ready for space in half an hour. There were delays, however, before she could lift off. Only two spacesuits were on board; others had to be borrowed from the Interstellar Transport Commission's stores. Luckily the storekeeper was able to find one large enough to accommodate the roboticist's corpulence. Meanwhile Pinnett got in touch, by radio telephone, with *Epsilon Scorpii's* ship-keeping officer to make arrangements for the reception of the boarding party.

Finally, with everybody and everything aboard *Little Sister*, the pinnace was buttoned up. Yosarian, not without diffidence, took the pilot's seat in the control cab. Grimes sat beside him. Billy Williams and Pinnett disposed themselves in the main cabin. Permission was received from Aerospace Control to lift off. Yosarian looked at Grimes, who nodded.

The fat man's pudgy hands hesitated briefly over the console, then turned on the inertial drive. *Little Sister* shuddered as the thrust built up. The drive hammered more loudly as the little ship lifted from the apron. Yosarian increased the rate of ascent and said to Grimes, "Can't you feel the difference? The innie needed tuning very badly."

It sounded the same to Grimes as it always had—but as long as Yosarian's tinkerings kept him happy that was all right by him. He did not interfere with the roboticist as he pushed *Little Sister* up and up, through wisps of high cirrus, into a sky which rapidly deepened to indigo, into the airless blackness where the unwinking stars were brightly shining. The pinnace's new owner seemed to know what he was doing and was not so arrogant as to attempt himself tasks that were better carried out by the computer. He fed the elements of *Epsilon Scorpii's* synchronous orbit, which he had obtained

24

from Pinnett, into *Little Sister's* electronic brain and switched control from manual to automatic. Before long a spark appeared on the radar screen, a point of light, tiny at first, that expanded into a glowing blob that grew steadily.

He turned to Grimes and said, "Well, there she is, Captain." He paused, then asked, "How did I do?"

"Very nicely, Captain," said Grimes.

Yosarian blushed happily and said, "Would you mind taking over now, Captain Grimes? You're more used to this sort of thing than I am."

"But you have to get some practice. Just match orbital velocity; it shouldn't be difficult. Edge her in until we're half a kilometer off target, then put her back on automatic. . . ." He transferred his attention to the NST transceiver. *"Little Sister* to *Epsilon Scorpii*. . . ."

"Eppy Scorpy to *Little Sister*. I read you."

A slightly effeminate voice, thought Grimes. Some very junior officer, he decided, not an old retired captain augmenting his pension with a shipkeeper's salary. (But he had been a shipkeeper himself although he had been neither old nor retired. He had needed the money.)

"Is your airlock ready?" he asked. "We will board as soon as we're suited up."

"Opening outer door now," came the reply.

Little Sister was on station, maintaining the correct distance off. In the cabin Pinnett was getting into his spacesuit; it was obviously not the first time that he had been required to wear such a garment. Yosarian, however, required assistance to get into the especially large outfit that had been borrowed for him. When the roboticist was at last suited up Grimes got into his own space armor. He realized, once he had sealed himself in the garment, that it was not the one that he had regarded as his own while he had been *Little Sister's* owner and master. The last person to have used it must have been Tamara Haverstock; after all this time a trace of her perfume still persisted. He allowed his memories briefly to take over his mind. Who else had worn this suit? Only Tamara, he decided—and she, now, was no more than a recollection of somebody whom he would never see again, any more than he would ever see again those other lost ladies— Jane Pentecost, Fenella Pruin, Shirl, Darleen, Susie, Una Freeman. . . . *I must be wanting a woman*, he thought, *if it takes no more than a fugitive whiff of scent to start me wandering down memory lane.* . . .

"Are you all right, Skipper?" asked Williams sharply, his

25

voice distorted but still recognizable as it came from the helmet speaker. The big man had seated himself in the chair vacated by Yosarian, was speaking into the NST transceiver microphone.

"Of course, Mr. Williams," said Grimes. He added, lamely, "I was just thinking." He continued, speaking briskly, "All right. You're in charge until we get back. We're locking out now."

The small airlock could accommodate two persons—but not when one of the pair was as bulky as Yosarian. Grimes and Pinnett, therefore, went out first after Grimes had told the roboticist that, according to protocol, he, as captain, should be last out of the ship. Before long the three men were hanging outside *Little Sister's* golden hull, staring at the great hulk of *Epsilon Scorpii* gleaming against the backdrop of stars. Sunlight was reflected from most of her shell but the open airlock door was in shadow. That was all to the good; it made it much easier to see the bright green light that illuminated the chamber.

"Grimes to Pinnett. Go!" ordered Grimes.

Pinnett went. He handled himself not unskillfully, launching himself into the void with an economically short blast from his suit reaction unit, making only one trajectory adjustment before he braked himself just outside the open airlock door. Grimes watched him, his figure in black silhouette against the green illumination, as he pulled himself into the chamber.

"You next, Mr. Yosarian," said Grimes.

"I . . . I don't think. . . ." Then, in a burst of embarrassed frankness, "This is the first time that I've done this sort of thing. . . ."

"So we take no risks," said Grimes.

He positioned himself behind the fat man, put both gloved hands on the other's armored shoulders, took a firm grip.

He said, "Whatever you do, don't touch your reaction-unit controls. I don't want a hole blasted in my belly. Just relax. . . ."

Pushing Yosarian before him, he jetted toward *Epsilon Scorpii*. The short flight was a clumsy one. He was grateful that there were not many witnesses. He managed to turn around when halfway to his objective, fired a short braking blast. He missed the open doorway, fetched up with a clang on the ship's side a meter from the rim. Fortunately Pinnett was spaceman enough—like most of the Interstellar Transport Commission's managers he had done his stint as a

26

ship's purser—to extend a helping hand, pulling Grimes and his bulky, ungainly tow into the chamber.

There was ample room for all of them in the airlock and they were able to get themselves sorted out, all standing the same way up, their magnetically soled boots holding them to the deck. The outer door closed and the illumination changed from green to red, indicating that they were in a hard vacuum environment. It acquired a yellowish tinge, became amber, showing that atmosphere was being fed into the chamber. It became green once more.

The inner door opened.

The shipkeeper was waiting to receive them.

She spoke into the little transceiver that she was wearing on her left wrist.

"Come in," she said sourly. "This is Liberty Hall. You can spit on the mat and call the cat a bastard. I hope that one of you is an engineer. The autochef is playing up again. I've lost count of the number of times that I've reported it. And isn't it time that I got some new spools for the playmaster? And. . . ."

Grimes stared at her. She was wearing a well-filled T-shirt and very short shorts. The sandals on her rather large feet were secured by string, the original straps being no more than broken ends. Her free-floating hair made a dingy green halo about her head. A pair of vividly green eyes glared at the boarders. Even her skin—and there was plenty of it on view—had a greenish tinge. She would have been a good-looking enough wench, thought Grimes, had she been cleaner (to judge from the state of her shirt and even her face she was a messy feeder), had her expression been less surly. But even after a bath and looking happy she would have been too strong featured to suit his taste in women.

A Donegalan, he decided. (He had visited New Donegal once, during his career in the Survey Service.) Human ancestry, but with a slight genetic drift from the norm. A woman-dominated society. No spaceships of Donegalan registry but, each year, a few promising girls sent to the Antarctic Academy on Earth—where the Commandant and his officers made sure that none of them did well enough to graduate into the Survey Service. Most of them, however, did qualify for entry into the Interstellar Transport Commission and other shipping lines. There was more than male chauvinism involved in the Academy's attitude toward the Donegalans. They were notorious for always carrying chips on their shoulders, and such an atttitude on the part of junior officers could seriously impair the efficient running of a warship.

Faceplates were opened.

"Ms. Connellan," said Pinnett, "this is Captain Grimes." Grimes nodded. "And Mr. Yosarian. . . ." The roboticist managed, even in his bulky spacesuit, a quite courtly bow. Pinnett went on, "Ms. Connellan is one of our second officers. . . ."

"Demoted to watchperson," she snarled. "I've a Master's ticket—and this is the best job that the bloody Commission can find for me!"

"Shipkeeping officer," Pinnett corrected her. "With very generous hard-lying money over and above your salary."

"Which I earn, in this rustbucket where damn all works the way that it should!"

"What exactly is not working, Ms. Connellan?" asked Grimes pleasantly.

"The autochef, for a start. And the NST transceiver only works if you know just where to give it a clout. You were lucky that it wasn't on the blink when you came up from Port Southern; the last time that you condescended to call on me, Mr. Pinnett, you had to hammer on the control-room viewports to attract my attention. Then, a couple of days ago, I tried to actuate the Carlotti transceiver, just so that I could find out what ships are around. It just spat sparks at me and died. Oh, and just to pass the time I've been browsing through the logs. It seems that Captain Taine had one helluva job establishing this wreck in orbit. I know that he's not the best ship handler in the universe but the fact that the innies were playing up made him even worse than usual. And. . . ."

"That will do, Ms. Connellan," snarled Pinnett. "That will do!"

"Like hell it will. What about the nutrient pumps for the tissue culture vats? I've had to dump the lamb and the beef and the pork. Would *you* like chicken for every meal?"

"That will do!"

"It will *not* do, Mr. Pinnett. I demand that you find me a deep space appointment."

"I am not the Commission's astronautical superintendent, Ms. Connellan."

"Too right you're not. But you're a planetary manager, aren't you? Somebody in the top office must listen to you sometimes."

"Captain Grimes," said Pinnett, trying hard to ignore the irate shipkeeper, "may I suggest that we start the tour of inspection?"

28

"It's what we came here for," said Grimes. "Ms. Connellan, will you lead the way? We'll start in the control room and work aft."

"Are you really thinking of buying this . . . *thing?*" asked the girl interestedly. "You must have more money than sense."

Perhaps I have, thought Grimes. *Perhaps it's always been that way, even when I've been flat broke.*

Grimes was glad that Yosarian had come along. Even though the roboticist was not an astronautical engineer he knew machines; too, there was his keen interest in spaceships.

"The people who were here," he complained, "just did not care. All over there is lack of proper attention. . . ."

"I should have been given the time to get the shore gang up here to do some cleaning up," said Pinnett stiffly.

Yosarian ignored him as he continued his inspection of one of the offending pumps on the farm deck.

"Look at this!" he spluttered. "Every lubrication point clogged! Small wonder that it seized up. . . ." He stared reproachfully at the woman. "Surely even you should have seen what was the trouble."

"I'm employed as a shipkeeping officer," she snapped, "not as a mechanic!"

Yosarian shook his head sadly. "But your own comfort. . . . Your own safety, even. . . ."

"I've told you that I'm not an engineer."

"That is glaringly obvious," he said.

"Mr. Pinnett," she demanded, "did you bring this man here to insult me?"

"But this is Mr. Yosarian," said Pinnett.

"And so what? Am I supposed to fire a twenty-one-gun salute? But if there were any guns in this ship they wouldn't be working, any more than the pumps are."

"So the pumps aren't working," snarled Pinnett. "You are at least partly responsible for that."

"The butterfly-brained Terry apes who were the alleged engineers of this scow on her last voyage were responsible, and you know it!"

"Let's get on with the inspection," said Grimes tiredly.

Throughout the ship it was the same story, a glaring example of the "she'll be all right" principle carried to extremes. There were many things, such as those nutrient pumps, that Ms. Connellan could have put right. And, with all the time on her hands, she might have done something about the state

29

of the inertial drive room. Hasty repairs of some kind seemed to have been carried out at the very conclusion of the voyage while the ship was being established in parking orbit—and then the tools employed had not been returned to their clips but had been carelessly dropped, were now, in these free fall conditions, drifting around dangerously in the air eddies set up by the body movements of the inspection party.

Grimes began to round up the wandering spanners and such, returning them to their proper places on the shadow board. Yosarian assisted. Although the roboticist was not used to working in the absence of gravity, he could not bear to see machinery neglected.

Neither Ms. Connellan nor Pinnett made any attempt to lend a hand.

Farther aft it was discovered that one of the propellant tanks for the auxiliary reaction drive had been leaking; that level would have been a suitable habitat for goldfish but not for human beings.

"*If* I am going to buy this ship," said Grimes, "I shall require new certificates of spaceworthiness."

"But the last annual survey," the manager told him, "was only five standard months ago."

"Then a lot happened in that five months," said Grimes. "And one helluva lot, in the way of maintenance, didn't happen!"

Back at his hotel in Port Southern Grimes conferred with Billy Williams and Magda Granadu.

"Pinnett will come down in price," he said. "But it was just as well that we had Yosarian along as a sort of independent witness. He can bring some pressure to bear."

"I'm sorry that I didn't get to meet that shipkeeping officer," said Williams. "To judge from what I heard of her on the NST radio it's a bloody good thing that she doesn't come with the ship!"

"I've shipped with Donegalans," said Magda. "They're bitter, resentful. On New Donegal they're on top. They're just not used to accepting men as equals, let along superiors. Too, this Connellan woman knows that the shipkeeping job was just the Commission's way of sweeping her under the carpet."

"Well," Grimes said, "they'll just have to find her another deep-space posting when they sell the ship from around her." He grinned. "And may the Odd Gods of the Galaxy help me unfortunate master who gets saddled with her!"

30

Chapter 5

The details of the sale were ironed out with surprising ease and for a sum quite a bit lower than the original asking price. Yosarian pulled considerable Gs on his home world and even the mighty Interstellar Transport Commission listened when he talked. One of his engineers, an ex-spacer, went out to *Epsilon Scorpii* to make sure that the ship's inertial drive was in proper working order, then acted as engine-room chief while Grimes, assisted by Bill Williams, brought the vessel down to the spaceport. (During this operation Ms. Connellan made it quite clear that she was employed as a shipkeeping officer only and was not required to lend a hand with any maneuvers.)

So Grimes had his "new" ship sitting on the apron, handy to the spaceport workshops whose facilities he was using. The obnoxious Ms. Connellan was no longer on board; she had left, with her baggage, as soon as the ramp was down. It was now up to Pinnett and the Commission to find for her suitable employment.

The next four weeks were busy ones. Grimes and Williams went through the ship from stem to stern with the Lloyd's and Interstellar Federal surveyors, pointing out the things that needed doing while Pinnett, who had reluctantly agreed that the Commission would bear the cost of making the vessel spaceworthy, tried to argue that many of the proposed repairs were only of a cosmetic nature. The trouble was that the Federation surveyor tended to side with him, saying more than once to Grimes, "You aren't in the Survey Service now, Captain. This isn't a warship, you know."

Grimes got his way (he usually did) but it was costing him much more than he had anticipated. For example, he had been obliged to foot the bill for making the auxiliary reaction drive fully operational, such an additional means of propulsion being no longer mandatory for merchant vessels. The charge for the work involved was not a small one.

He had been temporarily rich but he was no longer so; what money had been left after the purchase of *Epsilon Scorpii* was fast being whittled away. If his luck ran out again he would be back where he started—only instead of having a golden white elephant on his hands it would be one constructed of more conventional and far less valuable materials.

Nonetheless he felt an upsurge of pride when she was renamed. To have the new nomenclature fabricated in golden letters was a needless extravagance but one that pleased him. It was a tribute to Big Sister, the almost too human computer-pilot of *The Far Traveler*. It was also a sort of memento of *Little Sister*. As for the second half of the name, it was just there because it went naturally with the first, Grimes told himself—although the lady so commemorated was part of what he was already thinking of as the *Little Sister* period of his life and about the only one from whom he had not broken off in acrimonious circumstances.

SISTER SUE. . . .

He stood on the apron looking up at his ship, at the golden name on the gray hull gleaming brightly in the afternoon sunlight. Williams joined him there.

"Very pretty, Skipper," he commented. Then, "Who was Sue?"

"Just a girl," said Grimes.

"She must have been somebody special to get a ship named after her. . . ." Williams shuffled his big feet, then went on, "I'm afraid I've bad news for you, Skipper."

"What now?" demanded Grimes. "What now?"

This was too much, he thought. He now had, not without a struggle, a spaceworthy ship, a sturdy workhorse, and all that he needed was a little bit of luck to make a go of things.

What had happened to his famous luck?

"It's the manning, Skipper," Williams said. "We're all right for engineers. We've old Crumley lined up; he's a bit senile but he's qualified, a double-headed Chief's ticket, inertial drive and reaction drive. For the Mannschenn Drive there's Professor Malleson. He passed for Mannschenn Chief before he came ashore to go teaching. As I told you before, he's taking his sabbatical leave from the university. Also from the university there'll be a couple of bright young Ph.D.s to act as his juniors. And we've a Sparks, another old-timer, retired years ago but wanting to get back into space. . . ."

"So what's the trouble?"

"In the control room, Skipper. According to the Manning Scale we should have three control-room watchkeeping officers—although we can lift with only two as long as we get a permit. Well, you've got me, as mate. You should have got old Captain Binns—he used to be in the Dog Star Line—as

32

second mate. But he got mashed in a ground-car accident last night. At his age it'll be at least six months before he's grown a new left arm and right leg."

"There are times," said Grimes, "when I strongly suspect that the Odd Gods of the Galaxy don't like me. So Binns is out. Is there nobody on this benighted planet to fill the gap?"

"Well, er, yes. There is."

"So what's all this talk of bad news?"

"The Green Hornet," said Williams, "has let it be known that she's had the Interstellar Transport Commission in a big way."

"The Green Hornet?"

"Kate Connellan. 'Green Hornet' is her company nickname. Anyhow, she had a knock-down-and-drag-'em-out row with Pinnett. She resigned—about a microsecond before Pinnett could fire her. And, as far as we're concerned, she's qualified and she's available."

"Oh," said Grimes. "Oh."

Could he possibly afford to wait until somebody more suitable turned up? He could not, he decided. He had been lucky enough to have a consignment of government cargo offered to him, but if he could not lift it by the specified date somebody else would be found to do the job.

"She has a master's ticket," said Williams.

"But she's still an eleven-trip officer," said Grimes.

"Eleven trips, Skipper? How do you make that out?"

"One out and one home," Grimes told him.

Chapter 6

Articles were opened.

Grimes, having done all the autographing required of him in his capacity as captain, stood behind the counter in the shipping office, watching his officers affixing their signatures to the agreement while the shipping master checked their qualifications and last discharges, if any.

Billy Williams was the first to sign. He said cheerfully, "I'll get back on board, Skipper. They should be just about ready to start the loading."

Magda Granadu signed and followed the mate out of the

office, Mr. Crumley, a frail, white-bearded, bald-headed old man, produced one of the old-fashioned certificates bound in plastic rather than in flexisteel and a discharge book held together with adhesive tape.

"You'll find that times have changed since you were Chief of the *Far Centaurus,* Mr. Crumley," said the shipping master cheerfully.

"A ship's a ship and engines are engines, aren't they?" grumbled the ancient spaceman.

His three juniors signed. They possessed neither certificates nor discharge books, only diplomas from the Port Southern College of Technology. One of them, Denning, had been employed by Yosarian Robotics, the other two, Singh and Paulus, by the Intracity Transit Corporation. They were squat, swarthy, youngish men who could almost have been triplets—competent mechanics, thought Grimes snobbishly, rather than officers.

Malleson, looking every inch the gray-haired, untidy, stooping, absent-minded professor, signed. His two juniors, tall young men, briskly competent, with fashionably shaven heads and heavily black-rimmed spectacles, signed.

Old Mr. Stewart, the electronic communications officer, signed. His certificate and discharge book were as antique as Mr. Crumley's. *Shave his head,* thought Grimes, *and stick the hair on his chin and he'd be old Crumley's double....*

"You don't have a doctor, Captain?" asked the shipping master.

"I've got three," said Grimes. "Ph.D.s."

"Ha ha. But you have tried to find one, haven't you? A medical doctor, I mean. So I'll issue you a permit to sanction your lifting off undermanned. You realize, of course, that you'll have to pay your crew an extra ten credits each a day in lieu of medical services. . . . Cheer up, Captain. You'll be getting it too."

"But *I'll* be paying it," growled Grimes. "Out of one pocket and into the other."

"Ha ha! Of course. It's not very often that I get masters who are also owners in here. In fact the only one before you was a Captain Kane. I don't suppose you've ever run across him." Grimes said nothing and the shipping master, who was checking the entries in the Articles of Agreement, did not see his expression. "H'm. We were talking of permits, weren't we? I take it that you still haven't been able to find a third mate. . . . And where *is* your second mate, by the way?"

"She was told what time she was to be here," said Grimes.

34

"She?" echoed the shipping master, looking at the preliminary crew list. "Oh. The *Green Hornet.* But I thought that she was with the Commission."

"She *was."*

"And now you've got her. Do me a favor, will you, Captain. Don't bring her back to Port Southern. I'll never forget the fuss she kicked up when she was paid off from *Delta Crucis,* threatening to sue the Commission, the Department of Interstellar Shipping and the Odd Gods of the Galaxy alone know who else! To begin with she was screaming wrongful dismissal—but, of course, she wasn't being dismissed but transferred. To *Epsilon Scorpii.* Then there was a mistake in her pay sheet—twenty cents, but you'd have thought it was twenty thousand credits. And. . . ."

Grimes looked at his watch.

"I certainly wish that I didn't have to have her," he said. "But I have to. Where *is* the bitch?"

"Do you know where she's staying?"

"Some place called The Rusty Rocket."

"Cheap," sneered the shipping master. "And nasty. You can use my phone, Captain, to check up on her. They might know where she's got to."

He showed Grimes through to his private office, seated him at the desk. He told Grimes the number to punch. The screen came alive and a sour-faced blonde looked out at them.

"The Rusty Rocket?" asked Grimes.

"This certainly ain't The Polished Projectile. Waddya want?"

"Is a Ms. Connellan staying with you?"

"She was. She won't be again. Ever."

"Where is she now?"

"In the right place for her. Jail. I hope they throw away the key."

After a little prodding Grimes got the story. The previous night there had been a nasty brawl in the barroom of The Rusty Rocket, the focus of which had been Kate Connellan. There had been damage, injuries. The police had been called. Arrests had been made.

Grimes thanked the woman and disconnected.

He said to the shipping master, "Now I suppose I'll have to pay her fine or bail or whatever." He sighed. "More expense."

"I'm afraid that's out of the question, Captain. In the old days the police authorities were only too pleased to get rid of drunken spacers as soon as possible—but not anymore. Not since the new Commissioner was appointed. Now any spacer who makes a nuisance of himself—or herself—is given a stiff sentence and has to serve it. Every minute of it."

Grimes sighed again. He owed no loyalty to the troublesome Ms. Connellan, he told himself. Had her name been on his Articles she would have been one of his people—but she had not yet signed.

He said hopefully, "I see no reason why I shouldn't lift off with only the mate and myself as control-room watchkeepers. After all, in *Little Sister* there was only me. I was the cook and the captain bold. . . ."

"Regulations," the shipping master told him. "A vessel of *Little Sister's* tonnage is classified as a spaceyacht, even though she may be gainfully employed. Your *Epsilon Scorpii*—sorry, *Sister Sue*—is a ship. The manning scale calls for a master and three mates. I can issue a permit to allow you to lift with only two mates. But you may not, repeat not, lift with only one qualified control-room officer in addition to yourself."

"And I must lift on time," muttered Grimes. "If I don't the penalty clauses in the charter party will beggar me." He filled and lit his pipe, puffed furiously. "Do you think that if I made a personal appeal to this Police Commissioner of yours, putting all my cards on the table, it might help?"

"It might," said the shipping master. "It might—but the Commissioner has a down on spacers. Your guild has already lodged complaints—which have been ignored. Still, you can try. As long as you watch your language you should be able to stay out of jail."

Grimes borrowed the telephone again and ordered a cab.

In a short time he was on his way from the spaceport to the city.

Like most of the other buildings in Port Southern, that housing Police Headquarters was a pyramid. But it was not a tall, graceful one, all gleaming metal and glittering glass, but squat and ugly. The material used for its construction looked like dark gray stone although it was probably some plastic.

Grimes walked in through the frowning main entrance, approached a desk behind which a heavily built man, with silver sergeant's stripes on the sleeves of his severe black uniform, was seated.

"Your business, citizen?" asked the police officer.

"I wish to see the Commissioner."

"Your name, citizen?"

36

"Grimes," said Grimes. "Captain Grimes."

"A spacer, eh? The Commissioner doesn't like spacers." The sergeant laughed briefly. "In fact. . . ."

A bell chimed softly from the telephone set on the desk. A female voice—that of a secretary, Grimes supposed, although it was oddly familiar—said, "Send Captain Grimes up, sergeant."

The policeman raised his heavy eyebrows in surprise. He growled, "So the Commissioner will see you. What have you got that all the other spacers haven't? The elevators are over there, citizen. The Commissioner's office is on the top floor." He laughed again. "The apex of our pyramid."

Grimes thanked the man, walked to the bank of elevators. As he approached the indicator, lights showed that a cage was descending. The door opened as he got to it. There was nobody inside. The door closed again as soon as he had entered and the lift started to rise before he could touch the button of his choice.

Service, he thought. *With a smile?*

The car stopped gently. The door opened. Grimes stepped out. The walls of the apex of the police pyramid were all glass, overhead automatically polarized to reduce the glare of the sun. There were elaborate arrays of screens, some of which displayed ever-changing pictures while in others numerals flickered into and out of being. There was a big desk behind which was sitting a woman, a large woman in black and silver uniform with what looked like commodore's braid on her shoulderboards.

She looked at Grimes. Grimes looked at her. Beneath her glossy brown hair, short cut, the face was too strong for prettiness, the cheekbones pronounced, the pale-lipped mouth wide over rather too much jaw.

"Una . . ." he said softly. "Long time no see."

"Commissioner Freeman," she corrected him harshly. "I knew, of course, that you were on this planet but I was able, quite successfully, to fight down the urge to renew our old . . . acquaintanceship. But now that you have come to see me I let my curiosity get the better of me.

"And what do you want? Make it quick. I'm a busy woman."

"I didn't know that you were the Police Commissioner here, Una. When did you leave the Corps of Sky Marshals? How. . . ."

"This isn't a social call, Grimes. *What do you want?*"

"Your men, Una. . . ." She glared at him. He started

37

again. "Your men, Commissioner Freeman, arrested one of my officers. I'd like her back. I'm willing to pay her fine." He added hastily, "Within reason, of course."

"One of *your* officers, Grimes? The only spacer at present in our cells is a known troublemaker, a Kate Connellan, whose most recent employment was with the Interstellar Transport Commission. She faces charges of assaulting a police officer, occasioning bodily harm. There are three such charges. Also to be considered, and compensated for, is the damage done to the uniforms of those officers. There are five charges of assaulting civilians. There are charges of violent and abusive behavior. There are charges of damage to property—mainly furniture and fittings of The Rusty Rocket. Need I go on?"

"It seems enough to be going on with," admitted Grimes glumly.

"But how is it that you can claim that this person is one of your officers, Captain Grimes?"

"I opened Articles today, Commissioner Freeman. Ms. Connellan was supposed to sign on as second mate. I'll be frank. She wouldn't have been my choice but she was the only qualified officer available."

"Still the male chauvinist pig, Grimes, aren't you?"

"Her sex has nothing to do with my reluctance to employ her. And, in any case, I must have her if I'm to lift off on time."

"You should have kept that *Little Sister* of yours. To judge from my experiences while under your command—ha, ha!—a glorified lifeboat is just about the limit of your capabilities. But you had to have a *big* ship, didn't you? *Epsilon Scorpii*—or *Sister Sue*, as you've renamed her. Who was Sue, by the way?"

"Just a girl," said Grimes.

"Spoken like a true male chauvinist pig. I hope that she has happier memories of you than I have. Even now I can't force myself to eat baked beans. And as for bicycles. . . ."

"You can't blame me for either," said Grimes hotly.

"Can't I? Well, after that most peculiar mess that you got me into I was allergic to space as well as to beans and bicycles. I resigned from the Corps—although I'm still supposed to be on their reserve list. And I've found that useful. Sky Marshals pull heavy Gs with most of the planetary police forces."

"So when you came here you started at the top," said Grimes as nastily as he dared.

"Not at the top, although my having been a Sky Marshal entitled me to inspector's rank. After that my promotion was strictly on merit."

"Local girl makes good," said Grimes.

"Do you want to be arrested too? I can soon think of a few charges. Insulting behavior to a police officer for a start. . . ."

"I can see that I'm wasting my time," said Grimes. He turned to walk back to the transparent tube in the center of the room that housed the elevator.

"Hold it, Grimes!"

Grimes halted in mid-stride, turned to face Una Freeman. "Yes, Commissioner?"

"I am disposed to be lenient. Not to *you*, Captain, but to Ms. Connellan. I have heard accounts of what actually happened at The Rusty Rocket. She was provoked. You aren't the only male chauvinist pig around, you know. It is unfortunate that she attacked my officers after dealing with those . . . *men* who had been taunting her. Nonetheless she is not a very nice person. I shall be happy if she is removed from this planet.

"Pay her fines to the desk sergeant on your way out and she will be released to your custody. Bear in mind that you will be responsible for her good conduct for the remainder of her stay on this world."

"Thank you," said Grimes.

She laughed harshly and asked, "Will you still thank me after you've been cooped up in a ship with The Green Hornet for a few weeks? Am I doing you a good turn, Grimes? Think that if you want. But I sincerely hope that by the time you get to Earth you'll have changed your tiny mind!"

Grimes stood there silently, looking at her. He remembered how things had been between them before everything had turned sour. He remembered the long weeks in the accommodation dome of that unmanned beacon station, the continual bickerings, the monotonous diet of baked beans, with which delicacy the emergency food stores had been fantastically well stocked.

It was a pity that things had gone so badly wrong. He, for a while at least, had loved her after his fashion. She had reciprocated. But when the beacon tender, making its leisurely rounds, had finally arrived to pick them up they were no longer on speaking terms.

Even so. . . .

"Thank you," he said again.

"For nothing," she growled and then, ignoring him, began to study the papers on her desk.

She ignored his good-bye as he left her.

Chapter 7

The Desk Sergeant must have been given his orders while Grimes was on the way down from the Commissioner's office. There were forms ready for signing. There was a receipt book.

"What have *you* got that other spacers haven't, citizen?" he asked. "But as long as you've got money that's all that really matters. Ha, ha. Now, the fines. . . . Grievous bodily harm to the persons of three police officers at five hundred credits a time. . . . That's fifteen hundred. Replacement of one complete uniform. . . . One hundred and seven credits and fifteen cents. . . . Repairs and dry cleaning to two other uniforms. . . . Twenty-three credits fifty. . . . Medical services to the assaulted officers. . . . One hundred and fifty credits. . . . Riotous behavior, breach of the peace etc. . . . Two hundred and fifty credits. One night's board and lodging in our palatial cells. . . . One hundred and twenty-five credits. Ten percent service charge. . . . Two hundred and fifteen credits and fifty-seven cents. Making a total of two thousand, three hundred and seventy-one credits and twenty-two cents."

"Is there no discount for cash?" asked Grimes sarcastically.

The policeman ignored this.

"A check will be acceptable," he said, "or any of the major credit cards."

Grimes pulled out his checkbook and looked at the stubs. He was one of those people who prefer to keep their own accounts rather than put himself at the mercy of the computers. He was still quite a way from being flat broke. He made out a check for the required amount, signed it and handed it over, was given a receipt in exchange.

"And now, citizen, if you'll sign these. . . ."

These were official forms, and by affixing his autograph to them he made himself entirely responsible for Ms. Connellan during the remainder of her stay on Austral. He would be liable for any debts that she had incurred. He would be liable,

40

too, for any further fines, for the costs of any civil actions brought against her and so on and so on and so on.

Una Freeman was striking a very hard bargain. It was a seller's market.

He signed.

When he straightened up from the desk he turned to see that the Green Hornet, escorted by two policewomen who looked even tougher than herself, had been brought up from the cells. She was not a prepossessing sight. One of her eyes had been blackened. Her green hair was in a tangle. Her clothing was soiled and torn.

She scowled at Grimes.

She said sullenly, "I suppose you're expecting me to thank you. But you're only helping yourself, aren't you? We both know that."

"That's the way of it," said Grimes. "And now we'll get you to the Shipping Office to sign on, and then you'll report straightaway to the chief officer, aboard the ship. He'll find you a job to keep you out of mischief."

"What about my gear?" she demanded. "All my things are still at The Rusty Rocket. I can't join a ship without so much as a toothbrush or change of underwear."

"We'll stop off on the way to the Shipping Office," Grimes told her.

There was a public telephone in this ground-floor office. Grimes used it to order a cab. He said a polite good day to the sergeant and the two female constables then went outside to wait, almost pushing Ms. Connellan ahead of him. He realized that he was afraid that Una Freeman might change her mind and was anxious to remove himself from close proximity to her as soon as possible.

The Green Hornet asked him for a cigarette. He told her that he did not use them. He produced and filled his pipe, lit it. She snarled at him, saying, "It's all right for *you*."

He told her, "Just stand to leeward of me and you'll be getting a free smoke." She snarled at him again, wordlessly.

The cab came. Grimes got in beside the driver so that she could sit in solitary state on the back seat. The ride to The Rusty Rocket was made in silence; the driver, unrepresentative of his breed, was not a conversationalist and Ms. Connellan seemed to be sulking. This suited Grimes, who was in no mood to be ear-bashed.

They arrived at the shabby hostelry, a small, pyramidal building with functionless vanes giving it a faint similitude to an archaic spaceship. Grimes asked the driver to wait for them. He and the Green Hornet went inside.

There were unpleasantries.

Ms. Connellan did not have—or said that she did not have—the money to pay her bill. Grimes had been expecting that. What he had not been expecting was to be presented with another bill, a heavy one, to cover repairs to the replacement of various pieces of equipment and furniture. It was obvious, he was obliged to admit, that the playmaster had had its face smashed in, and recently. On the other hand the thing looked as though it had been on the point of dying of old age when it had been put out of its misery. There were two broken bar stools. There was a dent in the stained surface of the bar. There was a bin of broken bottles which, according to the sour-faced manageress, had been swept off the shelves behind the bar by the berserk Green Hornet.

"Did you do this damage?" asked Grimes exasperatedly.

"I did not!" snapped Ms. Connellan.

"She did!" yelped the manageress. "Like a wild beast she was! Screaming and shouting. . . ."

"I had to scream to make myself heard! I had to fight to defend myself!"

"If there was a fight, *you* started it!"

"I did not!" She turned to Grimes. "Pay no heed to her, Captain. She's lying like a flatfish!"

"Lying, you say, you deceptive bitch! Who's lying, I ask. Not me. And I'm holding on to your bags until I'm paid for all the wanton destruction!"

"You'll let me have my baggage," snarled the Green Hornet, advancing threateningly on the landlady, "or . . ."

"Ladies, ladies," admonished Grimes, interposing himself between them.

"Ladies. . . ." sneered Ms. Connellan. "I'll thank you not to tack that archaic label on to me!"

"She admits it!" jeered the other woman. "She's no lady!"

"Who are *you* calling no lady, you vinegar-pussed harridan? I'll. . . ."

"You will not!" almost shouted Grimes, pushing Ms. Connellan to one side before she could strike the manager. "Now, listen to me! Unless you behave yourself I'll put you in the hands of the police again. The Commissioner's an old friend of mine. . . ." (Well, she had been a friend, and rather more than a friend, once, a long time ago.) "I'll ask her to keep you under lock and key until I'm ready to lift ship. And as for you, madam. . . ."

"Don't talk to me like that, buster. I'm not one of your crew."

"Can I see that bill again, madam?" She thrust the sheet of dirty and crumpled paper at him. "Mphm. I see that you're charging for a *new* playmaster. And that I am not paying. One quarter of the sum you've put down should buy a good second-hand one, one far better than that . . . wreck. The bar stools? I'll let that pass, although I still think that you're overcharging. The dent in the bar? No. That's an old damage, obviously. And now, all these bottles. . . . Were they all *full* bottles? I'll not believe that, madam. I note, too, that you've charged retail price. Don't you buy your liquor at wholesale rates?"

"I'm an honest woman, mister!"

"Tell that to the Police Commissioner," said Grimes. "I've no doubt that she's already well acquainted with your honesty." He began to feed figures into his wrist companion. "One second-hand playmaster. . . . I've seen them going for as low as one hundred credits, quite good ones. . . . Six bottles of Scotch at four credits each wholesale. . . . Twenty-four credits. . . . But as they were almost certainly no more than half full, that makes it twelve credits. . . ." He raised his eyebrows. "Brandy, at twenty-four credits a bottle? Even as a retail price that's steep."

"Either you pay," said the woman stubbornly, "or I call the police."

"Do just that," Grimes told her. "As I've said already, Commissioner Freeman is an old friend of mine."

"Like hell she is. She hates spacers."

"In general, yes. But in particular? Ask yourself why she released Ms. Connellan to my custody, although usually she insists that spacers serve their full sentences, with no fines and no bail."

"All right," said the woman suddenly. "All right. I'll take your word for what you say you owe me. Just don't come back in here again, ever. And tell that green bitch of yours to keep clear of my premises."

"Who are you calling a green bitch, you draggle-tailed slut?" screamed Kate Connellan. "I'll. . . ."

"You will not!" snapped Grimes. "Collect your bags and put them in the cab. And now, madam, if you'll make out a receipt for two hundred and ten credits. . . . That covers the

43

playmaster, the bar stools and a very generous estimate of the cost of liquor lost by breakage."

Check and receipt changed hands.

Grimes went out to the waiting cab in which the Green Hornet, two battered cases on the seat beside her, was sullenly established. He got in beside the driver, told him to carry on to the spaceport.

Chapter 8

The cab brought them into the spaceport, to the foot of *Sister Sue's* ramp.

Grimes was pleased to see that the loading ramps had been set up around his ship, that already streams of crates and cases were being whisked up from the apron to the yawning cargo ports. This was *real* freight, he thought, not the little parcels of luxury goods that he had been carrying in *Little Sister*. He could read the consignee's title stenciled on each package: SURVEY SERVICE RECORDS, PORT WOOMERA.) There had once been a major Survey Service Base on Austral, which had been degraded to a Sub-Base. Finally, only a short while ago, it had been closed down altogether. The transport *Robert A. Heinlein* had lifted off personnel and all the really important stores and equipment. There had been no great hurry for the rest of the stuff, mainly records going back almost to man's first landing on Earth's moon, until the warehouse accommodating the material was required for a factory site.

So perhaps, thought Grimes, this was not real freight after all, except in terms of tonnage. Anybody with any sense would have ordered all that junk destroyed—but the Survey Service, as well he knew, was a breeding ground for planet-based bureaucrats whose dusty files were the temples of whatever odd gods they worshipped.

Nonetheless he had been lucky to get this cargo.

Quite fantastically it had tied in with Magda Granadu's reading of the *I Ching*. She had thrown the coins and constructed a hexagram on the afternoon of the day that Grimes had renamed the ship. *Huan*, it had been. *Dispersion. There will be progress and success. The king visits his ancestral temple. It will be advantageous to cross the great water and to act with firm persistence.* And in the first line there had been the reference to "a strong horse"—and the Epsilon Class tramps had long been known as the sturdy workhorses of the Interstellar Transport Commission.

Yet Grimes had been dubious, at first, about the wisdom of carrying *that* cargo to *those* consignees. He had left the Survey Service under a cloud, had resigned hastily before he could be brought to face a court-martial. But, apart from the obnoxious Delamere's attempt to drag him back to Lindisfarne Base from Botany Bay, there had been no moves made to arrest him, although more than once, as a civilian shipmaster, he had been in contact with Survey Service vessels and personnel.

He had gone to Captain Taberner, Resident Secretary of the Astronauts' Guild on Austral, for advice.

"Not to worry, Captain," that gentleman had told him. "You're one of ours now. We look after our own. You'll get the finest legal defense if—and it's a big 'if'—the Admiralty takes any action against you. We fought an illegal arrest case a few years back—you may have heard about it—when some officious destroyer skipper seized a ship called *Southerly Buster.* Captain Kane's ship. You must have heard about *him.* Anyhow, we won and Drongo Kane was awarded very heavy damages."

So that was that, Grimes thought. If the Guild's legal eagles could save the bacon of an unsavory character like Kane they should be able to do at least as well by him.

He let the Green Hornet board first while he walked around the ship. He told her to report as soon as possible to Mr. Williams.

Finally he climbed the ramp to the after airlock, took the elevator to the No. 3 cargo compartment. Williams was there with a human foreman stevedore who was directing the spidery stowbots. The mate was harassed looking and his slate gray uniform shirt was dark with perspiration. "Tell those bloody tin spiders of yours," he was shouting, "that it's the heavy cases bottom stow and those flimsy crates on top!" He turned to face Grimes. "I had to chase the Green Hornet out of here. Her idea of stowage was big packages under and little packages over, regardless of weight." He switched to a falsetto voice. " 'That's the way that we always did it in the Commission. . . .' " He snorted. "It certainly ain't the way we did it in the Dog Star Line!"

45

"Where is she now?"

"I told her to make a check of the navigational equipment."

Grimes left the mate attending to the stowage, carried on up to Control. There he found Ms. Connellan sulkily tinkering with the mass proximity indicator. She was still dressed as she had been when released from jail.

"Why aren't you in uniform?" he asked.

"What uniform am I supposed to wear?" she countered. "All my trappings are Interstellar Transport Commission."

"Then find out," he told her, "the name of a local uniform tailor. Mr. Williams should know. Get on the telephone and order full sets of uniform trappings for all hands."

"Including you, Captain?"

"Not including me."

Some time in the past Grimes had had his own Far Traveler Couriers insignia made up—the cap badge a stylized rider on a galloping horse, in silver, with two golden comets as the surround; the same horse and rider, but in gold, over the four gold stripes on his epaulets. When he could afford it he would put his people into Far Traveler Couriers uniform but it could wait.

"I suppose you know, sir," said Ms. Connellan, the tone of her voice implying that he didn't, "that the shipowner is responsible for supplying his personnel, at his expense, with uniform trappings."

"I know," said Grimes.

After she left him he began to reassemble the MPI. Luckily she had done no more than to remove the hemispherical cover.

A spacelawyer . . . he thought.

In any astronautical service, naval or mercantile, such are crosses that their commanding officers have to bear.

Chapter 9

Yosarian came to see Grimes shortly before *Sister Sue* was scheduled to lift off. He was carrying a parcel, a gift-wrapped box. Grimes, taking it from him, was surprised at how heavy it was.

"Just a small gift, Captain," said the roboticist. "From myself, and from another . . . friend. I hope that you will like it."

"Thank you, Mr. Yosarian. But the other friend . . . ? Apart from you I don't have any friends on this planet."

The fat man laughed.

"Open the parcel," he said, "and you will see."

Grimes put the package on his desk. The tinsel ribbon around it was tied with a bow that came undone at the first tug. The metallic paper fell away to reveal a box of polished mahogany with brass fittings. The two catches holding down the hinged lid were easy to manipulate. Inside the box was foam plastic packing. Grimes pulled it out carefully, saw the rich gleam of metal, of gold.

He stared at what was revealed. There was a tiny bicycle, perfect in every detail. Seated upon it was one of Yosarian's mechanical dolls, a miniature golden woman, naked and beautiful. He recognized her—or, more correctly, knew whom she represented.

"Una Freeman . . ." he murmured. "Commissioner Freeman."

"As I said, Captain, an old friend of yours. And a friend of mine for quite some years. A charming lady."

"Mphm."

"When I mentioned to her that I was going to give you one of my dolls as a farewell gift she said that she would like it to be from both of us. But I got the impression that the combination of naked lady and bicycle was some sort of private joke."

"At least she didn't ask you to include a golden can of baked beans. That's another private joke."

"But what is the meaning of this?" asked Yosarian. "I was able, easily, to make the lady and her steed to her specifications. But a bicycle . . . ?"

"Miss Freeman and I were working together. It was when she as a member of the Corps of Sky Marshals and while I was in the Survey Service. It's a long story; you must get her to tell it to you some time. But, fantastic as it may sound, the two of us were cast away on an almost desert planet with two bicycles for company. Mphm. Rather *special* bicycles."

"I gathered that."

Carefully Grimes lifted the exquisitely made models from the box, the little woman still sitting on the saddle, her tiny hands grasping the handlebar, her feet on the pedals. He set the toy—or the toys; he did not think that the assemblage

47

was all in one piece—down onto the desk. He let go of it hastily when one foot lifted from the pedal, went down to make contact with the surface on which the bicycle was standing.

"It—she—is attuned to your voice, Captain," said Yosarian. "Tell her to ride around the desk top."

"Ride around the desk top," ordered Grimes dubiously.

The golden foot was back on the golden pedal after giving a backward shove; both feet were on the pedals and the golden legs were working smoothly, up and down, up and down, and the golden filaments that were the wire spokes of the wheels glittered as they turned, slowly at first, and then became a gleaming, transparent blur.

Round the desk she rode, balancing on the very edge of its top, cutting no corners, faster and faster. And then she was actually over the edge with the wheels running on the shallow thickness of the rim, machine and rider no longer vertical to the deck but horizontal.

This was fascinating, but Grimes had to think about getting his ship upstairs in the very near future.

He asked, not taking his eyes from the fascinating golden figurine, "Are there batteries? How is she powered?"

"From any light source, natural or artificial."

"How do I stop her?"

"Just tell her, Captain."

Grimes restrained himself from saying Stop, realizing that if he did so the golden toy might fall to the desk, damaging itself.

"Back onto the desk top," he said. (Sometime, he thought, he must make a slow motion recording of that graceful gymnastic maneuvering.) "Back into the box." (The bicycle ran up the vertical side of the container with ease, hovered briefly in the air before plunging downward.) "Stop."

"You're getting the hang of it, Captain," said Yosarian.

"All I can say," said Grimes, "is thank you. Thank you very much."

"You should also thank Commissioner Freeman. The nature of the gift was her idea—and she was the model for part of it."

"Then thank her for me, please."

"I will do so." Yosarian got up from the chair on which he had been sitting. "And now I must go. There is still work for me to do aboard *my* ship." He extended his hand. Grimes shook it. "Bon voyage, Captain. And good fortune. Oh, I

48

have a message from the Commissioner. She told me to tell you that bicycles aren't always what they seem, and to remember that." Something seemed to be amusing him. "Bon voyage," he said again, and left.

Grimes pottered about his day cabin, making sure that all was secure. He lifted the box containing Yosarian's—and Una's—farewell gift down from the desk, stowed it in his big filing cabinet. (There was room for it; the ship, under her new ownership, had yet to accumulate stacks of incoming correspondence and copies of outgoing communications.) He made sure that the solidograph of Maggie Lazenby was secure on the shelf on which he had placed it while he was settling in. He would have to find a suitable site for Una and her bicycle, he thought; it would be a crime to leave her to languish unseen in the box. He remembered another gift from another woman, the miniature simulacrum of Susie. He remembered, too, the troubles that it had brought him. But the mini-Una, he told himself, for all her motility would be no more dangerous than the image of Maggie.

His telephone buzzed. The fleshy face of Williams appeared on the screen.

"Mate here, Skipper. Mr. Yosarian's ashore now. I'm sealing the ship."

"Thank you, Mr. Williams."

"And Aerospace Control confirms that we're all set for lift-off at 1400 hours."

Grimes looked at the bulkhead clock. The time was 1350. He left his quarters and went up to the control room.

Chapter 10

Sister Sue lifed from Port Southern.

It was not, of course, the first time that Grimes had handled her; he had brought her down from the parking orbit to the spaceport. This, however, was his first lift-off in the ship. He could not help thinking that she appreciated his touch on the controls—and inwardly laughed at his subscription to the pathetic fallacy. But he persisted in his imaginings. *Little Sister* had been little more than a girl, eagerly responsive to his lightest caress. *Sister Sue* was a woman, no longer

49

young, an experienced woman. She required—demanded, even—a heavier hand.

She lifted steadily, accelerating smoothly. Below her the glittering city dwindled and the horizon began to display curvature. Up through filmy upper clouds she drove, up through the last, tenuous shreds of atmosphere, into the blackness and the hard vacuum of space.

Soon it was time to set trajectory for the interstellar voyage. Grimes cut the inertial drive, then used the directional gyroscopes to swing the vessel about her axes. He brought the bright star that was Sol directly ahead, then made the small correction for galactic drift. He started the inertial drive.

The temporal precession field built up.

As always there was disorientation, visually and aurally, while colors sagged down the spectrum and perspective was distorted. As sometimes, although not always, happened there was prevision, a consequence of the warping of the fabric of space and time.

Grimes stared at what, at first glance, had seemed to be his reflection on the inner surface of one of the viewports. With a shock he realized that it was the image of a much older man than himself that was staring back at him. There were the same prominent ears, there was a foul-looking pipe clamped between the teeth. (The here-and-now Grimes' pipe was still in his pocket.) The apparition was gray-haired. He was, like Grimes, in uniform but the gold braid on his shoulderboards was a single broad stripe, not four narrow ones. Above it was a winged wheel device, not the Far Traveler stylized courier. Somehow the name of the ship was in the background but the letters were wavering, squirming as though alive, dissolving, reforming. They stabilized and no longer spelled *Sister Sue* but *Faraway Quest*. . . . And was that Williams there beside this other—this future—Grimes? An older Williams, just as it was an older Grimes in the reflection.

Then, the field established and holding, things snapped back to normal—or as normal as they ever could be in a ship running under interstellar drive. The pseudo reflections vanished. Outside the control room the warped continuum now presented an uncanny, even to a seasoned spaceman, aspect with every star no longer a sharp point of light but a writhing, coruscating spiral nebula, slowly but visibly drifting across the field of vision.

Grimes looked at Williams. Williams looked at him. There was mutual acknowledgment that their futures were somehow interlinked. Then Williams looked at the Green Hornet, slumped and sulky in her chair. He grinned at Grimes as though to say, *Whatever happens, whatever is going to happen, we won't be saddled with* her, *Skipper*.

With slow deliberation Grimes filled and lit his pipe. He said, "Deep space routine, Mr. Williams." He turned to the girl and told her, "You have the first watch, Ms. Connellan."

"I still haven't had time to unpack properly. Sir."

"That will have to wait until you come off duty. The chief officer has been watch on and stay on ever since we opened Articles."

She glowered at him but said nothing. Grimes wondered if, should he log and fine her for the crime of dumb insolence, he could make it stick. He looked back at her coldly, then released himself from his chair and walked to the hatch leading down to the axial shaft. Williams followed him.

"A stiff drink before you get your head down, Number One?" asked Grimes.

"Thank, Skipper. I could use one."

Grimes led the way into his quarters. He went to the liquor cabinet. Williams asked for beer. Grimes mixed himself a pink gin. Seated, the two men faced each other across the coffee table.

The mate raised his condensation-bedewed can in salutation. "Here's to a long and prosperous association, Skipper."

"I'll drink to that, Mr. Williams. Oh, by the way, when the time-twister was warming up did *you* see anything?"

Williams laughed. "I saw myself as a frosty-faced old bastard—and you even frostier faced! I've had these glimpses of the future before and, just between ourselves, they're more reliable than Magda's *I Ching!*"

"On one occasion," Grimes told him, "I was treated to the prevision of a naked lady riding a bicycle. . . ."

"I doubt if *that* came true, Skipper!" laughed Williams.

"But it did. By the time it was all over I was allergic to both the wench and her velocipede!"

He got up, went to the filing cabinet and brought out the mahogany box. He opened it, lifted out the beautiful . . . toy, set it down on the deck. "Ride around the cabin," he ordered. "Slowly."

Williams stared as the naked cyclist made her leisurely rounds.

"Where did you get that, Skipper? One of Yosarian's specials, isn't it?"

"Yes," said Grimes. "A parting gift. From him, and. . . ."

51

"And?" Williams bent down in his chair to look more closely at the tiny, golden cyclist as she glided past him. "And? Surely not! Isn't that our beloved Police Commissioner?" He laughed. "But she is a friend of Yosarian's. And I know that she was a Sky Marshal before she settled down on Austral. Don't tell me, Skipper, that she was the lady in your, er, vision!"

Grimes allowed himself a small grin.

"Gentlemen don't tell," he said.

"Come off it, Skipper! We aren't in the wardroom of a Survey Service warship; this is a merchant ship. Religion, politics and sex are quite permissible topics of conversation. In any case it's highly unlikely that any of us will ever be seeing Commissioner Freeman again—and thank the Odd Gods of the Galaxy for that!"

"All right," said Grimes. "I met Sky Marshal Freeman, as she was then, when she was supposed to be taking possession of the pirated, then abandoned *Delta Geminorum*. You may recall the case. The ship was just wandering around, going nowhere in particular, with her Mannschenn Drive in operation. Ms. Freeman called upon the Survey Service for assistance. I was between ships at the time and was put in charge of the prize crew. We—Ms. Freeman, the people in the prize crew and myself—went out in the Lizard Class courier *Skink* to intercept the derelict. We found her and synchronized temporal precession rates. It was arranged that Ms. Freeman and I would be the first to board her; we left *Skink* in a Class A boat, practically a spaceship in miniature, complete with mini-Mannschenn, Carlotti radio, life-support system and all the rest of it. As far as we could work things out afterward there was some sort of interaction between the temporal precession fields of the ship, *Delta Geminorum*, and the boat as we made a close approach. This caused the detonation of the bomb which the pirates had left as a booby trap. It was a thermonuclear device. We were as near as dammit at ground zero—and, as I've said, there was this interaction between temporal precession fields.

"We weren't killed. . . ."

"That's obvious, Skipper!"

"It wasn't at the time. Not to *Skink*'s captain and his crew, and to my prize crew, who were still aboard his ship. They all thought that Sky Marshal Una Freeman and Lieutenant Commander John Grimes had been well and truly vaporized, together with the boat and the derelict. It was so reported. Of course I was able to report differently some time later, after our return to this universe."

"I've heard all these stories about alternate universes," said Williams, "but I've never quite believed them. Oh, there were a few odd stories about *Delta Geminorum* and Ms. Freeman and yourself—but most people thought that they were some sort of Survey Service smokescreen, covering up something with serious political implications, or. . . . When Ms. Freeman first came to Austral—with her Corps of Sky Marshals background she started in the police force with senior inspector's rank—a few of the local rags and stations tried to interview her. All that she'd say about the *Delta Geminorum* affair was that it was classified. I hope that you won't say the same."

"I'm a civilian shipmaster now," said Grimes. "I don't even hold a reserve commission. But if I tell you, keep it to yourself, will you?

"We were flung, somehow, into a more or less parallel universe. There had been a galaxy-wide war, resulting in the destruction of all organic life. Life, of a sort, had survived—the intelligent machines. The ruling entity, regarded as a god and with godlike powers, wanted to give his late creators, the human race, a fresh start. (Not that they'd been human, as we understand the term. They'd been more like centaurs.) Una—Ms. Freeman—and I were captured. We were set down in an oasis on an otherwise desert planet. There were plants, animals. There was water and a wide variety of edible fruits and nuts. The implication was that we were to become the Adam and Eve of the new race. Una wasn't all that keen on the idea—and neither was I. After her last contraceptive shot wore off we were very, very careful.

"There were guardian angels in this Garden of Eden—although we didn't realize that they were until they tried to force us to do the bidding of the robot god. . . ."

"What form did they take, Skipper?"

"Bicycles," said Grimes.

Williams' eyes followed the little golden Una as she rode around the day cabin on her graceful golden steed. He laughed.

"So she has a sense of humor! The only time that I met her personally I thought that she was humorless. But what happened in the end?"

"I don't like uppity robots," said Grimes. "I never have. After we discovered the true nature of those bicycles I . . . disposed of them. It wasn't all that easy. If you've ever been

53

a cyclist you'll know that even an ordinary bicycle can be quite vicious at times. The robot god made his appearance. He'd decided that we were not fit and proper persons to be the parents of the new race. He banished us from the garden. He slung us back into our own universe. Luckily he had us put back in the boat first.

"We found ourselves in orbit around a world—Tamsin IV, as a matter of fact—with one of those unmanned beacon stations. I tried to convert the beacon into a transmitter so that I could send a call for help. Frankly, I rather buggered it up. So we had to wait until the beacon tender dropped by on its normal rounds. The station had emergency stores, luckily. Unluckily there wasn't much variety. Can you imagine a steady diet of baked beans in tomato sauce for seven weeks?"

"What was wrong with honeymoon salad, Skipper?" asked Williams. "Just lettuce alone, with no dressing."

"The honeymoon was over, Mr. Williams, before we were expelled from the garden. Conditions weren't right for its resumption."

"From what I've seen of Commissioner Freeman," said Williams, "I'm surprised that conditions were ever right." He looked again at the unwearying golden cyclist. "But, to judge by that, she doesn't look too bad out of uniform."

Chapter 11

The voyage from Austral to Earth was a relatively short one—long enough, however, for Grimes to get the feel of his ship and to make an assessment of his crew. The ship he liked. He knew that during her service under the Commission's flag she had been regarded as a notoriously awkward bitch; he did not find her so. Perhaps the change of ownership had sweetened her nature. Already—at least insofar as Grimes was concerned—she was as comfortable as an old shoe.

Regarding his personnel he was not so happy. Only the mate, Billy Williams, and the Catering Officer, Magda Granadu met with Grimes' almost unqualified approval although he was developing a liking for a few of the others.

One day he amused himself by making out a Voyage Staff

Report. Had he been still in the Survey Service this would have been required of him, as it would have been had he been in command of a vessel owned by any of the major shipping lines. As owner/master he could report only to himself.

Williams, William, he wrote. *Chief Officer. A very good second in command. A tendency to be overzealous. Competent spaceman and navigator. Pleasant personality.*

He filled and lit his pipe, cogitated on what he had written. If this were a real report he would have no hesitation in signing it and sending it in.

He resumed writing. *Connellan, Kate. Second Officer. A typical Donegalan female chauvinist bitch. Carries a perpetual chip on her shoulder. Is perpetually complaining about the ship, her shipmates, the meals, etc., etc. and etc. Barely competent as spaceperson and navigator.*

And that, he thought, would be letting her off lightly. If Billy Williams or Magda Granadu were called upon to make a report on her their words would scorch the paper. At every change of watch she would annoy the Chief Officer with her complaints and comparisons. "In the Commission's ships we used to get so-and-so and such-and-such. In the Commission's ships we used to do it *this* way. . . ." The Catering Officer had tried her best to please everybody, but the Green Hornet could not—would not—be pleased. There was no Donegalan whisky in the bar stores. Donegalan national dishes never appeared on the menu. (Among the edible vegetables grown on the farm deck were no potatoes.) She was allergic to paprika. Sour cream made her come out in spots.

But there would be no need to put up with her any longer once *Sister Sue* got to Port Woomera. There should be no trouble in filling any vacancies on Earth.

Stewart, Andrew. Radio Officer. Conscientious and competent. Has no interests outside his profession.

Just an old-time Sparks, thought Grimes, and none the worse for that.

Crumley, Horace. Chief Engineer, Reaction and Inertial Drives. Another old-timer. Extremely conscientious.

And as boring as all hell, thought Grimes. All his conversation is along "when I was in the old so-and-so" lines.

Denning, Fred. Second Engineer. A refugee from a bicycle shop but reliable. Not, unfortunately, officer material.

Snobbish bastard! he admonished himself.

Singh, Govind. Third Engineer. A refugee from the Port

55

Southern Monorail. Would be happier aboard a train than a spaceship—and, possibly, a little more useful.

Mr. Singh had endeared himself to Grimes by fixing the playmaster in the captain's day cabin; after his ministrations the thing would present a picture only in black and white with sound no louder than a whisper. Fortunately old Mr. Stewart had been able to get the thing working properly.

Paulus, Ludwig. Fourth Engineer. Another refugee from the Port Southern Monorail. Has not yet been given the opportunity to demonstrate his incompetence but when the times comes will not be found lacking.

Come, come, Grimes, he thought reprovingly. Your innies are working, aren't they, and working well. So are the life-support systems. Just because people haven't been through the Academy and learned which knives and forks to use at table and how to wear a uniform properly it doesn't mean that they're no good as spacemen.

Malleson, Phillip. Chief Engineer, Mannschenn Drive. Very much the academic but he knows his job. Good conversationalist. . . .

But he's being paid to run the time-twister, isn't he, not to be the life and soul of the party. Still, it always helps when an officer is a good shipmate as well as being highly efficient.

Federation Survey Service, then Trans-Galactic Clippers. A typical big ship engineer of the better kind.

Watch that snobbery, Grimes!

Trantor, George. Second Engineer, Mannschenn Drive. And Ph.D., and makes sure that everybody knows it. As snobbish in his way as I am in mine. Must know his job, otherwise Malleson wouldn't tolerate him.

Giddings, Walter. Third Engineer, Mannschenn Drive. Another Ph.D. Like Mr. Trantor tends to hold himself aloof from the low, common spacemen.

Granadu, Magda. Catering Officer/Purser/Acting Bio-Chemist. An extremely capable person and a good shipmate. An inspired touch with the autochef. Farm deck always in perfect order. Works well with members of other departments—as, for example, with the engineers in necessary maintenance of LSS. Very popular with almost every member of the crew. I have no doubt that if this vessel becomes known as a happy ship she will be largely responsible.

Somebody was knocking at his door.

"Come in," he called.

It was the Green Hornet.

56

"Yes, Ms. Connellan?" asked Grimes, trying to hide his distaste.

"Sir. It is bad enough having to keep watch and watch. But when I am not being fed properly the situation becomes intolerable!"

Grimes looked at her. The sealseam at the front of her uniform shirt was under great strain. So was the waistband of her shorts. And it was obvious that she had not been feeding herself properly; there was a splash of half-dried sauce over her left breast and another on the right leg of her lower garment.

"Lunch," he said, "was very good."

"All right for people who like mucked up food with the real flavor disguised by garlic and pepper!"

"There is always choice, Ms. Connellan."

"What choice, sir? I've raised the point with Ms. Granadu, our so-called Catering Officer, time and time again."

"There was a perfectly good steak, to order, with French fried potatoes."

"French fried potatoes my a . . ." She caught herself just in time, finished the sentence with "foot." "Potatoes reconstituted from some sort of flour, molded into shape and then fried. But not *potatoes*. On New Donegal we know our potatoes. I'll say this for the Commission—in their ships you get real potatoes!"

"Your last ship was *Delta Crucis*, wasn't she?" asked Grimes.

"Yes. What of it?"

"A cargo-passenger liner, Ms. Connellan. You get luxuries aboard passenger ships that you don't get in Epsilon Class tramps. You have a bio-chemist on the Articles who is practically a full-time gardener, who can amuse himself by growing all sorts of things in the hydroponics tanks. Here, Ms. Granadu has plenty to occupy her time without bothering about things that are hard to grow in aboard-ship conditions."

"You could have carried a few kilos of potatoes in the stores."

"Storeroom space is limited, Ms. Connellan."

"Everything in this bloody ship is limited. I should have had my head examined before I signed on here."

"I shall be happy to release you as soon as we get to Port Woomera," said Grimes coldly.

"Oh, will you, sir? Isn't that just typical. You use me, exploit me, and then you cast me aside like a worn-out glove."

57

"If it hadn't been for me," Grimes told her, "you'd still be in the Port Southern jail."

"And probably feeding a damn sight better than I am here."

"Ms. Connellan, you have made your complaint. I have listened to it. You are the only person aboard this ship who has found fault with the food. You are at liberty to make further complaints—to the Guild, to the Shipping Master, to whoever will listen to you—after we get to Port Woomera.

"That is all."

"But. . . ."

"That is all!" snarled Grimes.

She glared at him, turned sharply about and flounced out of his day cabin. Looking at her fat buttocks straining the material of her shorts almost to bursting Grimes thought that it was exercise she needed rather than more starch in her diet. If *Sister Sue* were a warship he would be able to order people to have a daily workout in the gymnasium. But *Sister Sue* was a merchantman and the powers of her captain, although considerable, were only a civilian shipmaster's powers.

Chapter 12

Sister Sue came to Port Woomera.

Grimes stared into the stern view screen, looking at what once had been a familiar view, the waters of the Great Australian Bight to the south and to the north the semi-desert, crisscrossed with irrigation canals, with huge squares of oddly glittering gray that were the solar energy collection screens, with here and there the assemblages of gleaming white domes that housed people and machinery and the all-the-year-round-producing orchards. Close inshore, confined in its pen of plastic sheeting, was a much diminished iceberg. Farther out to sea a much larger one, a small fleet of tugs in attendance, was slowly coming in toward what would be its last resting place.

Grimes applied lateral thrust to bring the ship directly above the spaceport. He could see clearly the white buildings, assemblages of bubbles, and the lofty control tower. And

58

there were the smaller towers, metallically gleaming, that were the ships, great and small.

His berth had been allocated. He was to bring *Sister Sue* down to the Naval Station, about five kilometers to the east of the commercial spaceport. He could identify a Constellation Class cruiser, a couple of Star Class destroyers and what he thought was a Serpent Class courier. *Adder?* he wondered. That little ship had been his first command. But he doubted if the long arm of coincidence would be stretched to such an extent. It was extremely unlikely that there would be any ships or any people whom he had known, during his days in the Survey Service, at Port Woomera. He had never been attached to the Port Woomera Base.

The triangle of brightly flashing beacons marking his berth was clearly visible. It showed a tendency to drift away from the center of the screen. Grimes put on lateral thrust again to counteract the effect of the light breeze, decreased vertical thrust. On the screen the figures of the radar-altimeter display steadily diminished.

He allowed his attention to wander briefly, looked to the towers of Woomera City in the middle distance. He watched one of the big dirigibles of Trans-Australia Airlines coming into its mooring mast at the airfield at the city limits. Soon, he thought, he would be aboard one of those airships. His parents, in Alice Springs, would be looking forward to seeing him again after his long absence from Earth.

Looking back to the radar altimeter read-out he stepped up vertical thrust. *Sister Sue* was not a Federation Survey Service courier, or a deep-space pinnace like *Little Sister*, in which a flashy landing would be relatively safe. It wouldn't do for a ship of this tonnage to drop like a stone and then slam on thrust at the very last moment. Nonetheless, he thought, she would be able to take it. She was a sturdy enough brute.

One hundred meters to go. . . .

Ninety-five. . . . Ninety. . . .

Slight drift, thought Grimes. *Lateral thrust again.* . . .

He turned to look at his officers. Williams, he noted, was watching him approvingly. The Green Hornet hastily wiped a sneer from her face. Without his being a telepath Grimes knew what she was thinking, *Anybody would think that the bloody ship was made of glass!*

To hell with you, he thought. *I won't have to put up with you for much longer.*

Deliberately he took his time over the final stages of the descent.

At last *Sister Sue's* stern vanes made gentle, very gentle contact with the apron. She rocked ever so slightly, then was still. Shock absorbers sighed as they took the weight when the inertial drive was shut down.

"Finished with engines," said Grimes smugly. He pulled his pipe from a pocket, filled it and lit it.

"Finished with engines, Skipper," repeated Williams and passed this final order on to the inertial-drive room. Then, "Shall I go down to the airlock to receive the boarding party? I see them on the way out."

"Do that," said Grimes.

Through a viewport he watched the ground cars scurrying out across the apron. Customs, he supposed, and Port Health and Immigration. One of them, however, was a gray vehicle looking like a minor warship on wheels—probably the Survey Service officer responsible for arranging for the discharge of *Sister Sue's* cargo. But what was that broad pennant fluttering from a short mast on the bonnet of the car? He got up from his seat, swung the big mounted binoculars to bear.

A black flag, with two golden stars. . . .

Surely, he told himself, a Rear Admiral would not be concerning himself with the offloading of an unimportant consignment of outdated bumf.

Was the Survey Service still after his blood?

But if they were going to arrest him, he thought, they would have sent a squad of Marines, not a flag officer.

Nonetheless there was cause for worry. In his experience Admirals did not personally welcome minor vessels, minor merchant vessels especially.

He went down to his quarters to change hastily into the least shabby of his uniforms and to await developments. As he left the control room he heard Ms. Connellan singing softly to herself—and at him.

"Sheriff and police a-coming after me. . . ."

Bitch! he thought.

Chapter 13

"So we meet again, Grimes," said Rear Admiral Damien.

"This is a surprise, sir," Grimes said. Then, "Congratulations on your promotion."

Damien laughed. "Once I no longer had *you* to worry about, once I wasn't always having to justify your actions to my superiors, I got my step up."

Grimes waited until his guest was seated then took a chair himself. He looked at Damien, not without some apprehension. Apart from the extra gold braid on his sleeves his visitor looked just as he had when he was Commodore Damien, Officer Commanding Couriers, on Lindisfarne Base. He was as thin as ever, his face little more than a skull over which yellow skin was tightly stretched. He still had the mannerism of putting his skeletal fingers together, making a steeple of them over which he regarded whomever it was he was addressing. So he was now looking at Grimes, just as he had so often looked at him in the past when Grimes, a lowly lieutenant, had been captain of the Serpent Class courier *Adder*. On such occasions he had either been taking Grimes to task for some misdeed or sending him out on some especially awkward mission.

"Coffee, sir?" asked Grimes.

"Thank you, er, Captain."

Grimes called Magda on the telephone. Almost at once she was bringing in the tray with the fragrantly steaming pot, the cream, the sugar and the mugs. She looked at Damien curiously, then at Grimes.

She asked, "Will that be all, sir?"

"Yes, thank you, Magda."

She made a reluctant departure. Probably everybody aboard *Sister Sue* would be wondering why an Admiral had come to visit Grimes, would be expecting her to have the answers.

Grimes poured. He took both sugar and cream in his mug. Damien wanted his coffee black and unsweetened.

He said, "I suppose you're wondering, just as your Catering Officer was wondering, what I'm doing aboard your ship."

"I am, sir."

"It all ties in with my new job, Grimes. My official title is Coordinator of Merchant Shipping. When I learned that a star tramp called *Sister Sue*, commanded by John Grimes, was due in I was naturally curious. I made inquiries and was pleased to learn that *Sister Sue's* master was, indeed, *the* John Grimes."

"You flatter me, sir."

"Nonetheless, Grimes, this is not altogether a social call. No, I haven't come to place you under arrest. Or not yet, anyhow. There were, of course, very extensive inquiries into the *Discovery* mutiny and you were more or less cleared of culpability. More or less. There are still, however, those in high places who would like your guts for garters."

"Mphm."

"Cheer up, Grimes. I haven't come to shoot you." He sipped. "Excellent coffee, this, by the way. But you always were notorious for your love of life's little luxuries." He extended his mug for a refill. "I suppose that this ship keeps quite a good table."

"I like it, sir."

"I must invite myself to lunch some day. But this morning we will talk business."

"Business, sir?"

"What else? You're not only a merchant captain, you're a shipowner. You're the one who has to arrange future employment for your ship, yourself and your crew."

"That thought had flickered across my mind, sir. Perhaps you could advise me. It is some many years since I was last on Earth."

"I've found you jobs in the past, Grimes. Whenever there was something too out of the ordinary for the other courier captains you were the one who got it. Now, I'll be frank with you. As Coordinator of Merchant Shipping I work very closely with Intelligence. And Intelligence doesn't consist only of finding out what's happening. Sometimes it's making things happen. Do you get me, Grimes?"

"Dirty Tricks, sir?"

"You can put it that way. Also countering other people's dirty tricks. You know El Dorado, don't you?"

"I was there once, sir, when I was a junior officer in *Aries*. And for a while I was yachtmaster to the Baroness Michelle d'Estang, one of the El Doradan aristocracy."

"And you know her husband, Commodore Baron Kane."

"He's hardly a friend, sir."

62

"But you know him. Well, I want *you* on El Dorado. There's a shipment of luxury goods to be carried there; wines, caviar, fancy cheeses and such. Normally one of the Commission's ships would be employed—but, as requested by the Admiralty, the Commission will not have a vessel available. So they will have to charter something. And that something will be your *Sister Sue*. Who *was* Sue, by the way?"

"Just a girl. . . ."

"The young lady on the bicycle exchanging glares with our Commander Lazenby?" Damien got up from his chair to look at, first of all, the solidograph of Maggie, then at the golden statuette of Una Freeman. "H'm. I seem to have seen that face before somewhere. . . . On Lindisfarne Base, wasn't it? That Sky Marshal wench you were supposed to be working with. But, unless my memory is playing tricks, her name wasn't Susan. . . ."

"It wasn't," said Grimes. "It still isn't."

"Of course, you've seen her recently. . . ."

(Was that a statement or a question?)

"She's the Port Southern Police Commissioner," said Grimes.

Damien seemed to lose interest in Grimes' art gallery, returned to his chair.

"Now, Grimes, this charter. . . ."

"What's the catch, sir?" asked Grimes. "I somehow can't believe that anybody in the Admiralty loves me enough to throw lucrative employment my way."

"How right you are, Grimes. You'll have to work your passage. To begin with, you will be reenlisted into the Survey Service—on the Reserve List, of course, but with your old rank. Commander."

And when I'm back in the Service, thought Grimes, *they'll have me by the balls*.

He said, "No thank you, sir. I'm a civilian and I like being a civilian. I intend to stay that way."

"Even though you have civilian status, Grimes, you can still be compelled to face a court-martial over the *Discovery* affair."

"I thought you said that it had been swept under the carpet, sir."

"Carpets can be lifted. Quite a number of my colleagues would rather like to lift that one."

"I'm a member of the Astronauts' Guild, sir. They've tangled with the Survey Service more than once in defense of their people—and usually won."

63

"They probably would in your case, Grimes—but you must know that the legal profession doesn't know the meaning of the word 'hurry.' While the lawyers were arguing your ship would be sitting here, idle, with port dues and the like steadily mounting, with your officers wanting their three square meals a day and their salaries. It'd break you, Grimes, and you know it."

Damien was right, Grimes knew.

He said, "All right. But if I do join the Reserve I'd like a higher rank, with the pay and allowances appertaining while on active duty."

Damien laughed. "Always the opportunist, Grimes! But there's no such animal as a Reserve Admiral and you'll find Reserve Commodores only in the major shipping lines." He laughed again. "Far Traveler Couriers can hardly be classed as such."

"Captain will do," said Grimes magnaminously. "But what exactly do you want me for, sir? How does it tie in with that charter to El Dorado?"

"I can't tell you that until you're officially back in the Service." Damien got slowly to his feet like a carpenter's rule unfolding. "But I'll not rush you. I'll give you until tomorrow morning to make your mind up. Don't bother to come with me, Grimes. I can find my own way down to the airlock."

As soon as he was gone Grimes rang for Magda Granadu. "And bring the coins and the book with you," he said.

Head and two tails . . . Yin. And again, and again, and again, and again, and again . . . K'un.

"The superior man," said Magda, "faithfully serves those who can best use his talents. There will be advantage in finding friends in the south and west, and in losing friends in the north and east. In quiet persistence lies good fortune. . . ."

"But I've already found friends in the south," said Grimes. "On Austral, at Port Southern. Yosarian. You and Billy Williams. Even Una Freeman. But where does the west come into it?"

"There are still southerly aspects to consider. Woomera, where we are now, is in Earth's southern hemisphere. And perhaps we should take initial letters into consideration. 'S' for south, 'W' for west. 'S' for Survey Service. 'W' for Woomera."

"Mphm? But finding friends here? Commodore Damien was never a friend of mine."

But wasn't he? Grimes asked himself. *Wasn't he?* Time and time again, during his captaincy of *Adder*, the little Serpent Class courier, Grimes had gotten away with murder, now and again almost literally. Damien, then Officer Commanding Couriers, must have stood up for him against those Admirals who wanted to make an example of the troublesome young officer.

"I think," Magda said, "that the Rear Admiral *is* a friend of yours. He looked into my office for a brief chat on his way ashore. He said, in these very words, 'You've a good captain here. Look after him.'"

"Mphm. Well, he's not such a bad old bastard himself. But we still have that prophecy about losing friends in the north and east. El Dorado is to the galactic north. And its name starts with an 'E'. . . ."

"And do you have friends on El Dorado, Captain?" she asked.

"Well, I did. The old Duchess of Leckhampton. . . . I wonder if she's still alive. And the Princess Marlene. . . . And the Baroness Michelle d'Estang. . . . All friends, I suppose. . . ."

She read again from the book. "The superior man finds a true master and chooses his friends among those whose natures are compatible with his own."

Grimes snorted. "There's one person aboard this ship whose nature is not compatible! The Green Hornet. I'd like you to get her pay made up so that I can get rid of her. There should be no shortage of qualified officers here, on Earth."

"On what grounds will you discharge her, Captain?"

"Just that her face doesn't fit."

She frowned thoughtfully. "I'm afraid that you'll not be able to make it stick. Hasn't Billy told you about the Guild on this world? It's just a junior officers' trade union. When I was late here, in *Borzoi*, the Old Man tried to get rid of the third mate, one of those really obnoxious puppies you get stuck with at times. He paid him off—and then the little bastard ran screaming to the Guild. The Guild not only refused to supply a replacement but brought a suit for wrongful dismissal. And slapped an injunction on us so that we couldn't lift until the case had been heard. Captain Brownlee didn't improve matters by saying, in court, just what he thought about the legal profession. It did not prejudice the judge in his favor. So he lost the case and we had to take the third mate back. The Dog Star Line was far from happy, of course. Their ship had been grounded for weeks. The captain

65

showed me the Carlottigram he got from Top Office. It was a long one, but one sentence sticks in my memory. 'We judge our Masters not by their navigation or spacemanship but by the skill with which they walk the industrial tightrope.' "

"And what happened to Captain Brownlee?" asked Grimes.

"Transferred to a scruffy little ship on one of the Dog Star Line's more unpleasant trades."

"At least," said Grimes, "I don't have any owners to worry about."

"But you have an owner's worries, Captain. You can't afford to be grounded by legal hassles when you should be flitting around the galaxy earning an honest living."

"That's true. But are you sure that Ms. Connellan will scream to the Guild if I try to pay her off?"

"She's already screamed."

"Oh. I'd have thought, to judge from the way that she's been complaining, that she'd be glad to see the last of us."

"She's not altogether a fool," said Magda. "She knows that she's virtually unemployable. She's got a job and she means to hang on to it."

Chapter 14

By the time *Sister Sue* was linked up to the Port Woomera telephone system. Grimes' intention had been to ring his parents in Alice Springs as soon as possible but, after his conversation with Magda, decided first of all to have things out with the Guild.

He got through to the local secretary, in Woomera City, without trouble. The face looking out at him from the screen was not a young one and at first Grimes hoped that he would be given a sympathetic hearing.

He said, without preamble, "I'd like to get rid of my second mate, Captain Davis."

"Ms. Connellan has already talked with me, Captain Grimes, and I must say that her complaints of sexual and racial discrimination seem quite valid."

"I'm not practicing discrimination. I just want her out of my ship."

"Then I must warn you, Captain Grimes, that the Guild will give full support to Ms. Connellan."

"I'm a Guild member too. Shouldn't you be looking after *my* interests?"

Davis smiled sadly. "You must realize, Captain, that shipmasters comprise less than twenty-five percent of Guild membership. Junior officers are in the majority. You might say that I am their employee. There is another point. You are a shipowner as well as being a shipmaster. As far as the majority of our members are concerned, shipowners are the natural enemies of all good spacemen. . . ."

"Ms. Connellan is not a good spaceman," growled Grimes. "She is a bad spacewoman."

"Perhaps, perhaps. But I've only your word for that, Captain."

"My chief officer will bear me out. And my catering officer. And my radio officer. And my senior engineers."

"Among whom only the chief officer is a Guild member."

"So you're not prepared to help me, Captain Davis?"

"I have heard Ms. Connellan's story. You were happy enough to engage her in Port Southern when you desperately needed an officer."

"That was then," growled Grimes. "This is now."

"As you say, Captain Grimes, this is *now*. You are no longer in Survey Service with godlike powers over your crew."

Grimes snorted. Any Survey Service captain who tried to come the heavy deity would very soon be smacked down to size by the real gods—not only the admirals but the bureaucrats and the politicians.

He asked, "Were you ever in the Service yourself, Captain Davis?"

"No."

"I thought not," said Grimes. "If you had been you wouldn't be talking such a load of crap."

That ended the call—and, no matter what the *I Ching* had told him, this was one friend that he had not found in the south and west.

He smoked a pipe and then put a call through to Alice Springs. His mother and father were pleased to hear his voice and see his face again—although not as overjoyed as he thought that they should have been. But they had their own interests, he thought, and he had long since ceased to be one of them.

"When are you coming out?" his father asked.

"As soon as I've got various pieces of business tidied up here. Things, quite suddenly, seem to have become a little complicated."

Grimes senior laughed. "I've always thought that you were a sort of catalyst. Things happen around you. But come as soon as you can."

"I will," promised Grimes.

His mother's face replaced that of his father on the screen. She had changed very little; slim, rather horse-faced women keep their looks far more successfully than do their more conventionally pretty sisters. She reminded him, fleetingly, of Shirl and Darleen. . . . (But surely she had no kangaroos in *her* ancestry. . . .)

"We'll be waiting for you, John," she said. "I'll see to it that we have a good stock of gin and a bottle of Angostura bitters."

"And ice," he said.

"And ice. Don't keep us waiting too long—otherwise the ice will melt."

"Or I'll drink all the gin," said his father, back on the screen.

"I'll have to hang up now," Grimes said. "I've things to see to. Look after yourselves."

"Listen to who's talking," his mother said.

Chapter 15

The next morning discharge of *Sister Sue's* cargo commenced under the supervision, from the shore end, of a bored Lieutenant Commander (S) and, aboard the ship, an increasingly exasperated Billy Williams.

"Damn it all, Skipper," he complained to Grimes, "did you ever see such a shower of nongs? Stowbots that Noah must have used to load the fodder for the animals aboard the Ark and brassbound petty officers running them who wouldn't be capable of navigating a wheelbarrow across a cow paddock! I'm not surprised that you resigned from the Survey Service if this is a fair sampling of their personnel!"

"That will do, Mr. Williams," said Grimes coldly.

He looked out from the cargo port and saw the ground car

wearing a Rear Admiral's broad pennant approaching the ship. So here, he thought, was Damien coming to ask him if he had made his mind up yet.

He went down to the after airlock to receive his visitor, stood waiting at the head of the ramp. Damien extricated himself from his vehicle, came briskly up the gangway. Grimes saluted him while Kate Connellan, who was just happening by, sneered. The admiral glared at the second mate, then allowed Grimes to usher him into the elevator cage. They were carried swiftly up to the master's quarters.

In the sitting room Damien, as though by right, seated himself behind the desk. Grimes looked at him resentfully, then took a chair facing the man who had once been his immediate boss. *He needs something to rest his elbows on,* thought Grimes, *so that he can make a really good production of steepling his fingers. . . .* Damien did just that and regarded *Sister Sue's* captain over the digital spire.

He said—and it was as much statement as question—"You have accepted the charter to El Dorado."

"Yes, sir. Conditionally."

"And your conditions?"

"My promotion to captain if I reenter the Survey Service."

"That has been approved. You are now Captain John Grimes, Federation Survey Service Reserve. The necessary documentation should be aboard shortly."

"I haven't finished yet, sir. I have a particularly awkward second officer and I'd like to get shot of her."

"That young lady in the airlock? A Donegalan, isn't she?"

"Yes. She's got the Guild on her side and I'll be involved in wrongful dismissal suit if I empty her out."

"Then you don't empty her out, Grimes. It is essential that you lift on time for El Dorado."

"Mphm. Well, I was hoping to pick up a third mate here. That would improve matters. At the moment the Green Hornet is fifty percent of my control-room staff. But the Guild doesn't seem to be in a mood to help me. . . ."

"I wonder why not," said Damien sardonically. "You know, of course, that all telephone calls made out from the Naval Station are monitored? No? Well, you know now. But not to worry, Grimes. I have already made arrangements for additional personnel for you. A Mr. Venner, who holds the rank of a Reserve Lieutenant Commander, will be applying to you for employment. He is a Guild member, of course, so there should be no difficulties. You will also be carrying a passenger—although actually he will be under your orders. If

69

merchant vessels still carried psionic communications officers he would be on your books—but if you signed him on as PCO it would look suspicious."

"A PCO, sir?"

"Yes. A Mr. Mayhew. Or Lieutenant Command Mayhew."

"Mphm. And I suppose that your Lieutenant Commander Venner has some skills not usually possessed by the average merchant officer."

"He has, Grimes. His speciality is unarmed combat—and combat using any and all material to hand, however unlikely, as a weapon."

"I remember one instructor, when I did a course," said Grimes, "who demonstrated on a lifelike dummy the amount of damage you can do with a pipe. . . ."

"Iron pipe? Lead pipe?"

"No, sir. This sort of pipe," said Grimes, filling and lighting his.

"By asphyxiation?" asked Damien.

"*No.*" Grimes made a stabbing gesture. "Used as a dagger."

"A poisoned dagger at that. Tell me, what arms do you carry aboard this ship?"

"A Minetti projectile pistol. Two hand lasers. That's all."

"And that's all that there will be. *Sister Sue* is not a warship."

"But, now, commanded by a Survey Service Reserve officer and with two other Survey Service officers on board."

"Agreed. But you must be wondering, Grimes, just what all this is about."

"Too right, sir."

"You've been to El Dorado, haven't you? You know the sort of people who live there. The filthy rich. You may have noticed that no matter how rich such people are they always want to be richer. And, too, there's the lust for power. Your old friend Drongo Kane is in many ways a typical El Doradan, although he was granted citizenship only recently. Before he became an El Doradan he attempted to take over an entire planet, Morrowvia. You were able to shove a spanner into his works. He tried again, on the same world, some years later. Again you were on hand, as master of the Baroness d'Estang's spaceyacht. The Baroness, an El Doradan, was well aware of Kane's criminality. Nonetheless she married him. . . ."

"I think that she rather regrets it now."

"Does she? Oh, she got you out of a nasty mess on New

Venusberg rather against her ever-loving husband's wishes, but that doesn't mean that a marriage dissolution is imminent.

"Well, we have learned that he has interested his El Doradan fellow citizens in another scheme of his, an ambitious one although not involving territorial acquisition. As you may know, El Dorado now has a navy. . . ."

"One ship," said Grimes. "An auxiliary cruiser, usually employed as a cruise liner, with Commodore Baron Kane as the captain."

"Correct. But El Dorado, through Kane, has been chartering sundry obsolescent tonnage and not so obsolescent weaponry."

"And upon whom is El Dorado going to declare war?"

"Nobody. But, as you know, there are always brushfire wars going on somewhere in the galaxy. Recently the Duchy of Waldegren put down a breakaway attempt by one of its colonies. The Shaara Galactic Hive has done the same, more than once. In such cases the rebel colonists have been outgunned and easily beaten. But suppose such rebels had been able to employ a mercenary navy?"

"Mercenaries like to be paid," said Grimes. "Mercenaries with warships expect much higher pay than do, say, infantrymen."

"Agreed. Now, just suppose that you're the king or president or whatever of some world that's decided to break away from whichever empire it's supposed to belong. Your imperial masters take action against you. Your trade routes are raided, your merchant ships destroyed or captured. And then somebody presents himself at your palace, cap in hand, offering his services. At a price. It's a price that you can't afford to pay, especially since the salesman makes it quite clear that he's not interested in the paper money that's being churned out by your printing presses. But he makes a proposition. He offers his services free. Free to *you*, that is. All that you have to do is to issue Letters of Marque to his ships, which then become privateers. As such they raid the imperial trade routes, capturing rather than destroying. Your own navy, such as it is, is then free to deal with the imperial navy while the privateers make their fortunes harrying the merchantmen."

"Mphm."

"Now I'm demoting you, Grimes. You're no longer this rebel king or prince or duke. You're just the owner/master of a scruffy star tramp, delivering a cargo to El Dorado and not knowing where the next cargo is coming from. Or going to. You know people on El Dorado. You know Kane. He knows you. It may surprise you to learn that he has quite a high opinion of you. Or a low opinion. He's been heard to say, 'They call *me* a pirate—but that bloody Grimes could give me points and a beating if he really set his mind to it!' " He laughed. "And he could be right!"

"I'm flattered," said Grimes, making it plain that he was not.

"I thought that you would be," said Damien. "And I don't mind telling you that Kane's opinion of yourself coincides with mine."

"Thank you. Sir." Grimes scowled even more heavily. "So the idea is that I join Kane's ragamuffin navy and then, somehow, switch sides."

"More or less, although I don't visualize any overt side switching. Hopefully you will contrive an incident, do something that will give us, the Federation Survey Service, an excuse to clamp down on the privateers. As you are aware, no doubt, the dividing line between privateer and pirate has always been a very thin one. You will, as instructed, break that line. You should be able to do so without any loss of life or injuries on either side, without, even, any serious damage to property—but you will commit an act of piracy. A suitable vessel to become the victim of your depredations has already been selected. She will, of course, carry a PCO who will, of course, be in telepathic touch with your Mr. Mayhew."

"Very ingenious, sir," said Grimes without enthusiasm. "And I suppose that I shall be secretly under Survey Service orders, as will be Mr. Venner and Mr. Mayhew. But what about the rest of my crew? Two refugees from an old men's home. University professors and glorified garage hands for engineers. I can't see any of them taking kindly to a career of piracy."

"Privateering, Grimes, privateering. And you'd be surprised—or would you?—at what people will do when the money is big enough. And they'll think that there's no risk involved, that it will just be a matter of capturing unarmed vessels."

"When a state of war exists, sir, merchant vessels are usually defensively armed."

"You needn't tell your people that."

"The real spacemen will know without my telling them. And Billy Williams, my chief officer, was in the Dog Star

Line—and *they* have always made a practice of arming their ships when they're running through trouble zones."

"So much the better. It will mean that you'll have three reasonably competent gunnery officers aboard *Sister Sue*—yourself, Williams and Venner."

"You're forgetting one thing, sir."

"And what's that, Grimes?"

"I have a conscience. I don't mind hiring myself out as a mercenary but I like to be able to approve of my employers."

"Until this mess has been cleaned up, Grimes, *we*, the Federation Survey Service, are your real employers."

"There have been times, Admiral Damien, when I have not approved of the Survey Service."

"You do not surprise me. Many times I strongly suspected that. Nonetheless, you have never approved of Kane. This will be your chance to pay off old scores."

And that, thought Grimes, was one quite good reason for accepting the assignment. Another reason was the prospect of making an honest, or a dishonest, profit. And—although he would never admit this to Damien—the Survey Service had been his life for so long that the prospect of returning to it, even as only a temporary reservist, was almost like coming home.

Chapter 16

Although the discharge of *Sister Sue's* inward cargo had been only two days' work, with no overtime involved, there was a delay of over a week before her loading for El Dorado could be started. Grimes took advantage of this respite to fly to Alice Springs to visit his parents. Williams could be trusted to look after things during the captain's absence and Damien had raised no objections. (Grimes wondered if legally the Rear Admiral could have done so but deemed it polite to ask his permission before leaving Port Woomera.)

The city of Alice Springs had changed little since Grimes' last time there. There were, he thought as the dirigible made its approach from the south and he looked out and down through the promenade deck windows, a few more white domes in the residential districts, an increase of the market garden acreage, vividly green in the desert, crisscrossed by shining irrigation canals. There seemed to have been a proliferation of the gray yet scintillant solar power collection screens.

His father and mother were waiting for him in the lounge at the base of the mooring mast. His maternal parent had changed very little; she was still tall and straight and slim, still with gleaming auburn hair that owed little to artifice. But his father had aged, more so than had been apparent in the small screen of the telephone when Grimes had called from Port Woomera. He, too, was tall but stooped and his abundant hair was white. His face was heavily lined. Yet the old boy, thought Grimes, looked prosperous enough. His historical romances must be paying him well.

They boarded the family electric runabout and drove to the Grimes home on the outskirts of the city, Matilda Grimes at the controls while the two men sat and talked in the back. His parents, Grimes discovered, had moved to a much larger house, one surrounded by a lush, sprinkler-fed garden. When the car stopped, a housebot of the latest model emerged to handle the baggage and contrived somehow to register disapproval of the single, small, battered case brought by the guest. *Another uppity robot*, thought Grimes, but said nothing.

Finally the three humans disposed themselves in the comfortably furnished sitting room, sipping the fragrant tea that Mrs. Grimes had made personally. "There are some things," she said, "that robot's just can't do properly." Her son agreed with her.

Afternoon tea gave way to pre-dinner drinks as the colors of the garden, seen through the wide picture window, dimmed and darkened in the fast gathering twilight. But not every plant faded into near invisibility. Grimes was pleased to see that the Mudooran sparkle bush that, as little more than a seedling, he had brought to his parents as a gift had not only survived but flourished, was now a small tree decorated with starlike blossoms, softly self-luminous, multicolored.

His mother saw what he was looking at.

She said, "We have always loved that bush, John. We've told ourselves that as it survived in what, to it, is an alien environment so you would survive. And, like it, you have not only survived but done well. A captain *and* a shipowner." She frowned slightly. "But I still wish that you could have become a captain in the Survey Service."

74

Grimes laughed. "So you still think that your illustrious ancestor. . . ."

"And yours!" she snapped.

" . . . would not have approved of my career. You'd have liked to have seen me become Admiral Lord Grimes, just as he became Admiral Lord Hornblower. But unless I emigrate to the Empire of Waverley I'll never become a lord. Not that I can imagine King James elevating me to the peerage."

"But John *was* a captain in the Survey Service," said the elder Grimes.

"At times," his wife told him, "you display an appalling ignorance of naval matters, inexcusable in one who is not only an historical novelist but who prides himself on the thoroughness of his research. John was captain of a Serpent Class courier—but his actual rank was only lieutenant. He was captain of bigger ships—first as a lieutenant commander, then as commander. But he never wore the four gold rings on his sleeve."

George Whitley Grimes laughed. "Anybody who is in command is a captain, no matter what he does or does not wear. What do you say, John?"

"I'm a captain," said Grimes. "I'm called that."

"But a *merchant* captain," said his mother. "It's only a courtesy title. And the uniform you wear is only company's livery."

"But *my* company," Grimes told her. "Far Traveler Couriers. And what Survey Service captain owns the ship that he commands or wears uniform trimmings of his own design?"

"But you still aren't a Survey Service captain," said his mother stubbornly.

But I am, my dearest Matilda, he thought. *I'm Captain John Grimes, Federation Survey Service Reserve. It's a pity that I can't tell you.*

Later during his stay Grimes talked with his father about the old-time privateers, trying to draw upon the old man's fund of historical knowledge.

"Perhaps the most famous, or notorious," said the author, "was Captain Kidd, although most people think that he was a pirate. He was tried as such, found guilty and hanged. For murder as well as piracy. During a heated altercation with his gunner, one William Moore, he broke that officer's skull with a wooden bucket."

"I murdered William Moore as I sailed," sang Grimes tunelessly.

75

"I murdered William Moore as I sailed,
I knocked him on the head
Till he bled the scuppers red
And I heaved him with the lead
As I sailed. . . ."

"So you know something of the story," said Grimes' father.

"Yes. But carry on, George."

"Kidd was commissioned as a privateer. He was authorized both to seize French vessels—at that time England was at war with France, a very common state of affairs—and to hunt down pirates. It was alleged that he joined forces with these same pirates and accumulated a huge treasure, which, to this day, has not been found. . . ."

"If you can't lick 'em, join 'em," said Grimes.

"Not a very moral attitude, young man. But it seems possible, probable even, that Kidd was framed. There were some very dirty politics involved. The Governor of New York, then a British colony, had his reasons for wishing Kidd silenced. Permanently."

"Mphm," grunted Grimes. What dirty politics would he be getting mixed up in, he wondered.

"And then," his father continued, "there was the literary buccaneer, Dampier. He was one of the first Europeans to reach Australia. He made his landings on the west coast and was impressed neither by the country nor its inhabitants. He actually started his seafaring career as a pirate but somehow acquired a veneer of respectability. He was actually appointed by the British Admiralty to command one of their ships on a voyage of exploration. After that he sailed as a privateer, making two voyages. On the second one he hit it rich. . . ."

"So there was money in privateering," said Grimes.

"Of course. Why else should a group of merchants buy a ship and fit her out and man her as what was, in effect, a privately owned man-o'-war? But the days of the privateer, on Earth's seas, were finished by the Second Hague Conference in 1907, Old Reckoning. Then it was ruled that a warship must be a unit of a national navy."

"You've been swotting this up," accused Grimes.

"As a matter of fact, I have. I'm working on an If Of History novel. About the Australian War of Independence, which started with the Massacre at Glenrowan, when the Kelly Gang slaughtered all the police aboard the special train. In actual history, of course, the special train was not

76

derailed—the Glenrowan schoolteacher, Curnow, flagged it down before it got to the torn-up track—and it was the Kelly Gang that was wiped out. . . ."

"I know, I know. And Ned Kelly is supposed to have been a freedom fighter. But he was a bushranger, not a privateer."

"Let me finish, John. Among the characters in my novel is a millionaire American shipowner who's very anti-British. And he has two of his ships fitted out as privateers to harry Pommy merchantmen."

"Cor stone my Aunt Fanny up a gum tree!" exclaimed Grimes. "The things you come up with! I'd just hate to be a character in one of your books!"

"I still think that the Australian War of Independence was a possibility," said the writer. "And, back in 1880, privateering was still legal. Anyhow, I got interested in the subject and carried on with more research. As far as I can gather, the 1907 Hague Conference ruling still holds good—but possibly only insofar as the Federated Worlds are concerned. It could be argued that any planet not in the Interstellar Federation can make its own rules. On the other hand, I have learned that the Federation's Interstellar Navigation Regulations are observed by just about everybody."

"I could have told you that," said Grimes. "They're taken as a model by all spacefaring races. But, getting back to the subject of privateering, there have been astronautical precedents. The notorious Black Bart, for example. He—like Captain Kidd—is widely regarded as having been a pirate. But he always maintained that he was a privateer. His planetary base was within the sphere of influence of the Duchy of Waldegren. The Duchy tolerated him, as long as he paid the taxes. They tolerated and, at times, used him. They weren't very fussy about whom they employed—they still aren't—any more than Black Bart was fussy about who employed him."

"Why all this interest in privateering, John?" asked his father.

"Oh, well, I guess that it's an interesting topic."

"You aren't thinking of going privateering?" asked the old man sharply.

"Who? *Me?*" countered Grimes.

"I wouldn't put it past you. But if you do, don't let your mother know. It's bad enough that you never got to be a four-ring captain in the Survey Service, but if you become a privateer she'd tell you never to darken her door again."

And what if I became both? Grimes asked himself.

But he said nothing.

Chapter 17

Grimes returned to Port Woomera; Billy Williams had telephoned to say that Rear Admiral Damien required his presence aboard *Sister Sue*. Grimes' father overheard some of the conversation.

He asked, a little suspiciously, "Why should an admiral be wanting you, George? You're a civilian shipmaster, aren't you?"

Grimes thought hard and fast, then said, "At the moment the ship is berthed in the Survey Service area of the spaceport. I will have to shift her to one of the commercial berths to load my outward cargo." (He probably would have to do just that but it would not be for a few days yet.)

He made his booking. His parents came to the airport to see him off.

"Look after yourself, John," his mother told him. "And try not to make it so long between visits."

"I'll try," he promised.

"And try to stay inside the law," said his father.

How much did the old man suspect? The author, Grimes well knew, at times had telepathic flashes and, more than once, while Grimes was still a schoolboy, had seemed to be able almost to read his mind. And there were others possessing psychic talents. Magda Granadu was one such.

She came to see Grimes as soon as he was back in his quarters aboard *Sister Sue*.

"Captain," she demanded, "what is happening?"

"We shall be carrying a cargo of luxury goods to El Dorado. That's common knowledge."

"But I feel uneasy. It's not the first time that I've had such premonitions."

"It must be the time of the month," said Grimes.

She flushed angrily and snapped, "It is not!"

"Sorry."

"I've brought the book," she said. "And the coins."

"Oh, all right," said Grimes. It would do no harm to humor the woman.

He took from her the three metal discs, shook them in his cupped hands, let them drop to the deck of his day cabin.

Two heads and a tail . . . *Yang.* Then another *yang.* And another. Then two tails and a head . . . *Yin. Yang* again, then a final *yin.*

"Well?" he demanded.

She consulted the book.

"Hsu," she murmured. "Biding one's time. Sincerity will lead to brilliant success. Firmness will bring good fortune. It will be advantageous to cross the great water."

"And what the hell's wrong with that?" asked Grimes.

"I haven't finished yet, Captain. Here's the commentary. Peril lies ahead, but despite the urge toward activity which is shown, he will not allow himself to be involved in a dangerous situation. Firm persistence in a right course of action will ensure great success. But strength and determination are needed to make the most of the progressive trends now operating. It is an auspicious time to commence a major undertaking. The strong man's inclination when faced with danger is to advance on it and combat it without delay; but here one would be wise to wait until success is assured."

Grimes laughed. "And what's wrong with that for a prognostication?" he asked. "It's an excellent weather forecast before the start of a voyage."

"But it counsels caution. It talks of danger."

"If we were afraid of danger, Ms. Granadu, we should not be spacers."

"My own reading," she said, "was much more ominous. It was *Po.* It will not be advantageous for me to make a move in any direction. The forces operating against me will be too great for me to prevail against them. I have to wait for a change for the better."

"And do you want to wait here, on Earth? I can pay you off, you know, although you should have given me more notice. But I don't want to lose you; you're a good catering officer and a very good shipmate."

"And I don't want to leave this ship, Captain. We shall just have to heed the warnings and be very, very careful."

You can say that again, thought Grimes. If all went as planned, he would find himself dealing with Drongo Kane—and he who sups with the devil needs a long spoon.

His door buzzer sounded.

"Come in," he called.

Damien was there, in uniform, and with him were two youngish men in civilian shirts and slacks. One of them was short, stocky, with close-cropped sandy hair over a broad, craggy face, with little, very pale blue eyes under almost non-existent brows. The other was tall, weedy almost, with fair hair that was more than a little too long, with sensitive features just short of being effeminate and eyes that seemed to vary in color.

"Here is your new third officer, Captain Grimes," said Damien. "Mr. Venner."

The short man bowed slightly and then took the hand that Grimes extended to him. His grip was firm and, Grimes knew, would have been painful had full strength been exerted.

"And this is Mr. Mayhew, an old friend of mine. . . ." *Like hell I am!* the words formed themselves in Grimes's mind. He looked at Mayhew suspiciously. "He asked me if I could arrange passage for him to El Dorado and beyond. He's spending his Long Service Leave traveling. . . ."

"And what's your line of business, Mr. Mayhew?" asked Grimes, genuinely curious as to what the cover story would be.

"Senior clerk, Captain, with Pargeter and Crummins, Importers. You may have heard of them."

Grimes hadn't—yet this Mayhew was suddenly looking like a senior clerk, like a man who had spent all his working life at a desk. Nobody would take him for a spaceman—nobody, that is, who was seeing the telepath as he wished to be seen.

"Magda," said Grimes, "will you see to it that the third officer's cabin is ready? And one of the spare rooms for Mr. Mayhew."

"Very good, sir."

She left.

When the door had closed after her, Mayhew's appearance underwent another subtle transformation. Now he looked like what he, in actuality, was—a Survey Service officer in one of that organization's specialist branches, a typical commissioned teacup reader. . . .

"I have often wished," said Mayhew, "that I could meet the man who first called us that."

"Probably an engineer," said Grimes.

"But *you* thought it, Captain. Just now."

"Don't bother to say that you're sorry, Captain Grimes," said Damien. "He'll know that you're lying."

"If he does," Grimes said, he'll be doing so in gross contravention of the Rhine Institute's code of ethics."

Mayhem smiled. It was a likeable smile. He said, "There

are some minds, Captain Grimes, into which I would no sooner probe than dive into a cesspit. Yours, sir, is not one of them."

"Thank you," said Grimes. "But I'll be greatly obliged if you don't make a habit of invading my mental privacy."

"Mr. Mayhew will be doing his job, Captain," said Damien. "I have no doubt that you will find his services extremely valuable. And Mr. Venner's. But I'll give you fair warning. Don't ever play cards with him."

This appeared to be some kind of private joke.

Grimes asked, "Does he cheat? Or is he just abnormally lucky?"

Venner grinned while Damien said, "Neither. You're the one who's notorious for having luck." He laughed. "Just stay that way."

"I hope I do," said Grimes. "But some famous privateers, such as Captain Kidd, weren't so lucky."

"Captain Morgan was," said Damien.

"Sir Henry Morgan," Grimes said, "wasn't a privateer. He was a pirate."

"What's the difference?" asked Damien.

Grimes sighed. It was all very well for the Rear Admiral to adopt such a could-hardly-care-less attitude. If things should go badly wrong it would not be he who would be left holding the baby.

Chapter 18

Sister Sue lifed from Port Woomera.

She had a full loading of commodities that even on their planet of origin were expensive, some of them hellishly so. Freight charges would make them even more costly. Beluga caviar, champagne, truffles, paté de foie gras. . . . Guiness Stout from Ireland, cheeses from Holland, France, Switzerland and Italy. . . . Whiskies from Scotland, Ireland, North America and Japan. . . . Salami sausages—Italian, Polish and Hungarian. . . . Smoked salmon, vintage sardines, anchovies, olives. . . .

To sit on top of such a cargo for a voyage of weeks' duration, thought Grimes, would be to suffer the tortures of

Tantalus. (He had not been nicknamed Gutsy Grimes for nothing.) In a ship with an uninspired catering officer and an ailing autochef the temptation to pilfer cargo would have been well nigh irresistible. Luckily *Sister Sue* was not in that class.

The lift-off was uneventful.

Venner, the new third officer, was obviously an experienced spaceman. Kate Connellan was slightly less surly than ususal; she must, thought Grimes, have been able to blow off steam in some way during the ship's stay in port. Williams was cheerfully competent. Old Mr. Stewart, manning the control-room NST transceiver, knew the drill. (At his age he should have.)

Mayhew occupied one of the spare seats, a privilege now and again accorded to passengers. He had assumed his senior-clerk-on-vacation persona and was asking stupid questions as part of his cover.

The ship drove up into the clear sky, her inertial drive thudding healthily. The altimeter readings displayed in the sternview screen shifted from meters to kilometers, mounted steadily. The picture of the spaceport diminished, faster and faster, became no more than white and silver specks on the ruddy desert. More desert, but with great green squares of artificial irrigation, came into view to the north while to the south were the dark waters of the Great Australian Blight. The horizon acquired curvature. Grimes looked out through the viewports. He thought that he could distinguish in the distance, the city of Alice Springs. In the opposite direction he could see the white glimmer of the Antarctic Ice Barrier.

Sister Sue was in space, clear of the atmosphere, plunging through the Van Allens. It was almost time to set trajectory.

The inertial drive was shut down; the ship had built enough velocity for her to continue to fall outward. The big directional gyroscopes turned her about her axes until the target star was lined up directly ahead. There was a small adjustment for galactic drift.

Grimes actuated the Mannschenn Drive.

There were the usual eerie effects as the temporal precession field built up—but, in Grimes' case, with a difference. He did not see anything but he heard a voice. His? It could have been, although it was not tuneless enough. It was singing the old song, The Ballad of Captain Kidd, with which he had afflicted his father's ears during that talk about privateers.

I murdered William Moore as I sailed, as I sailed,
I murdered William Moore as I sailed,
I knocked him on the head
Till he bled the scuppers red
And I heaved him with the lead
As I sailed. . . .

The voice faded to a whisper as inside the control room colors returned to normal and the warped perspective straightened itself out. The only sound was the thin, high whine of the ever-precessing rotors of the interstellar drive. Grimes restarted the inertial drive machinery and again there were *up* and *down* and the sensation of weight engendered by the steady acceleration.

He realized that Mayhew was looking at him. An ironical smile quirked the telepath's lips.

See you on Execution Dock, Captain. . . .

The words formed themselves in Grimes' mind.

He glared at Mayhew and thought, willing himself to transmit, *Very funny. Very bloody funny.*

Mayhew grinned.

After watches had been set Grimes invited Mayhew down to his cabin for a drink.

Before either man could set glass to lip he demanded, "What did *you* see, Mr. Mayhew? What did *you* hear?"

"What you did, Captain. Oh, I wasn't snooping. I wasn't trying to get inside your mind. But you were . . . broadcasting so strongly that I couldn't help picking up the words of that song. If it's any comfort to you I've looked through your crew list and there aren't any William Moores."

"There could be," said Grimes, "at some future date. But I hope not."

Mayhew sipped his gin then said, "I'm assuming, sir, that you wish me to function as a PCO does aboard a Federation Survey Service warship."

"I suppose that that's one of the reasons why Admiral Damien seconded you to me. But snooping is part of a PCO's duties of which I've never approved. Especially when it's against my own crew, my own shipmates."

"If you hadn't been so squeamish, sir, the *Discovery* mutiny might never have happened."

"You could be right, Mr. Mayhew. Mphm. But I still wish you to adhere to the Rhine Institute's Code of Ethics, at least insofar as this ship is concerned."

83

"If you insist, Captain."

"And as for your real duties, Mr. Mayhew, how is it that you don't have a psionic amplifier with you? I've never liked those naked dogs' brains in their tanks of nutrient fluid but I know that you can't function without them, not over any great range, that is."

Mayhew smiled. "It would hardly do for a mere passenger, a chief clerk blowing his life's savings on an interstellar voyage, to have such a pet. But I do have a psionic amplifier." He tapped his forehead with a long index finger. "Here. You know, of course, that there are such things as telepathic robots. There aren't many of them, mainly because they're so fantastically expensive. And the tiny piece of miniaturized circuitry that I now carry was more expensive still. And it has a limited life."

"Will it last until such time as you have to get in touch with your colleague aboard the . . . incident ship?"

"I hope so." Mayhew held out his empty glass. Grimes refilled it, topped up his own. "I hope so."

"Now, Mr. Mayhew," said Grimes, "I'm going to break one of my own rules. Your mention of the *Discovery* mutiny is why. I'm going to ask you what you, as a professional telepath, think of this ship, of her people."

For what seemed a long time Mayhew said nothing, sipping his drink thoughtfully.

Then he murmured, "You've a good second in command, sir. He's one of those men who must have a leader to whom to be loyal—and now you're it. But he's loyal, too, to his principles. Never forget that.

"Your second officer. The Green Hornet. She's a vicious bitch. Her only loyalty is to herself. Watch her.

"Your third, Venner, I know him personally. He's not really a Reservist, you know. That's just part of his cover. Oh, he ships out as a merchant spaceman, just as he has with you, but he's really employed, full time, by the Intelligence Branch of the Survey Service. As a hit man. His loyalties are to his real employers, not to you. If he were ordered to terminate you with extreme prejudice he would do just that."

"I'd guessed as much," said Grimes.

"And now, your catering officer," went on Mayhew. "In her you have a gem. Like Williams, she's loyal. And—this could be of real value—she has the power."

"What power?"

"Prevision. Some of her kind use cards, either ordinary playing cards or the Tarot pack. Some read teacups. Some

84

look into crystal balls. Oh, as you know, there are all sorts of lenses that can be used to focus attention on the future, on to the most probable of an infinitude of possible futures. She uses the *I Ching*."

"I know. She threw the coins for herself before this voyage started. She told me about it. Something about it's not being advantageous to make a move in any direction. And small men multiplying and having far too much to say for themselves. And the only course of action being just to ride it out and to hope for better times. . . ."

Mayhew laughed. "And it's true—but in a funny, quite trivial way. She's a good catering officer but the way that she programs the autochef the meals are too fancy for some of the juniors. And every time that she tried to turn out something plain it's . . . uninspired. For example. . . ." He frowned in concentration and said, "I'm snooping, Captain. With your permission, I hope. Two of your junior engineers are wondering what they're going to get for lunch. One of them has just said to the other, 'I suppose that the Romany Queen will be giving us more of her foreign, mucked-up tucker!' And the other's replied, 'I must have lost at least ten kilograms since I joined this bloody ship!' "

"If that's who I think it is," growled Grimes, "he's as fat as a pig. And getting fatter."

"It could be glandular," said Mayhew.

"Once you've seen him eating you'll not think that."

"And now he's saying, 'Of course, she's the Old Man's pet. . . .' "

"Enough," said Grimes. "Enough. Carry on with the run-down, please."

"All right, sir. Listeners seldom hear good of themselves, do they? Now, old Mr. Stewart. My electronic rival. As long as he has his toys to play with, he's happy. He'd be radio officer for anybody, in any ship in any service, and ask no questions. If Sir Henry Morgan had been blessed with radio your Mr. Stewart would have been as content in his ship as he is here, just sending and receiving as ordered.

"The other old-timer, Mr. Crumley, your inertial/reaction chief. . . . A rather similar type to Stewart. A ship, any ship on any trade, is no more than a platform on which his precious engines are mounted.

"Now, his juniors. Denning, Singh and Paulus. They're all little men. Not physically little necessarily—but *little*. They resent having to take orders—yours, their chief's, anybody's. They hate having to wear a uniform and mutter about your

Survey Service bullshit. But I don't think you'll have any trouble with them on El Dorado when—if?—Drongo Kane recruits you and the ship for his privateer navy. Privateering can be a very lucrative business and, when the victims are unarmed merchantmen, almost without risk.

"Malleson, your Mannschenn Drive king . . . Similar to Crumley and Stewart but—he kids himself—on a far higher plane. He's a master mathematician whereas the other two are mere mechanics. He likes money, so he'll not object to privateering. His loyalty? Essentially only to that weird, time-twisting contraption in the Mannschenn Drive room.

"Trantor and Giddings. . . . Little men again, hating authority, intellectual snobs who look down on rough, half-educated spacemen such as yourself. And Malleson they regard as an old has-been. But for all their intellectual veneer they're out of the same barrel as Denning, Singh and Paulus.

"All in all, Captain, not the best of crews to go privateering with."

Grimes laughed. "Competence at their jobs is all I can ask. As for their characters—well, the average privateersman must have been actuated by greed rather than by patriotism. But Billy Williams and Magda. . . . *They* have principles. . . ."

"As you do. You'll just have to convince them that we shall be fighting on the right side."

"I shall have to convince myself as well."

"No. You, sir, will just be taking orders—as Venner and myself will be. You're an officer of the Reserve recalled to active duty. You should have thought of all the implications when you accepted that commission."

"It seemed a good idea at the time," said Grimes.

Chapter 19

The voyage from Austral to Earth had been a short one, barely long enough for *Sister Sue's* people to get to know the ship and each other. That from Earth to El Dorado occupied all of two standard months. Dislikes that had been engendered on that initial trip now had ample time to develop, to fester. Grimes did not need Mayhew's psionic snooping to make him aware of the lack of harmony. Continually, it seemed, there was somebody at his door to complain about somebody else. The Green Hornet was a frequent visitor. According to her everybody aboard the ship was a male chauvinist pig, with the obvious exception of Magda Granadu. She was even more contemptible; she had sold out to the enemy, was a traitor to her sex. Then there were the inertial/reaction drive juniors with their never-ending whinges about the food, and the Mannschenn Drive juniors to lay complaint about the table manners, in the duty engineers' mess, of those whom they despised as mere mechanics. There were squabbles all the time about what programs should be shown on the playmaster. Even Williams—and it took a lot to ruffle him—said his piece. He practically demanded that Kate Connellan be paid off on El Dorado.

"I'd like to do it, Billy," said Grimes. "By all the Odd Gods of the Galaxy I'd like to do it! But she's a Guild member, just as you and I and Mr. Venner are. Unless she does something justifying instant dismissal we're stuck with her. Even then, I doubt if the El Doradans would allow us to turn her loose on their precious planet. They're very fussy."

"You've been there, Skipper, haven't you?"

"Yes. Once, years ago. When I was a very junior lieutenant in the cruiser *Aries*. The El Doradans were polite enough but they made it quite plain that we, from the Old Man down, were no more than snotty-nosed kids from the wrong side of the tracks. . . ."

That wasn't quite true, thought Grimes, remembering. The old Duchess of Leckhampton had been kind enough to him—and the Princess Marlene von Stolzberg rather more than kind. But they had used him, nonetheless. Still, he had been told that he could return to El Dorado to become a citizen once he had made his first billion credits. . . . The two main requirements for citizenship were noble ancestry and money—and of them money was by far the more important. Titles can be purchased. Grimes wondered how much Drongo Kane, Commodore Baron Kane, had paid for his. . . .

"But you're a shipowner, now, Skipper," said Williams, "not a mere hairy-arsed spaceman."

"But I'm not a *rich* shipowner, Billy. . . ."

And Drongo Kane, of course, was a rich shipowner. And, being Drongo Kane, wanted to be richer still."

"What's El Dorado *like*, Skipper?"

"It's a garden world, Billy. Huge estates, with mansions and even castles. At least one of those castles was shipped,

87

stone by stone, from Earth, Schloss Stolzberg. I was a guest there."

"And who was your host? Some crusty old Prussian baron?"

"No. As a matter of fact it was a very charming princess."

"And yet you say that you were treated like a snotty-nosed kid from the wrong side of the tracks?"

"No. Not *treated* like. After all, aristocrats have very good manners when they care to exercise them. *Regarded as* would be a better way of putting it. And we were welcome only because they wanted something from us. Once they got it, it was on your bicycle, spaceman!"

The telephone on Grimes' desk buzzed sharply.

"Yes?" he demanded.

Keyed to his voice the screen came alive. Looking out from it was Magda Granadu. She was pale, her expression worried.

"Captain, can you come down to the general room? There's trouble. A fight. . . ."

"Who's involved?"

"Mr. Venner and two of the engineers. It's two of them, the engineers, against one. . . ."

"We'll be right down," said Grimes.

Williams followed him out into the circular alleyway around the axial shaft. As usual, when there was any hurry, the lift cage was decks away. It came up at last—but then was reluctant to commence its descent.

The fight was over by the time that they hurried into the general room. Venner was standing there, scowling ferociously. There were the beginnings of a bruise on his right cheek. Also standing were Malleson, the Mannschenn Drive chief, and Giddings, one of his juniors. Not standing were Singh and Paulus. They were sprawled on the deck and making a mess on the carpet. Blood mingled with vomit.

"Captain!" Malleson stepped forward. "That man is dangerous! He should be put under arrest!"

Magda Granadu came back into the general room, overheard what Malleson was saying.

"It was two against one!" she cried. "It was self-defense!"

"But Mr. Venner was fighting to hurt, to kill," stated Malleson.

Venner said, "Why else should one fight?" He turned to Grimes. "I was watching the playmaster, sir. As a matter of fact I had it hooked up to the computer so that I could learn something about El Dorado. Mr. Malleson was watching it

88

too. Mr. Giddings was reading. Then Mr. Singh and Mr. Paulus came in. Mr. Paulus said, 'Who the hell wants this? What about one of those good sex spools we got at Port Woomera?' He switched off the playmaster. I made to switch it back on. Then he struck me."

"Is that true, Mr. Malleson?" asked Grimes.

"Yes, Captain. But it still doesn't justify the savagery of Mr. Venner's counterattack. He used his feet, and the edges of his hands. . . ."

"And why not?" asked Venner. "I do have certain skills. Why should I not use them?"

"A fist fight is a fair fight," insisted Malleson.

"When it's two against one?" asked Venner. "You saw how Singh was taking a swipe at me before I'd finished with Paulus. And what's all this rubbish about fist fighting being somehow manly, even noble? The noble art of self-defense? Why don't you grow up?"

"Mr. Venner!" snapped Grimes.

"Sorry, Captain. But I just don't like being mauled by drunks while I'm quietly minding my own business."

"Were Mr. Singh and Mr. Paulus drunk?" Grimes asked.

"They may have been drinking," admitted Malleson.

Meanwhile Magda, carrying a first-aid box, had come back into the general room, was wiping clean the faces of the two half-conscious engineers, and spraying their cuts and bruises with antiseptic syntheskin.

She said, "I'd like to get these two to the dispensary so that I can look at them properly."

"Will you give me a hand, Mr. Giddings?" asked Williams.

He and the Mannschenn Drive engineer got Paulus to his feet, supported him as he staggered out into the alleyway. After a short while they returned for Singh. Him they had to carry.

"I'll see you in my day cabin," Grimes said to Venner.

"And do you want me, Captain?" asked Malleson. "I was a witness."

"I may want to see you later," Grimes said. Then, to Venner, "Come with me."

"You realize, Mr. Venner," said Grimes, "that I shall have to make an entry in the Official Log."

"Of course, sir."

"You realize, too, that this could blow up into an interunion dispute. Mr. Paulus and Mr. Singh are members of the Institute of Interstellar Engineers. They were required to join before they signed Articles at Port Southern. I shan't be at all surprised if they send a Carlottigram to the Institute as soon as they're recovered."

"You seem to be remarkably well versed in industrial matters. Sir."

The man wasn't quite insolent although he was not far from it.

"I've been reading through the industrial files left by my predecessors on this ship," said Grimes. "They had their worries."

"The sort of worries, sir, that need not concern us. We're Survey Service, not civilians."

"As far as this ship is concerned, Mr. Venner, we *are* civilians. We must comport ourselves as such. I am asking you— no, ordering you—to apologize to the engineers. I know that they asked for trouble, and got it, but I don't want to get involved in any legal/industrial hassles after we've set down on El Dorado."

Venner scowled. "All right," he said at last. "I'll apologize. Under protest."

"Just say that you're sorry," advised Grimes, "for having used overmuch force to protect yourself. After all, you did not strike the first blow."

Somebody was hammering on the door. The Green Hornet, thought Grimes. She would be coming off watch now—and she, for some reason, hated to use the buzzer.

"Come in," he called.

She came in. She looked at Grimes coldly, glared at Venner.

"Captain," she almost shouted, "there are times when the Guild must stand by the Institute and this is one of them. I have heard how this man beat up Mr. Singh and Mr. Paulus. I demand that you *do* something about it."

"Mr. Venner is a member of the Guild," pointed out Grimes mildly. "As Mr. Williams is. As I am. Mr. Williams feels, as I feel, that Mr. Venner was merely defending himself from an unprovoked assault."

"There must be a proper inquiry," said Kate Connellan. "There must be punishment, a heavy fine at the very least."

"Yes," Grimes said thoughtfully, "I suppose that I could fine Mr. Paulus for his unprovoked assault on Mr. Venner. . . . Although, possibly, he has been punished enough."

"Are you mad?" she demanded. "It is Venner who should be punished."

"*Mr.* Venner," Grimes corrected her.

90

"There must be an inquiry," she insisted, "with proper entries in the Official Log."

"There will be log entries," said Grimes at last. He had better make such, he supposed, just to clear his own yardarm, if nobody else's. Neither the Guild nor the Institute would have representation on El Dorado but *Sister Sue*, as a merchant ship, would in the future be visiting worlds on which the Astronautical unions maintained officials. "Get back up to the control room, Ms. Connellan, to relieve Mr. Williams for a few minutes. I shall want him to countersign what I put down."

"But why the mate? I can write, Captain."

"You were not a witness to any of what happened. Mr. Williams was."

"Then I insist that I be allowed to read the entry."

Grimes sighed. "You, Ms. Connellan, as second officer of this vessel, as part of your duties, make all the routine log entries—arrivals, departures, drills, inspections. The log is, therefore, accessible to you at any time. Relieve Mr. Williams, please."

"Aye, aye, Captain, sir!" she replied sardonically and was gone.

Grimes used his telephone to call Malleson, the main witness, and old Crumley, who was the department superior of the two injured junior engineers. He called Magda Granadu, who told him that Mr. Singh had been fit enough to go on watch and that Mr. Paulus was also fit for duty. Grimes asked her to come up with the two senior engineers.

Williams came down from control. He seemed to be amused about something. Malleson, Crumley and Magda arrived shortly afterward. The engineers took seats as far away from the scowling Venner as possible.

Grimes said, "I am making a log entry on these lines. I shall say that in my opinion, Mr. Venner overreacted to the threat against his person. He is prepared to apologize to Mr. Paulus and Mr. Singh for this overreaction. I am stating that Mr. Paulus struck Mr. Venner after a slight argument over the playmaster programing, that Mr. Venner acted in self-defense. Mr. Singh came to the assistance of his friend and was also dealt with by Mr. Venner.

"Is that a fair statement of the facts?"

"Yes, sir," said Venner.

"Two of my engineers were badly injured, Captain," complained Crumley.

"They're fit for duty, aren't they?" demanded Magda.

"Mr. Malleson?" asked Grimes.

"It is, I suppose, a statement of the facts," admitted the Mannschenn Drive chief grudgingly. "But it takes no account of the . . . the. . . ."

"Poetic justice of it all," supplied Williams.

"*No.* The unwarranted savagery exercised by Mr. Venner."

"I have training in the martial arts, Chief," said Venner. "I possess skills—and I use them. My intention was to punish, not to incapacitate."

"That will do, Mr. Venner," said Grimes sharply.

He made the entry in the official log, signed, with a flourish, *John Grimes, Master.* Venner, the engineers and the catering officer left the day cabin. Grimes looked at Williams and asked, "Just why should our female chauvinist bitch be getting her knickers in a twist over the well-deserved misfortunes of mere males, engineers at that?"

Williams grinned.

"Don't you *know,* sir?"

"I'm only the captain," said Grimes. "Nobody tells me anything."

"Our Green Hornet is a woman. Mr. Paulus is a man. Personally, Skipper, I regard an affair between a control-room officer and an engineer as miscegenation. Early in the trip dear Kate tried to indicate to me that she was ready and willing. I wasn't interested. . . ."

"Why not?" asked Grimes interestedly.

Williams flushed, then said, "I'd have thought that that would have been obvious. I've known Magda for a long time. Well, she tried it on with me, then with Mr. Venner. Once again, no dice."

"Oh. One day," said Grimes, "somebody will make a regulation requiring ships with mixed crews to maintain an even balance of the sexes."

"It still wouldn't work," said Williams. "Apart from anything else there're all the in-betweens . . . Like the old joke. The male sex, the female sex, the insex and the Middlesex."

"It's time you got back on watch. But sign the log before you go." Leaving a generous space he printed, in capitals, the word MATE under his own signature. He turned the book around, pushed it toward the chief officer.

Williams signed.

William Moore Williams instead of his more usual *W. M. Williams.*

But he should have known, thought Grimes. He had sighted Williams' Certificate of Competency when Articles had been opened at Port Southern. On it the mate's name was given in full, and had been entered in full in the Articles by the Shipping Master. On the crew list, however, it was *Williams, W. M.* And Mayhew had seen the crew list but not the Articles.

I murdered William Moore as I sailed. . . .

"What's wrong, Skipper?" asked Williams concernedly. "Somebody walking over your grave?"

"No," Grimes said.

Not mine, he thought.

But what about the flash of prevision when he had seen himself, much older, with a much older Williams, the pair of them obvious shipmates?

He went on, "These aboard-ship squabbles always upset me."

"You aren't as upset as those two pig-iron polishers!" Williams laughed.

He went up to the control room to resume his watch.

Chapter 20

Venner's justifiable beating up of Paulus and Singh was not the only outbreak of physical violence on the ship before her arrival at El Dorado, although it was the most serious one. There was the fight between Paulus and Trantor, no more than an undignified exhibition of inexpert fisticuffs. The reason for it, Grimes discovered, was the transferal of Ms. Connellan's affections from one engineering department to the other. He lectured all those concerned, telling them sternly that even while he did not subscribe to archaic moral codes he was still a strong believer in the old standards of shipboard discipline and good conduct.

Paulus muttered something about Survey Service bullshit.

Grimes said coldly, "I'm inviting you to say that again. louder, Mr. Paulus—and warning you that if you do I'll throw the book at you. Insolent and contemptuous behavior toward a superior officer will do for a start—and that carries a fine of one hundred credits."

The engineer lapsed into surly silence.

93

Grimes dismissed the bruised combatants and the glowering Green Hornet. Williams remained with him.

"Billy," asked Grimes, "what am I going to do with that bitch?"

"You could have her fitted with a chastity belt, Skipper," suggested the mate.

"Yes. And a scold's bridle. But would the engineers make them?" He laughed. "Old Mr. Crumley might. I think that he's past it as far as women are concerned."

Williams laughed too. "Could be. But suppose he does make a belt. . . . Who's going to fit it about dear Katie's female form divine? The fat. . . . And that sweaty, greasy, green skin of hers. . . ." He glanced at the bulkhead clock. "But I must ask you to excuse me, Skipper. I promised Magda that I'd lend her a hand thinning out the lettuces on the farm deck."

Grimes felt a stab of envy. The engineers—or some of them—were getting theirs. Williams was getting his. And what did *he* have? A solidograph of a naked woman on one shelf, an animated golden statuette of another naked woman on a ledge on the opposite bulkhead. And both ladies were light-years distant. . . .

He said, "All right, Mr. Williams. Go and do your gardening. The Green Hornet for Second Mate . . . Mr. Greenfingers for Mate. . . ."

And the Captain green with envy?

Williams said, "Magda's promised us that Vietnamese dish for dinner, Skipper. You know. The one where you scoop up the pieces of meat, fish and whatever with lettuce leaves."

"I can hardly wait," said Grimes a little sourly although the meal was one of his favorites. He, in fact, had told the Catering Officer how to prepare, cook and serve it. "Off you go, then."

He buzzed Mayhew, who was in his cabin, asked him to come up for a drink and a talk.

"Well, Mr. Mayhew," asked Grimes after glasses had been filled and sipped, "what do *you* think of this shipload of malcontents? Will they be any good as the crew of a privateer?"

"You told me, sir, that I was not to snoop."

"But even if you aren't snooping you must pick things up, without trying to or wanting to."

"But I am not supposed to pass what I . . . hear on to anybody else." He laughed softly. "All right, all right. I know, and you know, that in the Survey Service the PCO is the captain's ears. It's no secret that we're fast getting to the stage where everybody hates everybody. Well, almost everybody. The honeymoon's not over yet for Mr. Williams and Ms. Granadu—and it's been going on for quite a while. Ms. Connellan? She despises the men she uses, just as they despise her. Oh, I know that she kicked up a song and dance when Mr. Venner made a mess of Mr. Paulus—but that was only because she resented having *her* property damaged by somebody else...."

"Never mind the moral issues, Mr. Mayhew. What I want to know is this. If—*if*—Admiral Damien's plot succeeds, if I'm admitted to Drongo Kane's gang of pirates, what about my crew?"

"No real worries there, Captain. Pirates and privateersmen have usually been malcontents. Of course, there *is* the danger of mutiny—but not even warships of the Federation Survey Service are immune to that."

"No need to remind me, Mr. Mayhew."

Mayhew ignored this. "In the case of the *Discovery* mutiny, Captain, there was an officer quite capable of taking over the command of the ship from you. Here there is not. Your Chief Officer, Mr. Williams, is personally loyal to his Captain. Your Third Officer, Mr. Venner, is loyal to the Survey Service—and to you, as long as you are his legally appointed commander. The Green Hornet? There's no loyalty there—but, assuming that the engineers do think of mutiny they have no confidence in Ms. Connellan's abilities. The feeling is that she couldn't navigate a plastic duck across a bathtub."

"No more could she. I have known many extremely capable women, but she is not one of them."

"*They* are, though," said Mayhew, looking from the solidograph to the golden figurine.

"Yes," agreed Grimes. He thought, *I could do with either one of them here, although not both at once....*

Mayhew said, "I don't think that a Police Commissioner, an ex-Federation Sky Marshal, would approve of privateering."

Grimes laughed. "Come to that, she didn't approve of me much. Although, if it hadn't been for her, I'd never have lifted from Port Southern on time."

"Perhaps," said Mayhew, "she had her orders."

"You mean that Damien—may the Odd Gods of the Galaxy look sideways at him!—was behind my getting the

95

contract to carry Survey Service records from Austral to Earth?"

"It is hard to keep secrets from a telepath," said Mayhew. "But our beloved Admiral had no hand in your purchase of this ship. He's just an opportunist."

And Damien, thought Grimes, could have had nothing to do with the truly beautiful gift that Yosarian and Una Freeman, jointly, had presented to him. He got up from his chair, carefully lifted the golden cyclist and her steed down from the shelf, set her gently on the carpeted desk.

"Ride," he ordered. "Ride. Round and round. . . ."

Fascinated, he and Mayhew watched as she circumnavigated the day cabin, slowly at first and then with increasing speed. Grimes remembered the real Una in the garden, the Eden from which they had been evicted by the robot deity. He remembered her graceful nudity in delightful contrast to the equally graceful machine that she had ridden.

"There's something *odd* about that bicycle. . . ." murmured Mayhew.

Keep out my memories! thought Grimes. Yes, there had been something odd about the bicycles that both of them had ridden on that faraway world in another universe. He recalled that final showdown when he had been obliged to fight the things. . . .

"Sorry, Captain," apologized Mayhew. "But I couldn't help getting pictures of you as a naked bullfighter, with a bicycle playing the bull!"

Chapter 21

There was the unpleasantness when Kate Connellan, who had taken too much drink before dinner, expressed her disapproval of the menu by hurling the contents of a bowl of goulash at Magda Granadu. It missed its target but liberally bespattered the unfortunate Mr. Stewart. For this assault by her upon a fellow officer Grimes imposed as high a fine as he legally could. There were mutterings from those who had been or were currently recipients of the Green Hornet's favors but even they knew that she had overstepped the mark. Then there was an undignified brawl between Mr. Singh, Mr.

Trantor and Mr. Denning, two of whom disapproved of Ms. Connellan's latest change of sleeping partners. This was broken up by Mr. Venner. There was the screaming match when the second mate discovered that the potato plants, installed in one of the hydroponics tanks before departure from Port Woomera, had died. Ms. Connellan alleged that these hapless vegetables had been murdered by Ms. Granadu so as to deprive her of New Donegal's renowned culinary delicacy.

"As long as *you* can have your stinking garlic," she had yelled at Grimes, "*you're* happy!"

There was another entry in the Official Log, another fine.

Grimes was not the only one relieved when, at long last, her interstellar drive shut down, *Sister Sue* was in orbit about El Dorado. His officers were at landing stations, Aerospace Control had granted permission for descent.

"All is ready for you at Bluewater Spaceport, *Sister Sue*," said the mechanical voice.

"Sounds like a robot, Skipper," commented Williams.

"Probably is," replied Grimes. "A small human population, living in great luxury, pampered by hordes of mechanical servitors. At least, that's the way that it was when I was here last, years ago. . . ."

"Bluewater Spaceport. . . . A pretty name," said Williams. "According to the directory there's another port, on the other side of the planet. Port Kane. . . ."

"That's new," Grimes told him.

"I don't suppose that we shall be seeing it," said Williams.

You've a surprise coming, thought Grimes.

He applied just enough thrust to nudge *Sister Sue* out of her orbit and she began her controlled fall, dropping down through the clear morning sky toward the almost perfect azure ellipse, visible even from this altitude, of Lake Bluewater. The last time that he had made a landing here it had been in an almost uncontrollable, rocket-powered reentry vehicle; in those days such archaic contraptions were still carried by major warships and some captains liked to see them exercised now and again. Grimes and another junior officer had been sent down in this dynosoar, as the thing was called, to be the advance landing party for the cruiser *Aries*. He had splashed down into the lake and had fallen foul of the Princess Marlene von Stolzberg, who had been enjoying an afternoon's water skiing, and her watchbirds.

He found that he was remembering that day very well. Would she remember him? he wondered. He had heard from her only once since that long ago visit to El Dorado. Would

97

she want to be reminded, now, of what had briefly flared between them? Would she have told her son who his father was? His thoughts drifted away from her to another El Doradan lady, Michelle, Baroness d'Estang. Was she on planet? He had last seen her, not so long ago, on New Venusberg and she had strongly hinted that there was unfinished business between them.

He envisaged a cozy little dinner party aboard his ship at which his only two guests would be the princess and the baroness. He chuckled.

"What's the joke, Skipper?" asked Williams.

"Nothing," said Grimes.

"Aerospace Control to *Sister Sue*," came the voice from the NST transceiver. "Surface wind northeast at three knots. Unlimited visibility. . . ."

"I can see tht," grumbled Grimes. Then, to old Mr. Stewart who was seated by the transceiver, "Acknowledge, please. Oh, just ask him—or it—not to foul up my landing with any flocks of tin sparrows. . . ."

"Sir?"

"You heard me."

Williams, Venner and Ms. Connellan looked curiously at Grimes as the radio officer repeated the request.

The reply was not long in coming.

"If your second landing on this world is as eventful as your first, Captain Grimes, the fault will be yours alone."

Williams laughed. "They seem to know all about you, Skipper!"

"The Monitor," said Grimes coldly, "sees all, hears all, knows all and remembers all."

"The Monitor?"

"The electronic intelligence that runs this world—although the human El Doradans are quick to point out that it is only a servant, not a master."

He returned his attention to the controls. *Sister Sue* was dropping fast, the arrhythmic beat of her inertial drive little more than an irritable mutter. Visible in the stern view screen was Lake Bluewater with, on its northern shore, the huddle of white buildings that was the spaceport, the tall control tower. A regular flashing of scarlet light indicated the position of the beacons; soon, now, they would be visible as three individual lights set in a triangle. Through the viewports could be seen the evidence of what great wealth and expensive technology can do to a once barren world. This planet, when first purchased by the El Dorado Corporation, had been

98

absolutely lifeless; now it was all park and garden, cultivated field and orchard. There were lakes and rivers, small seas, ranges of snow-capped mountains, forests. There was only one city, named after the planet, about fifty kilometers north of the spaceport, but there were chateaux, castles and manor houses sparsely scattered throughout the countryside. There were mines and factories—El Dorado was rich in valuable minerals—but all industry was underground.

"What was all that about tin sparrows, Skipper?" asked Williams.

"Watchbirds," replied Grimes. "Every El Doradan has his team of personal guardians. The flying ones have modified and improved avian brains in mechanical bodies."

"So if you made a pass at a local lady," said Williams, "you'd be liable to have your eyes pecked out."

"You've got a one-track mind. . . ." Grimes was going to say, but the Green Hornet got in first with, "No more than you'd deserve!"

Venner laughed and old Mr. Stewart chuckled.

"Quiet, all of you!" snapped Grimes. "Keep your eyes on your instruments. Let me know at once if you pick up any flying objects on the radar, Mr. Venner. Let me have frequent radar altimeter readings Ms. Connellan." (This last was not really necessary as there was a read-out in the stern view screen.) "Maintain an all round visual lookout, Mr. Williams."

"Anybody would think this was a bloody battle cruise," muttered the second mate.

Grimes glared at her. "I've still plenty of pages in the official log," he said.

Sister Sue continued her controlled fall. The marker beacons showed now as a triangle of three bright, blinking lights. Grimes brought this configuration to the very center of the screen. He stepped up the magnification. There were no other ships in port; the apron was a wide, empty stretch of gray concrete. A long streamer of white smoke was now issuing from a tall pipe at the edge of the landing field. It became particolored—an emission of white, then of red, then black, then white again. It gave an indication of wind velocity as well as of direction.

Compensating for drift was no problem. The inertial drive became louder as Grimes increased vertical thrust, slowing the rate of descent. He watched the diminishing series of figures to one side of the screen, noted irritably that the Green Hornet, reporting those same readings from the radar altimeter, was lagging badly. But this was not, after all, a battle cruiser.

Yet.

Down crawled the ship, down, at the finish almost hovering rather than falling. The tips of her vanes at last gently kissed the concrete. Grimes cut the drive. *Sister Sue* shuddered and sighed, then relaxed in the tripodal cradle of her landing gear. There were the usual minor creakings and muted rattlings as weight readjusted itself.

"Finished with engines," said Grimes, then refilled and relit his pipe.

Chapter 22

At a normal spaceport, on a normal planet, ground cars would have brought the various officials—Customs, Immigration, Port Health and all the rest of them—out to a newly arrived ship. Here, at Port Bluewater, there was only a solitary figure walking out from one of the white office buildings, pacing slowly over the gray apron. It was wearing a uniform of some kind, black with gold trimmings. It looked human.

Grimes went to the big mounted binoculars, swung and focused them. He looked at the dull-gleaming, pewter-colored face under the gold-embellished peak of the cap. A robot. So none of this world's human inhabitants considered it worth their while to receive him and his ship.

He said to Mr. Venner, "Go down to the after airlock to meet that . . . that tin Port Captain. Take him—no, *it*—up to Ms. Granadu's office. She'll have all the necessary papers ready for our Inward Clearance." He allowed himself a laugh. "At least I shan't be put to the expense of free drinks and smokes for a pack of bludging human officials!"

"He might want to plug into a power point, Skipper, to get a free charge," said Williams.

Venner left the control room. The Green Hornet began, in a desultory manner, to tidy things away.

Williams said, "I suppose I'd better go down to the office myself. There might be some word about discharging arrangements."

"I'll come with you," said Grimes.

Anywhere but here he would have waited in his day cabin for the ship's agent, there to discuss matters over coffee or something stronger. He did not, however, feel like entertaining in his own quarters what he had already categorized as an uppity robot.

The elevator was not immediately available so Grimes and Williams made their descent into the body of the ship by the spiral staircase. Magda was waiting in her office. All necessary documentation was arranged neatly on her desk, as also was a box of cigarillos. On a table to one side was a steaming coffee pot with the necessary crockery and containers of cream and sugar.

"You can put those away," said Grimes, gesturing.

"Not so fast, Skipper," said Williams. "*We* can use some coffee. And I'm never averse to a free smoke."

"All right. Pour me a cup while you're about it."

"Why should the coffee and the smokes not be required, Captain?" asked the catering officer.

"You'll see," said Grimes.

Venner appeared in the doorway.

"The Port Captain, sir," he announced, then withdrew.

The robot entered.

It said, in a quite pleasant, not overly mechanical voice, "Yes. That is my title. I am also Collector of Customs, Port Health Officer and Immigration Officer. If I may be allowed to scan your papers I shall soon be able to inform you whether or not all is in order."

Grimes had seen the thing's like before, both on El Dorado and aboard the Baroness d'Estang's spaceyacht. It could have been a handsome, well-made human being with a metallic skin. Williams and Magda, however, were familiar only with the common or garden varieties of robot, only crudely humanoid at the best. (They had seen, of course, the exquisite, golden figurine that had been given to Grimes before lift-off from Port Southern—but she was only a beautiful miniature, not life-size.)

The automaton moved to the desk, went through the papers like a professional gambler dealing playing cards. It seemed to have no trouble reading things upside down. After only seconds the documents were back in their original order.

The subtly metallic voice said, "You are cleared inwards."

"Don't I get certification?" asked Grimes.

"That, Captain, is not required. The Monitor has cleared you. You will, however, be issued the usual Outward Clearance documents prior to your departure."

"When will discharge be started?" asked Grimes.

"Your cargo is not urgently required, Captain. Perhaps to-morrow the shipment of caviar will be off-loaded. The other items? At the moment there is no warehouse space available."

"So I have to sit here," exploded Grimes, "with my ship not earning money, paying wages to my crew and feeding them. . . . And you, I suppose, will be charging port dues."

"Of course, Captain."

"Demurrage . . . ?" wondered Grimes aloud. "Compensation for delay?"

"That is not applicable in your circumstances."

Perhaps, perhaps not, Grimes thought. He would have to make a careful study of *The Shipmaster's Business Companion*.

"Another point," he said. "I was last here as an officer of one of the Survey Service's cruisers."

"We are aware of that, Captain Grimes."

". . . so I had no cause to find out what facilities are available to merchant vessels. Is there a Shipping Office here? I may have to pay off one of my officers."

"There is no Shipping Office here. In any case, as you should know, outworlders may not be dumped on this planet. And that seems to have concluded all immediate business. Should you require stores, repairs or other services you may call the Port Master's office on your NST. I wish you good day."

"Is my NST hooked up to the planetary telephone service?" asked Grimes.

"It is not, Captain. You may, however, use the telephonic facilities in the reception area in the main office. Such calls will be charged against you. Again I wish you a good day."

The Port Captain turned, strode out of the office. They could hear his (its) footsteps, too heavy to be those of a human being, in the alleyway outside—and, for quite a while, on the treads of the spiral staircase leading down to the after airlock.

Grimes, Billy Williams and Magda Granadu looked at each other with raised eyebrows.

Williams said, "I don't think that I shall like this world, Skipper, where even robots treat us like dirt."

"The last time I came here," said Grimes, "there was a human Port Captain. The Comte Henri de Messigny. He wasn't must better than his tin successor."

"What happened to the . . . Comte?"

"He . . . died."

102

"Were you involved, Skipper?"

"Yes," said Grimes shortly. "And now, Mr. Williams, you'd better see to it that the caviar is ready for discharge when somebody condescends to send a team of stowbots out to us. And you, Ms. Granadu, can let the Port Captain's office know what stores you require. Try to confine yourself to inexpensive items, will you? That is, if anything here *is* inexpensive . . . Mphm." He poured himself another mug of coffee, sipped it thoughtfully. "I think I'll take a stroll ashore," he went on. "I might make one or two phone calls. . . ."

"Looking up the old girl friends, Skipper?" asked Williams cheerfully.

"Surely you don't think, Mr. Williams," said Grimes coldly, "that any El Doradan lady would have anything to do with a mere spaceman?"

"There are precedents," said the Mate. "Drongo Kane, for a start. . . ."

And me before him, thought Grimes—but maintained his sour expression.

Chapter 23

The spaceport was almost as he remembered it, with only a few minor additions and alterations. And regarding these, he thought, his memory could be playing him tricks. He walked slowly across the apron to the Port Control building, a gleaming, white truncated pyramid topped by the graceful latticework pylon of the control tower. The main door was composed of two huge panels of opalescent glass which swung inward, to admit him, as he approached. He walked over the highly polished floor with its swirling inlaid designs toward the spiral staircase that rose from the center of the huge, high-ceilinged room. He stepped on to the bottom tread. Nothing happened. The last time that he had performed this action—how many years ago?—he had been borne smoothly upward to what were to be his temporary quarters and to much appreciated refreshment. This time, obviously, there were to be no free meals and drinks.

He turned away from the spiral staircase, walked to an

open booth against one of the walls. There was no panel with dials or buttons but he could recall the procedure. Inside the booth, facing the rear wall, he said, "Get me the Princess Marlene von Stolzberg."

The rear wall became a screen, three dimensional. From it stared a robot servitor, pewter-faced, clad in archaic livery, black, with silver braid and buttons and white lace ruffles.

"Who is calling?" asked the metallic voice.

"John Grimes. Captain John Grimes."

The servant moved away from the screen. Grimes was looking into a room, dark paneled, with antique suits of armor ranged against the walls. *So she's still living in the same place*, he thought. *That gloomy Schloss of hers. . . .*

The picture flickered, faded, was replaced by that of one of the other rooms in the castle, a boudoir, frumpishly feminine in its furnishings.

And she . . . she was not quite a frump, Grimes decided, although she was no longer the golden girl whom he had known. She was not quite fat, although the fine lines of her face were partially obscured by the overlay of fatty tissues. The padded robe that she was wearing concealed her body but, Grimes thought, it must have thickened. (When he had known her she had been a hearty eater.) Her hair was still golden but somehow dulled.

She looked out at him through blue eyes that were clear but cold, cold.

"Grimes," she said without enthusiasm. "John Grimes. Captain John Grimes. Should I congratulate you on your having achieved command? But I see from your uniform that you are no longer in the Survey Service. You are a commercial shipmaster?"

There was a note of disdain in her voice as she asked the question—or made the statement.

"Yes, Marlene. But I'm also a shipowner. I own my ship."

"The correct form of address, Captain Grimes, is Your Highness. As you should remember."

"Your Highness," repeated Grimes, his prominent ears flushing angrily.

"And why have you called me, Captain Grimes?"

"I . . . Well . . . Surely you remember, M . . . Sorry. Your Highness. You sent me a solidograph of yourself and . . . And a baby."

"Yes. I remember. *My* son. The Graf Ferdinand von Stolzberg."

"I . . . I wonder if I could see him. . . ."

104

"To satisfy your idle curiosity? The Graf and yourself would have nothing in common. Are you trying to tell me that you have paternal instincts, Captain Grimes? Ferdinand has never felt the need for a father—and even if he did would not wish to acknowledge a common spaceman as such."

"I apologize for wasting your time, Your Highness," said Grimes at last.

"The pleasure, if any, was all yours," she said.

The screen went blank.

Grimes filled, lit and smoked a soothing pipe. Then he said, slowly and deliberately, "Get me the Baroness Michelle d'Estang."

The screen came alive. This time the robot servitor had the appearance of a human female, a pretty, golden girl in severe black and white lady's maid uniform.

"Who is calling, please?"

"Captain John Grimes, late of *The Far Traveler* and *Little Sister*, now master/owner of *Sister Sue*."

The face and upper body in the screen were replaced by those of a man.

"Micky's out, Grimesy," said Drongo Kane. "Will I do?"

Grimes stared at his old enemy, at the face that looked as though it had been shattered at some time and then reassembled by a careless plastic surgeon, topped by an untidy shock of straw-colored hair.

"Please tell the Baroness that I called, Commodore Kane," said Grimes.

"I'll do that. You're looking quite prosperous, Grimesy. And I hear that you've got yourself a real ship at last. But I warn you—you'll not find it so easy to find cargoes to fill her. I should know."

"I've managed so far," said Grimes.

"And how many voyages have you made in that rustbucket of yours? Two, to date. Well, if you get stuck here you can always give me a call. I might, I just might, have something for you."

"That'll be the sunny Friday," said Grimes.

(For him to have replied otherwise would have been out of character.)

"Don't go looking gift horses in the mouth, Grimes. I'm prepared to let bygones be bygones. But I can always change my mind. And remember—sunny Fridays have a habit of coming around."

The screen went blank.

There was one last call that Grimes thought that he would make.

"Get me," he ordered, "Her Grace the Duchess of Leckhampton."

The robot servant looking out from the screen was, save for his gray metal face, a traditional English butler.

"Good morning, sir. Who shall I say is calling?"

"Captain John Grimes."

"Very good, sir. I shall ascertain if Her Grace wishes to speak with you."

After a very short wait the butler was replaced in the screen by the Duchess. She looked no older. (But she had never looked young.) Her thin white hair was carelessly arranged. Her cheeks were painted. She was wearing a gaudy emerald and scarlet shirt. There was a necklace of glittering stones that looked far too large to be genuine diamonds—but which almost certainly were genuine—about her wrinkled throat. Her black eyes sparkled from among the too liberally applied eye shadow.

"Young Grimes," she cackled, "but not so young any longer. And a captain. This is a pleasure."

"It is a pleasure," said Grimes, not untruthfully, "seeing you again."

"And when are you coming out to see me, John Grimes? What about this evening? Can you get away from your ship? But of course you can. You're the captain now. It is short notice, but I should be able to arrange a little party. I'll ask Marlene. . . ."

"I've already talked to her," said Grimes. "She didn't seem all that pleased to see me."

"Too bad. She's a silly girl, and dotes on that useless son of hers. But I shouldn't have said *that*, should I? After all, he's yours too. But whom else can I ask? Michelle? You know her, of course. And that husband of hers. And Baron Takada. And Chief Lobenga and the Lady Eulalia. . . . Just leave it to me. And perhaps you could bring one or two of your senior officers. . . ."

"But where do you live, Your Grace?"

"In El Dorado City, of course. I'll send a car for you. Can you be ready to leave your ship at 1800 hours?"

"I can, Your Grace."

"Good. I am looking forward to meeting you again, Captain Grimes."

He left the Port Control Office, walked back to the ship. He saw that a conveyor belt had been set up to connect with one of the upper cargo ports and that at its base a medium-sized air truck and a couple of spidery stowbots were waiting. As he watched, the first of the cartons slid out of the aperture in the hull, was followed by others in a steady stream. With a smooth economy of motion the robot stevedores loaded them into the body of the truck.

He walked up the ramp into *Sister Sue's* after airlock, took the elevator to the cargo compartment in which the shipment of caviar was stowed. He found Williams there and also the Port Captain, the agent or extension of the Monitor, who, wordlessly, was supervising the activity of the pair of stowbots which were loading cartons onto the top of the belt.

"Mr. Williams," said Grimes, "I think that our friend here can be trusted to function as a master stevedore. Come up to see me, please, and collect Ms. Granadu on the way."

"Aye, aye, Skipper. I'll just see the next tier broken—it's rather tightly stowed—then I'll be with you."

Grimes carried on up to his quarters, sat down in his day cabin to wait. Before long the mate and the catering officer had joined him.

"Sit down," he said. Then he asked, "Are you free this evening?"

"Free, Skipper? You have to be joking. We're confined to the vicinity of this blasted spaceport. There's no public transport. I asked the so-called Port Captain if we could use of the ship's boats to take a run into the city and I was told that intrusion into El Doradan air space by outworlders is prohibited."

"I've been asked to a dinner party, Mr. Williams, by the Duchess of Leckhampton. She suggested that I bring two of my senior officers with me. Does the Dog Star Line run to mess dress?"

"Only in their passenger ships, Skipper, and I was never in them. But I've a civilian dinner suit."

"That will do nicely. I won't be wearing uniform myself. And you, Magda?"

"I've an evening dress, Captain."

"Good. The Duchess's air car will be calling for us at 1800 hours."

Magda Granadu appeared to be thinking deeply. She said at last, "I feel that this will be an *important* meeting. . . ."

"Too right it is," said Williams. "It'll be the first time in my life that I've had dinner with a Duchess!"

"More important than that, Billy," the woman told him.

107

"Important for all of us. I think that we should consult the *I Ching,* Captain."

"We can wait until we get to Her Grace's mansion," said Grimes, "and she can read the Tarot pack."

"Does this Duchess have the gift?" asked Magda.

"I . . . I think so. When I was here before she came up with a rather uncanny prediction."

"And was she working for you—or for herself?"

"For El Dorado, I suppose," said Grimes.

"And my *Book of Changes* will be working for you, Captain. For us. Would you mind if I went down for the book and the coins?"

"Go ahead," said Grimes.

"She really believes it," said Williams when she was gone. "Do you, Skipper?"

"Do you, Mr. Williams?"

Magda came back, holding the black silk-covered book. She handed the three silvery coins to Grimes. He shook them in his cupped hands, let them fall to the deck. Two heads and a tail. The second throw produced the same result, as did the third. Two tails and a head, then two heads and a tail again. The last throw was a head and two tails.

"Upper trigram, *K'an,*" said the woman. "Lower trigram, *Ch,ien.* The hexagram is *Hsu. . . .*" She read from the book. "Biding one's time. . . . Sincerity will lead to brilliant success. Firmness will bring good fortune. It will be advantageous to cross the great water. . . ."

"That's our job, isn't it?" asked Grimes.

"I suppose so," she said. "But the Image is . . . interesting and possibly apposite. 'Clouds drift across the sky as if biding their time. The superior man, in accordance with this, eats and drinks, feasts and enjoys himself.' "

"There's no reason," said Grimes, "why we should not enjoy a free meal."

After they had left his cabin he called Ken Mayhew.

"Mr. Mayhew," he said, "I suppose you know that I've been invited to dinner with the Duchess of Leckhampton. I'm taking Mr. Williams and Ms. Granadu with me. I'd have liked to have taken you—for obvious reasons—but the old bat said that I could bring two of my officers with me. And unless we break your cover you're not one of my officers. You're a passenger, and only a senior clerk on holiday. They're a snobbish bunch here."

"I have already gained that impression, Captain. I have

108

been . . . eavesdropping, receiving unguarded thoughts from all over, trying to pick up something concerning *you.* There was a woman who came through quite strongly. She was vocalizing her thinking. *Should I see him again? But if I invite him here he will be almost certain to meet Ferdinand—and Ferdinand could notice the facial resemblance, even though I had his ears fixed while he was still only a baby. He believes that Henri was his father and I want him to go on believing that. Better a dead aristocrat than an impossibly bourgeois spaceman. . . .*"

"Mphm," grunted Grimes indignantly. "Am I impossibly bourgeois, Mr. Mayhew?"

"I don't think so, sir," said the telepath diplomatically. "Then there was a man, a spaceman I would say, like yourself. Would it have been this Drongo Kane? *So Grimes, of all people, is here. In a real ship. I could use him. After all, he held command in the Survey Service. He's been in a few naval actions. The only laws for which he has any respect are those he makes himself. But he's a prickly bastard. I'll have to handle him carefully. But, first of all, I'll have to see to it that there's a shortage of cargoes for his* Sister Sue—*what a name for a ship!—in this sector of the galaxy. I'll have to get old Takada on to it. He's our financial wizard. . . .*"

"The Baron Takada," said Grimes, "is El Dorado's financial wizard. And am I a prickly bastard?"

"You are at times, sir. But to continue. . . . There was a woman, elderly. *Just imagine that young Grimes turning up here after all this time . . . I wish that I were a few years younger. Marlene's a fool; she should have kept him once she'd got her claws into him. She's enough money for two and she could afford genealogical research to turn up some sort of patent of nobility for a commoner husband. Michelle wasn't so absurdly fussy—although you could hardly say that Kane married her for her money. He's plenty of his own. And he'll have plenty more—as we all shall!—if that private navy of mercenaries does as well as he says it will. . . .*"

"I always rather liked the Duchess," said Grimes, "although she's a ruthless old bat. So she's an investor in Kane's Honorable Company of Interstellar Mercenaries. Probably everybody is on this world. I've noticed that the very rich never miss any opportunity to become even richer. And Baron Takada will be pulling his strings and exporters and importers will be dancing to his tune, and I'll be sitting here on the bones of my arse, ffat broke and getting broker. . . .

And then Drongo Kane will bob up like a pantomime Good Fairy and offer me, and the ship, a job. . . ."

"You have some peculiar friends, sir," said Mayhew dryly.

"Don't I just. Can you sort of tune in to the dinner party tonight? Let me know, when I get back, if you heard anything interesting."

"I think I can manage that, sir."

"Good." He looked at the bulkhead clock. "It's time I was getting changed."

Chapter 24

Grimes and Williams, dressed in what the mate referred to as their penguin suits, stood at the foot of the ramp watching the Duchess's air car coming in. With them was Magda Granadu, also wearing a black outfit, high-necked, long-sleeved and with an ankle-length skirt. Its severity was offset by a necklace of opals, by a blazing, fire opal brooch over her left breast and by what was almost a coronet of opals in her piled-high auburn hair.

You can put an inertial drive unit into any sort of body, of any shape at all, and it will fly. If you want speed through the atmosphere streamlining is desirable. If speed is not the main consideration the streamlining may be dispensed with.

The Duchess's car was not streamlined. It was an airborne replica of one of the more prestigious road vehicles developed during the twentieth century, Old Reckoning, on Earth, even to the silver nymph decorating the square bonnet. It drifted down through the evening air, touched, then rolled the last few meters on its fat-tired wheels. The chauffeur—a gray-faced robot clad in black, high-collared, silver-buttoned livery—got down from the forward compartment, marched stiffly to the three humans and saluted smartly.

"Your transport, gentlemen and lady," he announced in a metallic voice.

He turned, walked back to the car and opened the rear door. Grimes held back to let Magda enter first but she said, "After you, Captain."

She followed him in, so as to sit between him and Williams. Williams entered. The robot chauffeur shut the door, returned to his own seat. There was a sheet of glass or some other transparency between him and his passengers. His voice came to him through a concealed speaker. "Gentlepersons, you will find a small bar in the panel before you. There is a single button in the padding, which you may press."

The car lifted. Grimes, whose mind was a repository of all manner of useless facts, recalled the proud boast of Rolls Royce on one of whose later cars this vehicle had been modeled. *The only mechanical sound you can hear is the ticking of the clock on the dashboard.* So it was here. The inertial drive is inevitably noisy, yet Grimes and his companions had heard only the faintest mutter as the car came in for its landing. Inside the passenger compartment there was not so much as a whisper to indicate that machinery was in operation.

"A drink, Skipper?" asked Williams.

"Just one," said Grimes. "We don't want to arrive doing an impersonation of drunken and dissolute spacemen."

When the button was pushed a section of panel fell back to form a shelf and to expose a compartment containing a rack of bottles, another one of glasses and a tiny refrigerator with an ice cube tray. There was a box of cigarettes and one of cigarillos. There was even a jar of pipe tobacco. (Grimes had smoked the local weed when on El Dorado, years ago, and enjoyed it.)

Magda dispensed drinks—whisky, genuine Scotch, for herself and Williams, gin and bitters for Grimes. She and Williams lit up cigarillos. Grimes scraped out his pipe and refilled it with the fragrant mixture. The three of them sipped and smoked, watching, through the wide windows, the landscape over which they were flying.

Here, between the spaceport and the city, it was well tamed, given over to agriculture. There were orchards, with orderly rows of fruit trees. There were green fields, and other fields that were seas of golden grain. In these the harvesters were working, great machines whose bodies of polished metal reflected the rays of the setting sun.

Ahead was the city, a small one, a very small one compared to the sprawling warrens found on the majority of the worlds of man. There were towers, only one of which was really tall, and great houses, oddly old-fashioned in appearance, few of which were higher than four stories. Every building stood in what was, in effect, its own private park. Lights were coming on as the sun went down, in windows and along the wide, straight avenues.

The air car was losing altitude. It dropped to the road

about a kilometer from the city limits, continued its journey as a wheeled vehicle. The landing was so smooth that had the passengers been sitting with their eyes shut they would never have noticed it. The vehicle sped on with neither noise nor vibration, a great orchard with golden-fruit-laden trees on either side of it. Then it was running along one of the avenues. There was other road traffic, ground cars which, like their own transport, were probably capable of functioning as flying machines.

Williams was enthusiastic. "Look, Skipper! A Mercedes! And isn't that a Sunbeam?"

That was an open car, with wire wheels and a profusion of highly polished brass. (Or gold, thought Grimes. On this world it could well be the precious metal.) A man in an archaic costume—belted jacket, high, stiff collar with cravat, peaked cap—was at the wheel. By his side sat a woman with a dust coat over her dress, with her hat secured to her head by a filmy scarf tied over it and beneath her chin. Both these persons wore heavy goggles.

The pseudo Rolls Royce slowed, turned off the avenue on to a graveled drive, made its way to a brilliantly illuminated portico beyond which loomed Leckhampton House, gray and solid, a façade in which windows glowed softly like the ranked ports of a great surface ship, a cruise liner perhaps, sliding by in the dusk. The car stopped. The robot chauffeur got out to open the door for his passengers, saluting smartly as they dismounted. In the doorway of the house stood a very proper English butler, pewter-faced, who bowed as he ushered them in. Another robot servitor, slimmer and younger looking than the first, led them to the drawing room, a large apartment illumined by the soft light from gasoliers, that was all gilt and red plush, the walls of which were covered with crimson silk upon which floral designs had been worked in gold.

It was all rather oppressive.

Following the servant Grimes and his companions walked slowly toward the elderly lady seated on a high-backed chair that was almost a throne.

"Your Grace," said the robot, "may I present Captain John Grimes, of the spaceship *Sister Sue*, and. . . ."

"Cut the cackle, Jenkins," said the Duchess. "I've known Captain Grimes for years. Shove off, will you?"

"Very good, Your Grace."

The servitor bowed and left.

"And now, John Grimes, let me have a look at you. You've changed hardly at all. . . ."

"And neither have you, Your Grace," said Grimes truthfully. He looked at her with admiration. She was dressed formally—and what she was wearing would not have looked out of place at the court of the first Queen Elizabeth, richly brocaded silk over a farthingale (Grimes wondered how she could manage to sit down while wearing such a contraption), ruff and rebato. A diamond choker was about her neck. There were more diamonds, a not so small coronet, decorating the obvious auburn wig that she was wearing over her own hair.

"Introduce me to the young lady and the young gentleman, John."

"Your Grace," said Grimes formally, remembering the style used by the rudely dismissed under butler or whatever he was, "may I present Miss Magda Granadu, my Catering Officer and Purser? And Mr. William Williams, my Chief Officer?"

"So you're the commissioned cook, Magda," cackled the old lady. "By the looks of John you ain't starving him. And you're his mate, Billy, somebody to hold his hand when he gets into a scrape. Do you still get into scrapes, John boy?"

"Now and again," admitted Grimes.

Then there were the others to meet—in Grimes's case to meet again. There was the Baron Takada, his obesity covered with antique evening finery, white tie and tails, the scarlet ribbon of some order diagonally across his snowy shirtfront with its black pearl studs. There was the Hereditary Chief Lobenga, tall and muscular, darkly handsome, in a high-collared, gold-braided, white uniform. There was his wife, the Lady Eulalia, her glistening black hair elaborately coiled above her face with its creamy skin, the nose too aquiline for mere prettiness, the mouth a wide, scarlet slash. Through the pale translucence of her simple gown her body gleamed rosily.

An under butler circulated with a tray of drinks. Grimes did not have to state his preference for pink gin; it was served to him automatically.

"You remember my tastes, Your Grace," he said.

"Indeed I do, John-boy. For drinks and for. . . ."

The butler made a stately entrance into the room.

"The Princess Marlene von Stolzberg," he announced. "Commodore the Baron Kane, El Doradan Navy. The Baroness Michelle d'Estang. . . ."

So she had come to see him after all, thought Grimes. It was a pity that Mayhew had not been able to warn him. She had put on weight, he thought, and remembered regretfully the slim, golden girl whom he had seen, skimming over Lake Bluewater, on the occasion of his first landing on this world. And yet she was more beautiful than she had seemed when he had talked to her by telephone. Like Eulalia she was simply but expensively attired in a robe of smoky spider silk—but her dress was definitely opaque.

She recognized his presence with a distant nod. He bowed to her with deliberate stiffness.

But Drongo Kane was cordial enough. Like Grimes and Williams he was in civilian evening wear; unlike them he gave no impression of being dressed up for the occasion. His suit looked as though it had been slept in. His black bow tie, obviously of the clip-on variety, was askew.

He seized Grimes' hand in a meaty paw, almost shouted, "Grimes, me old cobber! Welcome aboard!"

"This happens to be *my* party, Baron, in *my* house," said the Duchess coldly.

"But *I* am the naval authority on this planet, Duchess," Kane told her cheerfully. Then, to Grimes, "Let by-gones be by-gones is my motto. I've even brought Micky along to see you again."

"I brought myself," snapped the Baroness. She looked at Grimes and he at her. Her dress was modeled on the Greek chiton—but of the style worn by artisans, warriors and slaves. It was short, very short, secured at the left shoulder by a brooch that was a huge diamond surrounded by smaller stones. Her arms and her right shoulder were bare. Her gleaming, auburn hair was braided into a coronet in which precious stones reflected, almost dazzlingly, the gaslight. Her fine features were illumined by a sudden smile.

"John, it's good to see you!"

"And it's good to see you. . . ." How should one address a Baroness? he wondered. "Your Excellency. . . ."

"Not here," she told him. "That was for when I was off planet, in my own ship, with ambassadorial status. Call me Michelle." She glared at her husband as she added, "But don't call me Micky!"

Grimes would have liked to have talked longer with her but Drongo Kane was an inhibiting influence. So he circulated. He tried to make conversation with the Princess Marlene but it was heavy going. And then he was unable to escape from Baron Takada who evinced a keen interest, too keen an interest, in the financial aspects of shipowning.

Then the Robot butler announced in sonorous tones, "Your Grace, dinner is served."

Grimes realized that he was supposed to escort the Duchess in to the dining room. She put her hand lightly into the crook of his left elbow, indicated that they should follow the stately mechanical servitor. They marched slowly into the dining room, a huge apartment the walls of which were covered with broad-striped paper in black and white. At the head of the table, covered with a snowy-white cloth on which the array of golden cutlery and crystal glassware glittered, was the tall-backed chair, of ebony, which was obviously Her Grace's. The illumination, from massed candles in golden holders, was soft but adequate.

The Duchess seated, Grimes stood behind his chair, at her right, waiting for the other ladies to take their places. Opposite him was Marlene. Below her was Baron Takada, then the Lady Eulalia, then Hereditary Chief Lobenga. Williams was at the foot of the table. On Grimes' right was Michelle, with Drongo Kane below her, then Magda.

There was no scarcity of robot footmen. In a very short time all the guests were seated, a pale, dry sherry was being poured into the first of the glasses, and plates, of fine gold-trimmed porcelain, were set down at each plate. Grimes looked at his curiously. Surely this could not be a rose, a pink rose? But it was not, of course. It was smoked salmon, sliced very thinly and arranged in convincing simulation of petals.

He raised his glass to the Duchess and said, "Your very good health, Your Grace."

"Down the hatch, Skipper!" she cackled in reply.

Across the table the Princess looked disapprovingly both at her hostess and at that lady's guest.

Course followed course, each one beautifully cooked and served. English cookery is often sneered at but at its best it is superb. There was a clear oxtail soup, followed by grilled trout, followed by game pie. There was a huge roast of beef, wheeled around on a trolley and carved to each diner's requirements. (By this time Grimes was beginning to wonder if he would be able to find any room for some of that noble Stilton cheese he had noticed on the ebony sideboard.) There was tipsy cake, with thick cream. And there were the wines—the sherry, obviously imported, a hock that was a product of the Count Vitelli's vineyards and none the worse for that. With the game pie came a delightfully smooth claret, and with the beef a heavier but equally smooth Burgundy. Vitelli Spumante accompanied the sweet.

After all that Grimes could manage only a token sliver of the delicious Stilton. He looked down the table a little enviously at Williams, who was piling the creamy, marbled delicacy high on to crackers and conveying them enthusiastically to his mouth.

During the meal the conversation had been pleasant and interesting—and at times, insofar as Grimes was concerned, a little embarrassing. The Baroness told a few stories of their voyagings together in *The Far Traveler*. "If I had let her," she said, "Big Sister—that was the name that we had for the yacht's pilot-computer—would have spoiled John as much as you've been spoiling him tonight. She even made pipe tobacco for him; I think she used dried lettuce leaves for the main ingredient. . . ."

"It was still a good smoke," said Grimes.

"Talking of smoking," said the Duchess, "shall we leave the gentlemen to their port wine and cigars?"

All rose when she did. She was escorted from the dining room by her majordomo, the other ladies by robot footmen.

The gentlemen resumed their seats.

Chapter 25

A servitor brought in a large decanter of port wine, another a box of cigars, a third golden ashtrays and lighters. When these had been set down on the table the robots retired. Drongo Kane got up from his chair, took, as though by right, the Duchess's seat at the head of the table. Baron Tanaka was now sitting opposite Grimes, with the Hereditary Chief next to him. Williams moved up to sit next to his captain.

The decanter circulated. Kane filled his glass to the very brim. So did Williams. Cigars were ignited.

"Perhaps we should have a toast," said Kane. He raised his glass. "Here's to crime!"

And it was a crime, thought Grimes, how that uncouth

bastard gulped that beautiful wine as though it were lager beer on a hot day.

"But it is not crime," said Baron Takada, "if it is legal."

"As a banker, *you* should know, Hiroshi," Kane said. "What do you think, Grimes?"

"I always try to keep on the right side of the Law," said Grimes.

"Don't you find it rather a strain at times? A man like you. I've always thought that you'd make a good pirate. I haven't forgotten what you did to my ship that first time on Morrowvia."

"I thought that you were letting by-gones be by-gones."

"I am, Grimesey-boy, I am. I might even put some business your way. Some *honest* crime. Or legal crime."

"You're contradicting yourself, Kane."

"Have you ever known me to do that?" He refilled his glass, to the brim again, looked over it at Grimes. "Tell me, have you never regretted having left the Survey Service? Have you never felt naked swanning around in an unarmed ship when, for all your spacefaring life prior to the *Discovery* mutiny, you've had guns and missiles and the gods know what else to play with?"

"Are you offering me a commission in the El Doradan navy?" asked Grimes.

Kane laughed. "To be an officer in our navy you have to be of noble birth and I don't think that you qualify."

"If you're a fair sample of nobility, Baron Kane, I'm glad that I don't."

"Temper, temper, Grimes!" Kane wagged his cigar reprovingly. "Anyhow, you're a trained fighting spaceman." He turned to Williams. "And so are you, Mister Mate. You're out of the Dog Star Line—and they've always made a practice of defensively arming their ships when necessary."

"I have been in action, sir," admitted Williams.

"And there's your Third Officer, Grimes," Kane went on. "Your Mr. Venner. A Survey Service Reserve officer."

"How do you know all this?" asked Grimes.

"From your ship's papers, of course. The data was fed into the Monitor when you were cleared inward."

"And what are you driving at?" Grimes demanded.

Kane did not reply but Baron Takada murmured, "In times of economic stress the armed and armored man survives."

It sounded profound, probably more so than it actually was.

"Economic stress?" echoed Grimes.

"Yes, Captain. A state of affairs to which you are no stranger. My reading of your character is that you are a man who would take up arms to defend what is his. And has it not been said that attack is the best defense?"

So, thought Grimes, the first feelers were being put out. It would be out of character for him to be too eager to take the bait.

He said, "This is all very interesting, gentlemen, but I don't see how it concerns me. I own and command a ship, fully paid for. I show a profit on my voyage from Earth to El Dorado. Presumably there will be some cargo from here to elsewhere in the galaxy."

"I am afraid that there will not be," said Baron Takada. "The Interstellar Transport Commission has the contract for the shipment of our metal products off El Dorado. Too, I can tell you that there are no cargoes for ships such as yours, independently operated star tramps, in this sector of the galaxy." He smiled apologetically. "It is my business to know such things. The Duchess asked me if I could be of help to you in finding you employment, or in advising you where to find employment. I command a fine commercial and financial intelligence service and I have set it to work on your behalf. All inquiries have been fruitless."

"Something will turn up," said Grimes.

"Still riding your famous luck, Grimesey-boy?" laughed Kane. "I sort of gained the impression that it had been running out lately. If I hadn't pulled you out of the soup on New Venusberg. . . ."

"I gained the impression," Grimes said, "that it was the Baroness who was largely responsible for my rescue."

"I was there too." Again he filled his glass, then sent the decanter on its rounds. Baron Takada waved it on. Hereditary Chief Lobenga helped himself generously. So did Williams. So did Grimes. He knew that he should be keeping a clear head but this wine was of a quality that he rarely encountered.

Kane continued, "Just suppose your luck does run out, Grimes. Just suppose that you're stuck here, waiting for news of employment somewhere, anywhere, with port dues mounting and your bank balance getting lower and lower. And just suppose that I, your old cobber, offer you and your ship a job. . . ."

"A charter?" asked Grimes.

"Sort of," said Kane.

"What cargo, or cargoes?" Grimes persisted.

"What you can pick up," Kane told him.

For some reason he found this amusing. So did Lobenga, who laughed loudly. Even Baron Takada smiled.

"Cards on the table, Grimesy-boy," said Kane. "I'll spill the beans and see if you're ready to lick them up. If you aren't now, you may be in a few days' time, when you're still stuck here, with bills piling up and nobody in any hurry at all to discharge your cargo. You may have heard that I'm assembling a fleet at Port Kane. Owner-masters, not too scrupulous, down on their luck. . . ."

"Like you," said Grimes.

"Not like me. I'm not down on my luck. But you are. There's *Pride of Erin*, Captain O'Leary. And *Agatha's Ark*, Captain Agatha Prinn. *Spaceways Princess*, Captain Mac-Whirter. . . . All of 'em, like your *Sister Sue*, one-time Epsilon Class tramps in various stages of decrepitude. All of them armed. Oh, nothing heavy. A laser cannon, a quick-firing projectile cannon, a missile launcher. All of them with temporal precession synchronization controls fitted to their Mannschenn Drive units. Small arms, of course, for the boarding parties. . . ."

It was Grimes' turn to laugh.

"Just who do you think you can fight with an armed rabble like that?"

"Unarmed merchantmen, of course."

"*Piracy?*"

"No. Not piracy. Privateering," stated Kane.

He went on to tell Grimes what he already knew, what Damien had told him back at Port Woomera. He made it all sound as though it would work, and work well. Williams, to whom all this was new, listened entranced. Grimes did his best to look both disapproving and doubtful.

"And meanwhile," he said, "your gallant, money-hungry captains are sitting snug in Port Kane, eating their heads off and being paid for doing nothing."

"There is a retaining fee, of course," admitted Kane. "And no port dues are charged. And the ships will soon be lifting." He nodded toward the Baron. "Over to you, Hiroshi."

"You will appreciate, Captain Grimes," said Takada, "that a successful interstellar financier must maintain an intelligence service. Do you know, or know of, the Hallichek Hegemony? Of course you do. A not very pleasant avian matriarchy. On one of the worlds under their control, one of their colonies, the males have succeeded in becoming domi-

119

nant. Soon, very soon, the Prime Nest will be endeavoring to restore the status quo. A punitive expedition will be dispatched to Kalla, the rebel planet. The Kallans have a space navy of their own, a small one and a good one. The Kallan government is prepared to issue Letters of Marque to outsiders, such as ourselves, so that the Hegemony's merchant shipping may be raided and seized, leaving their own fighting ships to defend the planet."

"As an idea," said Grimes, "it's strictly for the birds!"

"But it could be fun, Skipper," said Williams.

It could be, Grimes thought. He was a human chauvinist at times and had never liked the Hallicheki, those cruel, dowdy, yet strutting and arrogant old hens. The males of their species were, by human standards, much more likeable.

"Think about it," said Kane. "Sleep on it. Remember that this is a golden opportunity to get in on the ground floor of what could be, what will be a very profitable business. Big profit, small risks. The arms that you carry will remain the property of the El Doradan Corporation so you will not have to buy them. The Corporation will make the necessary modifications to your ship, free of charge. We can also provide gunnery training facilities—although in your case it should not be necessary. You, and your mate and your third mate, already have experience with weaponry. . . ."

"Give it a go, Skipper!" urged Williams who, obviously, had overindulged in the excellent port wine.

"Mr. Williams," said Grimes, "seems to be enthusiastic. But what about my other officers?"

"Any merchant spaceman left by his ship on El Dorado," said Kane, "is regarded and treated as a criminal, jailed until such time as somebody can be persuaded to take him off planet. Such few unfortunates as have experienced the hospitality of our prison system have not been pampered. We do not believe in needless expense."

"No?" asked Grimes sardonically, looking around at the rich appointments of the dining room.

"Unless," went on Kane, "it is for ourselves." He got to his feet. "Shall we join the ladies?"

Chapter 26

The ladies were playing bridge, with the exception of the Princess Marlene. She was sitting by herself, idly leafing through a magazine. Kane looked at the dedicated quartet about the card table, turned to the other men and asked, "What about making up another four, Grimes?"

"I'm not a millionaire," Grimes said. "I can't afford to play with El Doradans."

"Your tabby's doing all right," said Kane.

And so she should be, thought Grimes. Magda was partnered with the Duchess, which lady was on the point of pulling off a Misere in no trumps. Was it fair, he wondered, that two women with psychic gifts should be allied? But Michelle and the Lady Eulalia could afford to lose money. Magda could not. Neither could he nor Williams. Too, he did not much care for the variety of bridge, with its Misere bids, that was being played. No matter what his cards were he played—not always successfully—to win. (And now, he thought wryly, he was being paid by Rear Admiral Damien to lose. . . .)

"All right," said Kane. "If you're chicken we'll adjourn to the music room." He called to the Duchess, "Is it okay to use your playmaster, Lecky? Could we watch those spools you've just got in from New Venusberg?"

The Duchess looked around and up to him, stared at him coldly. "You may use the playmaster, Baron Kane. It will exhibit whichever programs you order."

"New Venusberg . . ." murmured Williams. "Hot stuff. . . ."

Too hot for me, thought Grimes. He had been an unwilling performer in New Venusberg entertainments and his memories of that period of his life were not among his happiest.

The Princess had closed her magazine and put it down on her lap. She was looking at Grimes. Was that invitation in her expression? Could her attitude toward him have changed so suddenly? And if so, why? The El Doradans, as he well knew, did not believe in giving something for nothing.

121

He sauntered over to her, bowed stiffly. Her nod in reply was not stiff. She dropped the magazine on to the low table by her chair, extended a plump hand to him. He took it, helped her to her feet.

She said softly, "I thought, John, that we might take a stroll in the conservatory . . ."

He said, "That will be a great pleasure, Your Highness."

She was very close to him as they walked slowly out of the drawing room, her rounded—too well padded?—right hip brushing against his left one. They passed the music room. Looking in through the open door Grimes could see the wide, deep screen of the playmaster, alive with a vivid depiction of the Colosseum arena where naked gladiators, men and women, were battling to the death. He was fortunate, he thought, that on his one appearance there he and the others on his team had been pitted only against wild beasts.

Marlene guided him through a labyrinth of corridors, gaslit tunnels, stone-floored, walled with panels of some dark wood, gleaming with satin polish. They came to a door which opened before them. Beyond it was a dimly illumined cavern—it seemed at first—a green gloom that was alive with the rustle of lush vegetation, the tinkling of falling water. The air was warm, moist, redolent with the scent of growing things. Gradually the intensity of the light increased, was reflected from fleshy, scarlet flowers, from the glowing, golden globes that were exotic fruit of some kind.

"The one part of Leckhampton House," remarked Marlene, "that's not a slavish imitation of Old England. Although, I believe, the conservatories of some of the ancient establishments maintained by the nobility were hothouses in which all sorts of foreign plants flourished. . . ." She waved an arm in the direction of a luminous display of great, polychromatic blossoms. "I'm sure that if Her Grace's ancestors could have gotten a specimen of Tandoro Spectrum Flowers they would have done so."

They paused by the fountain, looked into the big basin in which the Locomotive Lilies—an ugly name for a quite beautiful plant—were cruising slowly around and around, each an almost circular pad of green leaves supporting a creamy blossom, with trailing root-tendrils that, as well as providing motility, snared the tiny, almost invisible water insects that were the lilies' food.

She didn't drag me in here to give me a lecture on botany, thought Grimes.

She had turned to face him, still standing very close. The

122

scent that she was wearing competed with the natural perfumes of flowers and foliage. It was not a losing battle.

She said, "At first, when I heard that you were coming back to this world, I was far from happy. Now I am not so sure. We had something once. I wonder if we still have it. . . ."

Her upraised face was an invitation for a kiss. He kissed her, on her open mouth. Her lips were warm, moist. He could feel her breasts against him, more full than they had been—how many years ago?—but still firm. His own body was showing signs of interest.

His right hand slid down her back, moving easily over the smooth, silky material of her dress, to the cleft of her buttocks. His fingers closed over a fleshy mound, squeezed gently.

She pulled away from him, quite violently. He thought that she was going to strike him but she did not. Then her face relaxed, the lines of emotion—but what emotion?—smoothing out. Her eyes, thought Grimes, were hard, cold, calculating.

Yet her voice was soft.

She said, "Not here, John. Not now. The Duchess knows everything that happens in this house of hers."

"She knew what happened before," said Grimes. "When. . . ."

"That was then," said the Princess. "This is now."

But she was close to him again, very close. There was another kiss. He restrained, with something of an effort, his hands from wandering.

She said, "You must stay with me again. At the Schloss."

He said, "As master I have considerably more freedom than I did when I was here before, as a junior officer."

"I wish that you could come out with me tonight," she told him, "but the castle is not in a fit state for the reception of a guest."

With hordes of robot servants on the job for twenty-four hours a day and seven days a week? he thought.

She sat down on the rim of the fountain basin, let her hand dangle in the warm water. The lilies clustered about her wrist, attracted by her body heat, by her perfume? Grimes submerged his own right hand. The drifting, motile plants avoided it.

She turned to face him again, looked at him with apparent frankness.

She said, "It is not in my nature to ask favors—but there is

123

one that I must ask you. You know that the Graf von Stolzberg is your son. He does not know that you are his father. He believes, as do many people on El Dorado, that he was sired by the Comte Henri de Messigny. I have made no demands on you until now. . . ." She paused. "No, I am not demanding. I am asking. This. If you enter Baron Kane's service will you, as it were, take Ferdinand under your wing?"

I wish that I'd had some say in naming the boy, thought Grimes.

He said, "But how can I?"

She said, "Then Baron Kane has not told you everything? But you will have to know sooner or later. Perhaps you have wondered what is to stop one of the privateers from deciding not to return to El Dorado with his spoils, from proceeding with all speed to, say, the Duchy of Waldegren or some other worlds or world where loot could be sold at a profit without too many questions being asked. This is what has been arranged. Each of the ships will carry an El Doradan supernumerary officer, seconded from our navy. These officers will make their reports, by Carlotti radio, at regular intervals, to our admiralty. Coded reports, of course."

"And if one of them fails to report, so what?" asked Grimes.

"I haven't finished yet. You know of our watchbirds. . . ."

"I do. But I just can't imagine such a contraption flapping around inside a spaceship."

"I should not need to tell you that our guardians are not necessarily in avian form. But guardians there will be, in the guise of some animal that might be carried aboard a spaceship as a pet. They will be programed to kill in defense of their masters. They will also be programed to self-destruct, catastrophically, should their masters be dead."

"And you think that young . . . Ferdinand will be appointed to my ship, to *Sister Sue*?"

"Of that I cannot be sure. It might be better if he is not. It could prove embarrassing. But this I do know. Baron Kane has said that his fleet of privateers must have a commodore and that you are the obvious man for the choice. As commodore you will have overall responsibility. You will be able to protect my son—*our* son—from danger."

"But he's a naval officer," said Grimes. "A spaceman. . . ."

And what was the El Doradan Navy? A rich men's yacht

club, its flagship a luxury cruising liner rated as an auxiliary cruiser. . . .

"He has never been in any sort of action," said the Princess. "But he's young and foolish. He hopes that there will be fighting."

"If I have my way," said Grimes, "*if* I join Drongo Kane's private gang, *if* I'm put in command of his ragtag fleet, there won't be. We shall keep well clear of real warships and confine our attentions to unarmed merchantmen."

"But you will enter Baron Kane's service," she pressed.

She was pressing in more ways than verbally. She was sitting very close to him on the basin rim, almost melting against him.

Damn you, he thought, *do you want it or don't you?* His arms were about her, hers about him. This time she made no objection to his straying hands. Her mouth was hot on his, open, her darting tongue busy. No matter what her motivations—anxious mother? Drongo Kane's recruiting sergeant?—she was as ready for him as he was for her. What if the conservatory were bugged? (It almost certainly was; on this world the Monitor saw all, heard all, knew all.)

He had worked her dress down over her shoulders, exposing her breasts. Her nipples were erect under his insistent fingers. She moaned, kissing him ever more hotly. One of her hands was at his crotch.

She. . . .

He. . . .

They overbalanced, fell with a loud splash into the fountain basin.

The water was neither deep nor cold but the sudden shock killed desire.

He scrambled out, then assisted her out of the pool. She glared at him as she hastily adjusted her clothing. Then she laughed. It was genuine amusement with nothing vicious about it. She was still laughing when two of the Duchess's robot lady's maids appeared, solicitously wrapped her in a huge white towel and led her away. Grimes, chuckling ruefully, followed.

"There *is* a swimming pool, John," said the Duchess when he made his dripping appearance in the drawing room, "but it is not in the conservatory. I hope that none of my lilies are damaged."

The footman's livery that had been found for him fitted well enough and, in fact, was of far better quality than any

125

of his own uniforms. Nonetheless he thought that it was time that he was getting back to his ship.

"What *did* happen, Skipper?" asked Williams as the air car bore them swiftly back to the spaceport.

"Nothing," grunted Grimes.

"But something must have happened, Captain," said Magda.

"All right," Grimes said. "I didn't cross the great water. I fell into it."

Chapter 27

Back aboard the ship, in his quarters, Grimes buzzed Mayhew and asked him to come up to see him.

The telepath looked sardonically at Grimes' borrowed livery and asked innocently, "Did you have a nice swim, Captain?"

Grimes glared at him and growled, "You know, of course, what happened in the conservatory. What else do you know?"

"I know, Captain, that *they* want you to play a major part in their venture. Your Survey Service background and training. Your reputation. You'll be an ideal figurehead, in more ways than one. . . ."

"How so?" asked Grimes.

"If things come badly unstuck, Kane thinks, you'll be left holding the baby. He looks forward to seeing that almost as much as he does to making another fortune or two."

"The bastard!" swore Grimes.

"Of course," went on Mayhew, "the Baroness is at least partly to blame for his attitude toward you. She's inclined to nag. 'John Grimes would never have done this. John Grimes would never have done that. . . .' She has a soft spot for you and she lets it show."

"I'm glad that somebody loves me," said Grimes.

And what about Marlene? he thought. Then—*No*, he decided. *I'll not ask. She's entitled to her privacy.*

"The old Duchess quite likes you," said Mayhew, "although she's quite prepared to use you. The Hereditary Chief Lobenga despises you—but he despises all honkies, as he thinks of white men. He is amused that the honkies, Baron

Kane, you and the others, will be going to all this trouble to put money into his bank account. The Lady Eulalia? She has no racial prejudices. Her blood line is so mixed that she can hardly afford them. She doesn't care where the money comes from, or how it is made, as long as it comes in. Baron Takada? A money man pure and simple—or not so simple. The Princess von Stolzberg? She is genuinely concerned about her son and wishes that he had not volunteered to become one of the El Doradan liaison officers with the privateer fleet. And there is something more. . . ."

"What?" demanded Grimes.

Mayhew smiled and said softly, "You were thinking very strongly on the subject of the Princess's privacy, sir. I respect that privacy, since it is your wish. But. . . . No matter. Just don't go looking gift horses in the mouth."

"And what about Trojan horses?" asked Grimes. "What about the El Doradan puppies, with their lethal pets, who'll be infesting our ships?"

"Those who have invested in the project," said Mayhew, "not unnaturally wish their investment to be protected. The Trojan horses, as you refer to them, are one means of doing this. There are other methods, less immediate but effective nonetheless. Baron Takada's net is flung wide, very wide. Should a liaison officer defect or be rendered ineffective, should his deadly pet be somehow destroyed without the subsequent destruction of all around it, then the lucky ship would find itself to be an extremely unlucky one, unable to find a market for its stolen goods, harried by officialdom throughout the galaxy."

"Perhaps," said Grimes. "Oh, you didn't include the Baroness in your run-down. . . ."

Mayhew laughed. "You have a friend there, John. A very good one. But like all the other El Doradans she loves money. Too, she is a jealous woman. For whose benefit did she dress the way she did for Her Grace's dinner party? And then—with whom did you go for a swim—sorry, walk—in the conservatory?"

"She was playing cards," said Grimes. "*And* she had her husband in tow."

"And as I said, she is a jealous woman. And now, sir, there are matters of immediate concern. The natives are becoming restless."

"What natives?"

"Your own crew, Captain. Oh, I didn't have to do any snooping. I just flapped my ears in what you would describe as the normal, human manner. The Green Hornet's the most outspoken. At dinner tonight she went off at the deep end. 'What about shore leave? It's all right for His Survey Service High and Mightiness, and his two pets, to go wining and dining with the snobocracy, but what about *us*? Stuck aboard this stinking ship and told that the entire bloody planet's off limits to us. I've a good mind to take one of the boats to fly to that city of theirs!' The junior engineers, both departments, were with her. Venner told her to shut up. She tried to pull rank on him. Then Malleson and Crumley ordered their people to have nothing to do with getting a boat ready. But even they are resentful at being confined to the ship. So is old Mr. Stewart."

"I'll see what I can do about it in the morning," said Grimes.

"You'd better, Captain. One of the things that the Green Hornet shouted was, 'If he's not bloody careful he'll have another bloody mutiny on his hands!' "

"Mutinies," said Grimes coldly, "are usually a result of too much shore leave. It happened to Bligh. It happened to me, in *Discovery*. But I admit that I should have raised the point with Kane. It'd be useless talking to that tin Port Captain about it."

Chapter 28

The next morning, after a leisurely breakfast in his quarters, Grimes went ashore to the Port Office to make his telephone calls. First he got through to the Duchess, thanking her for a very enjoyable evening and apologizing for any inconvenience that he may have caused. She thanked him for the pleasure of his company and assured him that no great damage had been done to the lilies and told him that his evening clothes, cleaned and pressed, would very shortly be sent out to him. She hoped that she would be seeing him again shortly and asked him to present her best wishes to Mr. Williams and Ms. Granadu.

Then he called Kane.

"Yes, Grimesy-boy? Are you dried out yet?"

Grimes ignored this. He said, "You're the naval authority

on this world, Commodore. I'm asking you if it would be possible for my crew to have any shore leave."

"It's a pity that you aren't at Port Kane, Grimesy. I've set up some quite good entertainment facilities there for the privateers. A bar, a cabaret . . . manned—or womanned—by volunteers. It's surprising how many of the local ladies don't mind a night's slumming among the drunken and licentious spacemen. But Port Kane's a long way from Port Bluewater, isn't it? Oh, how's your discharge going, by the way?"

"It isn't," said Grimes.

"Too bad. Haven't you made your mind up yet? If you did, *the right way, that is*, you and your boys would soon be wallowing in the fleshpots of Port Kane. *And* you'd be a commodore, like me. Doesn't that tempt you?"

"Not especially," Grimes said.

"Stubborn bastard, aren't you?" remarked Kane. "Face the facts, Grimes. As an owner/master you're finished—unless you charter your ship and hire your services to me. You don't like the Hallicheki. (Who does?) Why not turn your dislike into money?"

"I'll think about it," said Grimes. "Meanwhile, what about shore leave for my personnel?"

"I'll fix it," said Kane. "I'm a spaceman myself and I know what it's like being stuck aboard the ship when you're in port."

Grimes called the Schloss Stolzberg.

The face of a pewter-visaged servitor appeared on the screen. Then the Princess put in her appearance. Grimes wondered how it had been that he had thought her dowdy. She had matured—but why should she not have done so? Her blue eyes were far from cold. (Whatever had given him the idea that they were?) She smiled at him from inside the screen.

"John! It was fun last night, wasn't it?"

"I trust that you suffered no ill effects, Your Highness."

She laughed. "Shall we forget the titles? I'll call you John, not Captain. You may call me Marlene. When can you come out to stay with me again?"

"My time is my own," said Grimes. "I'm owner as well as master."

Her expression clouded briefly. She said, "At the moment I'm rather tied up. Perhaps after you've shifted your ship from Port Bluewater to Port Kane. . . ."

He said, "I have to finish discharge first. In any case I still haven't said that I'm willing to join Drongo Kane's private navy."

"But you've no option," she said. "Have you? There is nobody else whom I can trust to look after Ferdinand."

Grimes winced. "Tell me," he asked, "why *that* name?"

"Don't you like it, John?"

"Frankly, no."

"It is one that has been in my family, on my mother's side, for a very long time. Even you will admit that the Graf Ferdinand von Zeppelin was illustrious. My Ferdinand—*your* Ferdinand—is descended from an aeronaut. He is an astronaut.

"Is it not, somehow, fitting?"

"Mphm," grunted Grimes.

Chapter 29

Shore leave was arranged for that evening.

"You'd better go with the boys, Captain," said Mayhew. "If it's going to be as grim as I think that it will be you'll have to be seen sharing the vicissitudes of your gallant crew. I'll come along too. I'm not officially on your Articles but I don't think that anybody will notice."

"Very noble of you," grunted Grimes.

"I shall find it interesting," said the telepath.

Williams—lucky man, although he did not know it yet—was shipkeeping. Magda Granadu had elected to keep him company. Mr. Singh, sulking hard, was remaining on board to look after the essential services. There was small likelihood that anything would fail, but Grimes had modeled his own, Far Traveler Couriers, regulations on those of the Federation Survey Service.

The liberty party, attired in a variety of civilian clothing, was waiting at the foot of the ramp when the Wilberforce air car came to pick them up. *Not the sort of company I'd choose for a night ashore*, thought Grimes snobbishly. The Green Hornet, in an outfit of slightly soiled scarlet flounces, was talking with Denning and Paulus, the first in a suit of garish plaid, the other in a shirt of poisonous green with a bright orange kilt and sagging socks of the same color. A not very high-class tart, Grimes thought, trying to entice two honest mechanics enjoying a night out in the big city into her brothel. . . . And Venner, in rusty black, could have been a bouncer from the same establishment. Trantor and Giddings, Malleson's juniors, were holding themselves aloof from the others, already trying to put the message across, *We don't really belong with this mob.* They were neatly, too neatly attired in conservative dark gray with gleaming white shirts and black cravats. Malleson was every inch the tweedy, absent-minded professor. Old Mr. Crumley and old Mr. Stewart, both coincidentally rigged out in dusty brown, looked as though they should be occupying rocking chairs on the porch of a senior citizens' home. Mayhew, gray-clad, was also wearing his senior clerk persona. Grimes himself was looking smart enough in sharply creased white trousers over which was a high-collared black tunic with, on its left breast, his own badge, the horse and rider worked in gold.

The big air car, almost an air bus, came bumbling in from the north. This was no fantastically silent, superbly styled, pseudo Rolls Royce. It was, essentially, only an oblong box on wheels. It dropped down for a clumping, graceless landing. The robot chauffeur remained in his seat although he did condescend to press the button that opened the doors. The officers boarded the vehicle, Grimes last of all. He sat with Malleson and Mayhew on the rear transverse seat. Before he was properly settled the air car lifted. The sonic insulation was of very poor quality and the cacophony of the inertial drive unit inhibited conversation. Nonetheless Malleson tried to talk.

"This Countess of Wilberforce, Captain. . . . Do you know her?"

"No," Grimes almost shouted. "But I know of her."

"What's she like?"

"Filthy rich, like everybody else here."

"Why has she invited us to her bunstruggle?"

"Charity."

"Charity?"

"She's a notorious do-gooder."

"What have you got us into, Captain?"

"You all wanted shore leave, Chief. This was the only way that I could arrange it."

Conversation lapsed.

Grimes looked glumly out of the window, at the twilit landscape below, sliding rapidly astern. He could not see ahead but he could tell that the car was now descending. Jar-

131

ring contact was made with the road surface and the vehicle rolled along the broad avenue with the mansions, each in its own extensive grounds, on either side. It turned into a driveway, shuddered to a halt.

Wilberforce Hall was a red brick building of three stories, graceless but without enough character to be actually ugly. Inside the open main doorway stood one of the inevitable robot butlers and with him a tall, thin woman, black-gowned but with touches of white at throat and wrists. Her dark hair was scraped back from a high, pale forehead. Her bulging, pale gray eyes were set too close together over a beaky nose. Her mouth was small, the lips wrinkled. Her chin was almost nonexistent.

"Come in, boys and girls!" she cried in a high, sickeningly playful voice. She tittered. "Sorry. Boys and *girl* I should have said!"

Grimes made the introductions. He and the others were led into a chilly hall where there were hard chairs and little tables, where a few girls, mercifully prettier than their hostess, brought them weak tea and plates of uninteresting sandwiches and hard little cakes.

Grimes, with Malleson, Crumley and Stewart, sat at a table with the Countess.

"It is so good to have you here, Captain," she gushed. "I have been blessed with wealth and I feel that it is my responsibility to bring joy to others."

"Mphm." Grimes pulled out his pipe and tobacco pouch from a pocket, began to fill the former.

"Please don't think me stuffy," said the Countess, "but I would be so pleased if you wouldn't smoke, Captain. You are doing your lungs no good, you know, and there is even the possibility of brain damage. . . ."

Grimes put his pipe away.

"And we have such a treat for you this evening. As you may know I am the patroness of a number of missionary societies. Bishop Davis has very kindly sent me records of the work of his people among the Carolines. . . ."

The Carolines? Yes, Grimes recalled having read about them. They were a lost colony, descended from the survivors of a long-ago wreck, that of the gaussjammer *Lode Caroline*. They had been fortunate enough to make their landing on an almost paradisal world, one on which nature was kind, too kind perhaps. They had lived there happily, latter day lotuseaters, until the Survey Service's exploration ship *Starfinder* had stumbled upon their planet. Their "lotus," a fleshy leaved

132

plant which was their staple diet, had been investigated by *Starfinder's* scientists. Its organic chemistry was such that synthesis of the complex amino acids would be almost impossible. Daily ingestion of the leaves—raw, or cooked in various ways, or mashed and fermented to make a sort of sweet beer—ensured longevity, freedom from all minor and some major ills and, as a not unpleasant side effect, a state of continuous mild euphoria.

New Caroline was now a commercially important world.

And, thought Grimes, almost certainly the El Dorado Corporation had a dirty finger in that financial pie.

Two robot servants pulled aside the heavy drapes that covered one of the walls of the hall, revealing a huge playmaster screen. As this came to glowing life, depicting a green, blue and gold sphere slowly spinning in space, the lights in the room dimmed.

A sonorous voice announced, "New Caroline—where every prospect pleases but only man is vile. Where only man *was* vile until our coming, until we, of the New Reformed Missionary Alliance were able to bring to the unhappy people the Way, the Truth and the Light. . . .

"The Federation Survey Service has made available to us records taken by the personnel of *Starfinder*. These we show you so that you may judge for yourselves the depravity of the Lost Colonists, the degradation from which we have rescued them."

The planetary globe faded from the screen, was replaced by a village by a wide river, huts of adobe, grass roofed. The time seemed to be late afternoon. A woman emerged from one of the huts, raised her arms and yawned widely. Her teeth were very white against the red of her mouth, the dark, golden tan of her face. She was naked, firmly plump rather than fat. (The Countess looked reprovingly at Grimes as, at one of the other tables, Denning whistled loudly and Paulus remarked, in a carrying whisper, "A lovely dollop of trollop. . . .") She sauntered to a clump of purplish vegetation, almost like a huge artichoke, growing between her hut and its neighbor. She broke off the tip of a succulent leaf, brought it to her mouth, chewed slowly. She spat out a wad of fibrous pulp.

"Observe," intoned the commentator, "the shamelessness of these people, living in filth and squalor. . . ."

(Grimes did not approve of people spitting chewed cuds all over the place but that village looked neither filthy nor squalid—and certainly that sun-tanned body looked clean enough.)

Other people were emerging from their huts—men, women, children of various ages, all innocent of clothing. There was an absence of anybody very old—but that, thought Grimes, could be attributable to the beneficial effects of their staple diet. All the men were heavily bearded. Each of them had a nibble of lotus leaf and then all of them strolled down to the slow flowing river, waded through the shallows and then swam lazily up and down. Grimes ignored the rantings of the commentator and did his best to enjoy the idyllic scene.

"That was *then*," came the annoying voice. "This is *now*. During the few years that we have been on New Caroline we have made great strides. The naked have been clothed. The people have been aroused from their sinful indolence and now experience the benefits deriving from honest toil. . . ."

There were shots of long, neat parallel rows of the artichoke-like plant between which overall-clad Lost Colonists, their clothing dark-stained with perspiration, were working—weeding, spraying fertilizer from backpack tanks, plucking tender young leaves and putting them into baskets. Strolling foremen—Grimes could not be sure, but these men had the appearance of Waldegrensians—supervised, at times seemed to speak harshly to the workers. (Apart from the commentary there was no sound track.)

"And after the day's gainful employment there is the joy that only true religion can bring. . . ."

There was an exterior shot of an ugly chapel constructed of sheet plastic. There was an interior shot of the same building—the pews with the worshippers, dowdily clad in what looked like cast-off clothing from a score of worlds in as many styles—although every woman's dress was long, high-necked and with sleeves to the wrist. There was the pulpit where the black-robed priest was holding forth. There was a small organ at which a woman sat, hands on the keyboard, feet pedaling vigorously. Although an agnostic, Grimes had a weakness for certain hymns, especially those of the Moody and Sankey variety. But what this dispirited congregation was singing failed to turn him on. Not only were the words uninspired but the wheezy apology for a tune was not one to set the feet tapping or the hands clapping.

For many a year we lived in sin
And never knew the Lord;

But now we have been taken in
And glorify His Word . . .

Oh for a good, honest, Salvation Army band, he thought,
*with blaring brass and thumping drums and the lassies with
their tambourines. . . .*

Grimes awoke with a start and realized that the film was
over.

". . . noble work, Captain," the Countess was saying.
"And the contrast! Those poor sinners wallowing in squalor,
and then the happy, industrious people at the finish. . . ."

"Mphm," grunted Grimes, who did not feel like telling any
lies.

"And now you must excuse me, Captain. I have my
humble part to play."

She got up from her chair, walked to the portable organ,
the harmonium that had been wheeled in to below the now
dark and empty screen. The pretty girls who had been helping to entertain the spacemen distributed hymn sheets. The
Countess played. The girls waved *Sister Sue's* people to their
feet and started to sing. Reluctantly, hesitantly, the spacemen
joined in. It was hard to say which was more dismal, the
words or the music.

Sinners all, we beg for grace
And grovel at Thy feet,
And pray that even in this place
We find Thy Mercy Seat!

Holding that thick sheaf of printed matter in his hands
Grimes feared that the ordeal would go on for hours. But the
fourth sheet was not part of a hymnal; it was the beginning
of a brochure.

THE HAPPY KANGAROO, Grimes read with some amazement.

MUSIC, DANCING AND GIRLS, GIRLS, GIRLS!

Meanwhile the portable organ had fallen silent and the
Countess had risen to her feet.

"Thank you all for coming!" she cried. "I am glad that I
was able to bring some happiness into your drab lives. The
air car is waiting for you outside, but before you leave there
will be a collection for the Mission. I am sure that you will
all welcome this opportunity to contribute . . ."

One of the girls was circulating with a collecting bag. She
grinned at Grimes and the others at his table.

"The party's over, spaceman," she whispered, "but if you

come to Port Kane the entertainment will be more to your taste!"

Grimes made to put the hymn sheets and the other literature down on the table.

"Keep all the paper, Captain," she said. "You may be needing it." She laughed softly. "It'll please old Florry no end if she thinks you're holding revival meetings aboard your ship. And now. . . ."

She shook the bag suggestively.

The smallest money that Grimes had on him was a fifty-credit bill. He sighed as he made his contribution to the good cause. He wondered who else had contributed, managed to peak inside the bag and saw that, apart from his note, it was empty.

The Countess stood at the door bidding her guests good night.

"Please come again. . . ."

"*Not bloody likely*," was a too audible whisper from the Green Hornet.

"It was so nice having you."

"*That's what you think*." muttered somebody, Denning, Grimes thought.

"And you have seen, now, what good work we do among the disadvantaged, how we have raised a backward people to full civilization. . . ."

"*I'm crying for the Carolines*," Grimes could not resist saying.

"But there is no need for you to cry for them now, Captain. They have been saved, *saved*. Good night, good night, and bless you all!"

Grimes, at last tearing himself away to board the air car, was met by the hostile stares of his officers.

Back aboard the ship he told an amused and sympathetic Billy Williams what the evening had been like, enjoyed coffee and *real* sandwiches with him and Magda before going up to his quarters. Mayhew joined him there.

"Well," growled Grimes, "what did *you* make of it?"

The telepath grinned. "The Countess is genuine enough, in her way. She's not the first example of a too wealthy woman who's tried to buy her way into heaven. Too, the missionaries have opened up New Caroline to exploitation—which has been a good thing for the El Dorado Corporation."

"Those girls," demanded Grimes. "And this bumf. . . ."

He pulled the hymn sheets and the brochure from his pocket, threw the papers down on the coffee table.

"The girls," said Mayhew, "were both spies and recruiting agents. They were circulating among the juniors, subtly sounding them out, not so subtly promising them a good time if the ship should come to Port Kane." He picked up the brochure, leafed through it to the picture of a dancer. "Recognize her?"

"Mphm. She was the one carrying the collection bag around, wasn't she? Who'd ever have thought that she was like that under the frumpish black dress?"

"Never judge a parcel by its wrapping," said Mayhew philosophically.

"Clothes make the woman what she really isn't," countered Grimes. "That cuts both ways."

"Too true. Anyhow, Captain, before long the boys will be asking why you can't shift ship to Port Kane where there's some real action. Too, I have the feeling that your old friend Commodore Kane will be calling around shortly, promising to expedite discharge if you agree to join his private navy. I suggest that you convey the impression that (a) you could use some money, preferably in great, coarse hunks. . . ."

"You can say that again, Mr. Mayhew!"

". . . and (b) that you're craving a spot of excitement."

"Which I'm not."

"Aren't you, sir? And, in any case, I should not need to remind you that you are acting under Survey Service orders as much as Mr. Venner and myself are. Your job, for which you are being paid a four-ring captain's salary and allowance. . . ."

"I haven't seen the money yet."

"You—or your estate—will receive it as a lump sum when the mission has been brought to its conclusion. You are being paid, as I say, to infiltrate, and then to contrive an incident."

"All right, all right. I have to take the plunge some time. I just don't want to appear too eager."

"Perhaps," said Mayhew, "you should allow the Princess von Stolzberg to talk you around. That would be in character."

"Would it?" demanded Grimes. "Would it? I think that you had better go now, Mr. Mayhew."

Chapter 30

Grimes was finishing a late breakfast—almost always he took this meal in his own quarters—when the telephone buzzed. He thought that it would be one of his officers wishing to tell him something.

"Captain here," he said, facing the instrument.

The little screen came alive. To his surprise it was the face of Drongo Kane looking out at him. He thought, at first, that the piratical commodore was aboard the ship, was calling from the mate's or the purser's office. That tin Port Captain had told him that it would not be possible for the ship's telephones to be hooked up with the El Doradan planetary communications system. But the background scenery was wrong. None of the bulkheads in *Sister Sue's* accommodation was covered with blue wallpaper on which, embossed in gold, was a floral design.

He said, "How did you get through to me? I was told that I could use the ship's telephones only to talk to the port office."

"We can make calls to you," said Kane smugly. Then, "I hope that you and your merry crew enjoyed last night's outing."

"Ha!" growled Grimes. "Ha, bloody ha!"

"Your people," Kane went on, "would be far happier at the spaceport that the corporation, in recognition of my services, named after me. And you'd be much happier too, knowing that your ship was earning money again. Once she's on charter she gets paid, even when she's sitting on her big, fat arse, at my spaceport, waiting for the balloon to go up."

"I'm thinking about it," said Grimes grudgingly.

"Just don't be too long making your mind up, Grimesy-boy. Until you do there'll be no cargo worked—and then only if you make your mind up the right way. I'll be waiting to hear from you."

The screen went blank.

Grimes poured a last cup of coffee, filled and lit his pipe. It was very fortunate, he thought, that Kane did not, as he did, have the services of a tame telepath. He had raised this point already with Mayhew, had been told that the El Dorad-ans would not tolerate the presence on their world of any-body capable of prying into their precious minds.

The telephone buzzed again.

"Captain here," he told it.

It was another outside call. It was the Princess Marlene.

"Good morning, John." She laughed prettily. "I hear that you had a very boring time last night. I feel that I should of-fer some small compensation. Are you free today?"

"I am, M . . . Sorry. Your Highness."

She smiled out at him. "Marlene would have been better. So you are free. Then I shall call for you at . . . 1100 hours? Will that be suitable? Good. Can you stay overnight at the Schloss? Excellent. Until eleven, then."

She faded from the screen.

"Mphm?" grunted Grimes, recalling Mayhew's advice. "Mphm."

He called for Williams.

The chief officer, as soon as he set foot in Grimes' cabin, started complaining.

"I've been on the blower to that so-called Port Captain," he said. "He—or it—just couldn't tell me when any more cargo would be worked. You've your contacts here, sir. Can't you do anything?"

"Just be patient, Mr. Williams," Grimes told him.

"Patient, sir? You should have heard the growls over the breakfast table. And the engineers were waving those pam-phlets about—*you* know, the advertising for all the fancy fa-cilities at Port Kane. I told them what it would mean if we did shift ship there, the privateering and all the rest of it. They got interested and wanted to know if there was any money in it. And *your* pet, the Green Hornet, said, 'Forget it! Our saintly captain would never dirty his hands with piracy! All that he's fit for is dragging us to prayer meetings, like last night!' "

"There have been pious pirates," said Grimes. "One of my ancestors was one such. But tell me, what would your reac-tion be if I accepted Commodore Kane's offer of employ-ment?"

"I'd be with you, sir," said the mate at last. "After all, pri-vateering is not piracy. It's legal. And there should be money in it. The way I understand it is that the people financing the venture—in this case the El Dorado Corporation—would be entitled to a large percentage of the take, the balance being

139

divvied up among the crew, according to rank. Something like a salvage award. . . ."

"Sound people out, will you?" Grimes looked at the bulk-head clock. "And now, you'll have to excuse me. I have to get packed."

"You're leaving us, sir?"

"Only for a day. The Princess von Stolzberg will be picking me up at eleven. I shall be staying at the Schloss Stolzberg overnight. You'll know where to find me if anything horrid happens."

"Will do, Skipper. And so Her Highness has forgiven you for the swimming party. . . . If you can't be good, be careful."

"I'll try," said Grimes.

He was waiting at the foot of the ramp when the Princess's air car came in. It was not the gaily colored mechanical drag-onfly in which he had ridden with her before, years ago. It was a far more sober vehicle, although conforming to the current El Doradan fad or fashion. "A Daimler . . ." whispered Williams reverently to his captain as the elegant black vehicle, its silver fittings gleaming in the late morning sun, came in to an almost noiseless landing.

"A bloody hearse," muttered Ms. Connellan. "It's even got vultures following it!"

But they were not, of course, vultures. The pair of watch-birds, circling alertly overhead, were more like ravens.

Two doors of the car opened, one forward, one aft. The Princess, Grimes saw, was sitting in the front seat. She turned her head to smile at him invitingly. She looked softly mater-nal in a frilly pink dress—and yet there was more than a hint of the slim, golden girl whom Grimes had once known.

He threw his overnight bag into the rear of the vehicle, wondering if he was doing the right thing as he made to board at the front end. Apparently he was; the inviting smile did not fade as he took his seat by his hostess.

The doors closed.

Marlene's hands remained demurely folded on her lap, were not lifted to take the controls.

"Home," she ordered.

The car lifted. Inside it was as silent as the pseudo-Rolls had been.

She broke the silence, asking, "Do you remember the last time, John?"

"Yes, Marlene."

"You will find little changed," she told him. "The Croesus Mines are still in operation. . . ."

Yes, there was the low, spotlessly white building in the shallow, green valley. Below it, Grimes knew, were the fully automated subterranean workings. He wondered over how great an area these now extended.

"And the Laredo Ranch. . . . Senator Crocker is still playing at cowboys, rounding up his herds and all the rest of it. He's conquered his prejudice against robot ranch hands now. . . ."

Looking down, Grimes saw that a round-up was in progress, a milling herd of red-brown cattle with horsemen keeping the beasts grouped together. Which one of them was Crocker and which were the robots? They all looked the same from up here.

"Count Vitelli's vineyards. His wines are improving all the time."

"The Baroness d'Estang," said Grimes, "kept a good stock of them aboard her yacht, *The Far Traveler.* . . ."

"I still find it hard to understand," she said, "how and why you—of all people!—became a yachtmaster. And to *that* woman, of all possible employers!"

"Mphm."

"Some people," she went on cattily, "think that she married beneath her. If anything, the reverse is the case. The Baron is descended from an English lord. He had no trouble at all establishing his claim to the title. . . ."

I wonder how much it cost him? thought Grimes.

"And she, of course, is descended from a French pirate. . . ."

"A privateer," said Grimes. He would have liked to have said, *And you, my dear, are descended from German robber barons.* . . . He thought better of it. He would not bite the hand that, hopefully, was going to feed him.

"A privateer," she repeated. "What's the difference? Oh, there is a difference now, of course. The Baron's fleet will do nothing illegal. If I thought otherwise I would not have allowed Ferdinand to volunteer to serve as a liaison officer. . . ."

"Will Ferdinand be at the castle?" asked Grimes, half hoping and half fearing that the answer would be in the affirmative.

"No. He is at Port Kane with the other El Doradan officers. Perhaps it is as well. It could be embarrassing if you

141

met him in my company." Her hands went up to the wheel, grasped it firmly. It was an indication, thought Grimes, that she was determined to control the course of events. "And it will be as well, John, if he never knows that you are his father."

"Will he be seconded to my ship?" asked Grimes. "Assuming, that is," he added hastily, "that I join the enterprise."

"No. If he were it is possible that the relationship would become public knowledge. He will be attached to *Agatha's Ark*, under Captain Agatha Prinn. A strange woman, John, but, I believe, a highly competent spaceperson. Meanwhile, I understand that Baron Kane intends to appoint you commodore of the privateers. As you will be in overall charge you will be able to keep a watchful eye on my son. Our son."

"I haven't decided yet," said Grimes, "if I'm going to take Kane's offer."

"But you will," she said.

She relinquished her hold on the wheel so that she could point ahead. There, on a hilltop, was the grim, gray pile, a castle that was straight out of a book of Teutonic mythology. Schloss Stolzberg. As before, Grimes wondered how much it had cost to transport it, stone by numbered stone, from Earth. *I wish that somebody would give me a job like that,* he thought. He tried to arrive at a rough estimate of what the freight charges would have been.

Chapter 31

Slowly, smoothly, the car drifted down to a landing in the central courtyard, dropping past flagpoles from which snapped and fluttered heavy standards, golden heraldic beasts rampant on fields of purple, past turrets and battlemented walls, down to the gray, rough flagstones. From somewhere came the baying of hounds. Then as the doors of the vehicle opened, there was a high, clear trumpet call, a flourish of drums.

"Welcome, again, to Schloss Stolzberg," said the Princess.

"It hasn't changed," said Grimes.

"Why should it have done so, John?" she asked.

To this there was no reply.

142

He got out of his seat, stepped to the ground, then helped the Princess down. Her hand was pleasantly warm and smooth in his. She thanked him, then turned to address the car.

"We shall not be needing you again," she told it. "You can put yourself to bed."

A melodious toot from the vehicle's horn was the reply. The thing lifted, its inertial drive unit purring almost inaudibly. It flew toward a doorway that suddenly and silently opened in the rough stone wall, then quietly closed behind it.

She put her hand in the crook of his left arm, guided him to a tall, arched portal. The valves were of some dark timber, heavily iron studded, and as they moved on their ponderous hinges they creaked loudly. Grimes did not think, as he had his first time here, that this was an indication of inefficiency on the part of the castle's robot staff. Those hinges, he had been told, were meant to creak. It was all part of the atmosphere.

They were in the main hall now, a huge barn of a place but, unlike a real barn, cheerless. Only a little daylight stabbed through the high, narrow windows and the flaring torches and the fire that blazed in the enormous hearth did little more than cast a multiplicity of confused, flickering shadows. Ranged along the walls were what, at first glance, looked like space-suited men standing at rigid attention. But it was not space armor; these empty suits had been worn by men of Earth's Middle Ages. By men? By knights and barons and princes, rather; in those days the commonality had gone into battle with only thick leather (if that) as a partial protection. Marlene's ancestors had fought their petty wars ironclad. Grimes wondered what they would think if they could watch their daughter being squired by a man who, in their day, would have been only a humble tiller of the fields or, in battle, a fumbling pikeman fit only to be ridden down by a charge of metal-accoutered so-called chivalry.

Grimes, you're an inverted snob! he chided himself.

She led him across the hall, past a long, heavy banqueting table with rows of high-backed chairs on either side. She took the seat at the head of it, occupied it as though it were the throne it looked like. In her overly feminine ruffled pink dress she should have struck a note of utter incongruity, but she did not. She was part of the castle and the castle was part of her.

She motioned Grimes to the chair at her right hand. It was far more comfortable than it looked. He saw that a decanter

143

of heavy glass had been set out on the table and with it two glittering, cut-crystal goblets. Marlene poured the dark ruby wine with an oddly ceremonial gesture.

She raised her glass to him, sipped.

Grimes followed suit. He remembered that on that past occasion she had given him Angel's Blood from Wilsonia, one of the worlds of the Denebian system. She was giving him Angel's Blood again. It was a superb wine, although a little too sweet for his taste. It was also far too expensive for his pocket. Even duty free and with no freight charges it was forty credits a bottle.

She said softly, "I'd like to think that we're drinking to us. Do you remember how, years ago, I told you that you could come back here to live, to become a citizen, when you had your first billion credits?"

"I remember," said Grimes. (That was not among his happier memories.)

"You're a shipowner now, not a penniless Survey Service lieutenant. . . ."

"And I'm still not worth a billion C."

"But you could be, John. If the privateering venture is successful."

"Mphm."

"*Must* you grunt?"

"Sorry."

"I'm telling you, trying to tell you, that now you have the opportunity to become a citizen of El Dorado. A title? Proof of noble ancestry? That's no problem." She laughed. "It has been said, and probably quite correctly, that everybody in England has royal blood in his veins. Some monarchs did their best to spread it among their people. . . ."

"Such as Charles the Second," said Grimes. "But I'm Australian."

"Don't quibble."

"I like me the way I am," said Grimes, "A shipmaster. A shipowner."

"And a father."

"Ferdinand," he said, "is *your* son."

"And yours, John. You were there too. Or have you forgotten?"

He had not. He accepted the fresh glass of wine that she poured for him. (The decanter, not a small one, was now almost empty.)

"You have a responsibility," she went on.

Why didn't you engineer my discharge from the Survey Service, as, with your wealth, you could so easily have done? he thought. *But, of course, I didn't have that billion credits and then it didn't look as though I ever would. . . .*

A robutler in black and silver livery removed the now empty decanter and goblets from the table. Another one set down mats on the polished wood. More wine was brought, a chilled Riesling. And there were fat, succulent oysters on the half shell and a plate of brown bread and butter. Despite his nickname, Gutsy Grimes, the spaceman rarely, these days, enjoyed a large lunch, preferring to start the day with a good breakfast and to finish it with a good dinner, with possibly a substantial supper if he were up late.

"From the beds in the Green River," said Marlene. "I think that you will find them to your taste, John. Their ancestral stock is the Sydney Rock Oyster."

Grimes enjoyed them. So did Marlene. He thought, patting his lips with a napkin of fine linen, *If that was lunch, I've had it. And liked it.* But there was more to come—steak tartare, with raw egg, raw onion sliced paper-thin, gherkins, capers and anchovies, with a Vitelli Burgundy to accompany it. There was cheese, locally made but at least as good as any Brie that Grimes had sampled on Earth. There was, finally, aromatic coffee laced with some potent spirit that Grimes could not identify.

He looked at Marlene through eyes that he knew were slightly glazed. She looked at him through eyes that, as his were, were indicative of the effects of a surfeit of good food and good wine.

She said, "You look rather tired, John."

He said, "I'm all right, Marlene. It's just that I usually have a very light meal in the middle of the day."

"But you *are* tired. Don't you have a saying, This is Liberty Hall, you can spit on the mat and call the cat a bastard? This is Liberty Hall. If a guest of mine wants an afternoon siesta, then he shall have one."

She pushed her chair back from the table. Grimes rose from his own, moved to assist her to her feet. For a second or so she hung heavily in his arms.

She said, "I'll show you to your room."

She guided him through corridors, then up one of the spiral staircase escalators that were a feature of El Doradan architecture. They came to a suite that consisted of sitting room, bedroom and bathroom, plainly but very comfortably furnished. The wide bed, seen through the open door of the sitting room, looked very inviting.

"Mix us drinks, please, John," said Marlene, indicating the bar to one side of the sitting room. "I would like something long and refreshing. Use your own discretion."

She went through into the bedroom, then to the bathroom.

Grimes went to the bar, studied the array of bottles. The labels of some of these were familiar, others were not. Those that were not looked very, very expensive.

He thought, *I'd better play it safe.*

He found gin. In the refrigerator there were bottles of tonic water, the real stuff, imported from Earth. There were ice cubes, and lemons. He busied himself quite happily and, before long had prepared two tall, inviting glasses, each with its exterior misted with condensation.

And now, where was his hostess?

She was in the bed, her plump, naked shoulders creamily luminescent against the dark blue bed linen, her golden hair fanned out on the pillow. Her smile was both sleepy and inviting.

Oddly, for him, Grimes was feeling guilty.

The censor who lived in his mind and who, now and again, made himself heard was telling him that he should not be enjoying himself.

Grimes, she's fat. She's not your sort of woman at all. : . .

But she was a most comfortable ride.

Grimes, she's just using you. . . .

And didn't women always use men?

Grimes, you're using her. You're letting her persuade you to do just what you've come to this world to do. . . .

But why shouldn't he, he thought rebelliously, enjoy whatever fringe benefits came with the job into which he had been press-ganged by Rear Admiral Damien?

The feeling of guilt diminished but did not quite go away.

All right, all right, the Princess was a mercenary bitch, a founding member of the money-hungry El Dorado Corporation. Grimes, as a privateer commodore, would be a valuable employee of the Corporation. But. . . . But she was also a mother, concerned about the safety of the son whom he, Grimes, had yet to meet.

They shared a shuddering climax after which she continued to hold him tightly, her body soft and warm against his. Now he really wanted to go to sleep.

146

But she said, "John. Darling. What we had so many years ago has not been lost after all. . . ."

"No . . ." he lied.

(Or was it the truth? After that heavy lunch and the strenuous bedroom gymnastics he did not feel inclined to analyze his feelings.)

"You will make me very happy if you agree to become commodore of the privateer squadron. I shall know then that Ferdinand will be safe."

"I've always wanted to be a commodore," said Grimes.

"Then you will become one? For us?"

"Yes," said Grimes.

He wondered if his consent had been registered by the monitor. It almost certainly had been. There was no backing out now.

"John, darling, you've made us very happy. . . ."

Her soft lips brushed his ear as she whispered the words.

"And I'm happy to be of service to you," he replied.

They drifted into sleep then, limbs intertwined. It was a pity, he thought, that she snored—but the almost musical noise did not prevent him from following her into sweet unconsciousness.

Chapter 32

When he awoke it was late evening. He was alone in the big bed.

Well, he thought philosophically, *it was nice while it lasted*.

Somebody had come into the sitting room of his suite. *Marlene?* he wondered. (Hoped?) But by the gradually increasing illumination he could see that it was one of the robot servitors, carrying a large tray which was set down on a low table visible through the bedroom door.

Tea? wondered Grimes. He hoped that it was. Then the robot moved away and he could see that it was a silver ice bucket from which protruded the slender neck of a tall bottle. There was a tulip glass—no, glasses. There was what looked like a dish of canapés.

Marlene appeared in the doorway. The subdued lighting was kind to her. She was wearing a diaphanous robe through

147

which her full—too full?—body was clearly visible. (But she was no plumper, thought Grimes, than fat Susie had been before her remodeling.)

"You are awake, darling," she murmured. "I had hoped to wake you in the time-honored way. . . ."

Nonetheless she billowed into the bedroom, planted a warm, moist kiss on his not unwilling lips. She seemed to be inclined to carry on from there—but Grimes had more urgent matters on his mind.

He said, as he tried to break away from her embrace, but not too abruptly, "You'll have to excuse me for a few moments, Marlene. I have to go to the bathroom. . . ."

"Then go."

She released him but remained seated on the bed.

Grimes got from under the covers, feeling absurdly embarrassed. (Had it not been for the knowledge that each of them was using the other his nudity would not have worried him.) He went into the bathroom, closed the door behind him, did what he had to do. He was relieved to find a dressing gown of dark blue silk—it seemed to be a new garment—hanging there. He put it on. When he emerged he found that the Princess was in the sitting room, sprawled rather inelegantly in one of the chairs by the low table.

"Open the bottle, John darling," she said.

Grimes untwisted the wire and eased the old-fashioned cork free, hastily poured before too much of the foaming wine was lost.

"To success," toasted the Princess.

"To success," repeated Grimes.

They clinked glasses. She regarded him over the rim of hers. He wished that he had missed the coldly calculating gleam in her blue eyes. He wished that she were loving him for himself, not for what he could do for her.

The telephone—an instrument that Grimes, until now, had not known was part of the sitting room's appointments— chimed. The Princess, facing the corner just beyond the bar, said, "Marlene here."

The air shimmered and then a holographic projection of the pewter-faced majordomo appeared.

"Your Highness, an officer from the ship, *Sister Sue*, is calling. He wishes to speak with his captain."

"Very well, Karl. You may put him through."

The image of the robutler faded, was replaced by that of Williams. He seemed to be looking directly into the room— as, in fact, he was. Grimes wished that he were wearing something more formal than a dressing gown, that Marlene's negligee were not so transparent. The mate—blast him!—was trying hard not to leer.

"Sorry if I interrupted anything, Skipper," he said cheerfully.

"What is it, Mr. Williams?"

"The Baron, sir. Commodore Kane. He's just been on board. He asked me to call a meeting of all hands—which, of course, I did. He treated us to a fine sales talk on the pleasures and profits of privateering. Yes, it was a sales talk all right. He could sell a pair of hairbrushes to a bald man. . . ."

"Get on with it, Mr. Williams. Are the people willing to join Kane's enterprise?"

"Too right, Skipper. Even Magda. She insisted on going through her ritual with the coins and the book and came up with the *Chieh* hexagram." He looked at a scrap of paper that he was holding. "Regulation. There will be progress and success. But if the regulation is too severe and difficult, its good effect will not last long. . . ."

"So? Is that a good forecast?"

"It is, Skipper. You'll just have to ride with a loose rein, that's all."

"Mphm. You all seem to be sure that I shall agree to charter my ship to the El Dorado Corporation."

"The commodore gave us to understand, Skipper, that you'd agreed."

Grimes looked at Marlene. She looked back at him rather too innocently. Grimes turned his attention back to the solid-seeming image of Williams.

"All right, all right. Then why call me to tell me about it?"

"There's more, Skipper. We're to complete discharge at Port Kane. The commodore wants you back so that you can shift ship so as to be at Port Kane tomorrow morning, their time. There's a twelve-hour differential."

Grimes looked again at Marlene. She looked back at him, shook her head ever so slightly. Did that mean what he thought it did?

He said, "Mr. Williams, must I make it clear to you that Drongo Kane is neither the owner nor the master of *my* ship? Furthermore, the charter party has not yet been signed. Until it is, I am a free agent."

"But the officers," Williams said, "are looking forward to getting away from this cheerless dump to Port Kane. . . ."

"My nose fair bleeds for them, Mr. Williams. I shall return

149

to the ship tomorrow morning. . . ." The Princess nodded almost imperceptibly. "I shall return to the ship tomorrow morning to make all the necessary arrangements. A very good night to you."

Williams flickered and vanished.

"I'm glad that you were firm, John," said Marlene.

"Now I suppose we'll have Kane on the blower," grumbled Grimes.

"We shall not." She spoke firmly toward the corner of the room, "Karl, you are to accept no more incoming calls."

"Very good, Your Highness," came a disembodied, mechanical voice in reply.

"What if he calls around in person?" asked Grimes.

She laughed. "My watchbirds never sleep. And they are vicious."

She drained her glass, held it out for the refill. She helped herself to a savory pastry, then to another. Grimes decided that he had better start nibbling too, otherwise he would not be getting his share. It would have been a shame to have missed out; the creamy filling in the flaky cases, some sort of fish, he thought, was delicious.

Then the dish was empty save for a few crumbs. The tall bottle, now standing to attention in the ice bucket, was a dead marine. The Princess sighed, inelegantly wiped her mouth on the back of her hand.

"I could order up more," she said, "but it might spoil dinner. I thought that we would have it served here. It would be such a waste of time getting dressed and then getting undressed again. . . ."

Grimes thought wryly of the evening dress that he had packed, the resplendent mess uniform that he had worn while he had been master of the Baroness d'Estang's space yacht. It had been altered only inasmuch as the gold buttons now bore the crest of his own company, Far Traveler Couriers. He had affected to despise what, privately, he had called his organ grinder's monkey suit but had been looking forward to giving it an airing in the proper surroundings.

She said, "I think that we shall be more comfortable on the settee."

He got up from his chair, helped her to her feet. He thought, *If I married her I'd rupture myself carrying her across the threshold* . . . He deposited her at one end of the sofa, sat himself down at the other. She pouted at him but before she could move toward him the robot servants came in, cleared the low table of the debris of the pre-prandial

150

snack and then set it down between them, laying out on its surface napery and cutlery, a selection of glasses. Then there was caviar, glistening black pearls piled high in a crystal bowl nestling in a larger vessel in which was crushed ice, with paper-thin toast and butter. With this there was vodka, poured by the attentive robot waiter from a bottle that was encased with an ice block.

Grimes made a pig of himself. So did Marlene.

There was paté, rich and flavorsome, in which a profusion of truffles was embedded. There was lobster, served in its split carapace and drenched with garlic-flavored butter. There was duck—or some bird like it—with a crisp, honeyed skin and a cherry sauce, with tiny new potatoes and green peas. (By this time Grimes' appetite was beginning to flag although Marlene, whose face had become quite greasy, was leaving nothing on her plate.) There was steak, tender and rare, smothered with mushrooms. There was a fruit tart, topped by a minor mountain of whipped cream. There were the wines—white and rosé and red with, at the finish, an imported champagne with the sweet.

There was coffee.

Grimes took his black, Marlene with cream, lots of it.

Grimes repressed a belch.

Marlene did not.

Grimes said, speaking with some difficulty, "Thank you for a marvelous dinner."

Marlene giggled and said, "The laborer is worthy of his hire. Besides, it is very rarely, on this world, that I can enjoy a meal in the company of somebody who appreciates good food as much as I do."

Grimes took a cigar from the box proferred by the major-domo—genuine Cuban, he noticed. Marlene selected a slimmer smoke, a panatella. The robutler presented, first to Grimes then to his mistress, a metal index finger from which white flame jetted.

Grimes inhaled, wondering dimly that there should be room for anything else, even something so insubstantial as smoke, in his overfed body. He sat back, watching the silent, efficient robots removing the final plates and glasses, the coffeepot and cups. The table was shifted back to its original position between the two chairs and a large ashtray was placed on the richly carpeted floor.

Marlene, grunting a little with the effort, slowly shifted herself along the settee toward him. She covered the distance and then fell on to him. Her still-burning panatella dropped between their two bodies. Frantically he fished it out before it could do any damage, put it into the ashtray. Regretfully he placed his own cigar beside it. He was drowsy, so very drowsy. Marlene was sleeping, imprisoning him beneath the soft weight of her body. He tried to extricate himself, then gave up the struggle.

It may have been a dream but almost certainly it was not.

Awakening in the morning, alone in bed, as a robot servitor set down the morning tea tray, he had a confused memory of warm, pale flesh in the semi-darkness, of plump, naked limbs that imprisoned him, of hot, moist lips on his face and body, of an explosive release. . . .

"And what do you wish for breakfast, lord?" asked the liveried servant.

"Some more tea will do nicely," Grimes said. "After I've had my shower and all the rest of it. . . ."

Surprisingly he did not feel at all bad. He just did not feel hungry.

"Very well, lord. Her Highness wishes me to tell you that the car will be ready, to return you to Port Bluewater, as soon as you desire."

The old brush-off, thought Grimes. *On your bicycle, space-man. She's got what she wants, had what she wanted, and that's it.*

He finished his second cup of tea, then got out of bed and went through to the bathroom.

Chapter 33

He emerged from the bathroom refreshed and rather less torpid. He saw that his bed had been made and that on the coverlet fresh clothing—slacks, jacket and underwear—had been laid out. Presumably his case was already in the car.

He dressed and was not surprised to find that the waist-band of his trousers was tight. He filled and lit his pipe; he would have a quiet smoke while waiting for the second pot of tea.

The majordomo entered the sitting room carrying a big tray. He (it) was followed by Marlene. Clothed—this morning in pale blue—she looked no more than pleasantly plump. She sat down in one of the chairs by the coffee table, motioned to Grimes to take the other. The robutler put down the tray and left.

She said, "I thought, perhaps, that we might partake of only a light breakfast. . . ."

On the tray were both teapots and coffeepots, with milk and cream and sugar. There was a large pitcher of some chilled fruit juice. There were croissants, with butter and a syrupy conserve with whole strawberries.

"Nothing for me, thanks, Marlene," said Grimes. "Or, perhaps, some fruit juice." She poured, handed him the glass. "And I think I've changed my mind. I told the servant tea, but that coffee smells delicious. . . . Yes, two sugars." She filled his cup. "And I wonder if I might have just a nibble of croissant. . . ."

She laughed. "What I liked about you when I first knew you was your hearty appetite. I've heard that your Survey Service nickname was Gutsy Grimes. . . . And what of it? Good food is meant to be enjoyed."

She managed four croissants to Grimes' three and was more generous with butter and conserve than he was. Satisfied, she lit a cigarillo. Grimes resumed his pipe.

"And now, my dear," she said practically, "we have to get you back to your ship."

She was friendly enough, thought Grimes, but little more than that. The events of the previous night might never have happened.

She got to her feet unassisted, walked toward the door. Grimes followed. She led him through corridors and down spiral staircases to the courtyard. The gleaming Daimler was awaiting them and, standing by it at stiff attention, were the majordomo and four liveried footmen. Grimes wondered wildly if he was supposed to tip them. (What sort of gratuity would a robot expect?) But they bowed stiffly as their mistress and her guest approached and the robutler assisted her through the open door of the car. Grimes sat down beside her. The doors closed. The car lifted and, escorted by the watchbirds, flew silently northward.

Its passengers, too, were silent. Grimes, at first, attempted to make conversation but the Princess made it plain that she did not wish to talk. There was not, after all, much to say. On a mental plane, he realized, they had little in common— yet he admitted to himself that he did feel some affection for her. The silence was not an uncomfortable one.

Lake Bluewater showed up ahead, and the white buildings of the spaceport on its farther shore. And there was *Sister Sue,* gleaming silver in the strong light of the late morning sun. And that was where he belonged, thought Grimes, not in the castle owned by a member of this planet's aristocracy.

She spoke at last.

"I've brought you back, John, to where you really want to be."

He said, "I wanted to be with you." Then, bending the truth only slightly if at all, "I want to be with you again."

She laughed—regretfully?

"Do you? I'm no Michelle, and I know it. If you were to settle on El Dorado—and if Commodore Kane's enterprise is successful you might well be financially qualified—you would range farther afield than Schloss Stolzberg. I should not be able to hold you. There's too much of the tomcat in you. You're capable of feeling cupboard love—but, until you meet the right woman (if ever you do) little more. . . .

"But it was good having you. . . ."

Grimes tried to believe that she really meant what she said.

She was facing him now, holding her face up to his. He put his arms about her, kissed her. Her lips tasted of strawberries.

They broke apart as the car began its descent. Probably Williams and several of the others would be watching. He did not wish to be the subject of ribald comment.

The vehicle grounded gently on the apron, ran silently to the foot of the ramp. (Yes, Williams was there, and the Green Hornet.) The door on Grimes' side opened. He inclined his head to the hand that she extended to him, kissed it lightly. He dismounted, then reached through the other open door to retrieve his bag. He heard her order, "Home," as the doors shut. The car rose swiftly, dwindled fast to a mere speck in the southern sky.

"Sorry to have called you back, Skipper," said the mate cheerfully while Ms. Connellan scowled at Grimes. "But the Commodore is very insistent. He wants us at Port Kane as soon as possible, if not before."

"Are the engines ready?"

"Yes. I told Mr. Crumley to be ready for the shift. Oh, and the Commodore told me to ask you to call him as soon as you got back. You'll have to use the phone in the office." He scowled. "*They* can call us aboard the ship but we can't call them from the ship. . . ."

"All right," said Grimes. "Would you mind taking my bag
154

aboard for me, Ms. Connellan?" The Second Mate scowled at him but wordlessly took his luggage. "And come with me, Mr. Williams."

Together they walked into the port office. In the doorless booth Grimes said, "Get me Commodore Baron Kane." The holographic image of a golden lady's maid appeared and told him, "The Commodore will speak with you shortly." She faded. Kane appeared.

"Ah, Grimes, back at last after your wallow in the von Stolzberg flesh pots. Anybody would think that you were not eager for gainful employment."

"I had a duty to my hostess," said Grimes stiffly.

"I'm sure you did. Now, listen. Port Kane is twelve hours ahead of Port Bluewater. The hop should take you four hours, at the outside; I imagine that your innies are capable of delivering enough lateral thrust. If you lift off at, say, 1400 your time you should be at Port Kane at 0600 my time, just before sunrise. There'll be the usual beacons to mark your berth. Keep in touch with Aerospace Control to confirm your ETA and all the rest of it. The Port Captain will bring you a gnomonic chart and a plan of Port Kane."

"And also the bill for my port charges here?" asked Grimes.

"They'll be just a matter of bookkeeping, Grimes, to be deducted from whatever profit you make as a privateer. After your arrival—not immediately after, of course; like you I enjoy my sleep—I shall call aboard you with the charter party for your signature. Also I shall be introducing you to the other captains. Is everything clear, Grimes?"

"Yes, Kane."

Drongo Kane scowled, then grinned sourly. "All right, all right. I should have called you Captain Grimes. Soon it will be Commodore Grimes. Does that make you happy?"

"I'm rolling on the deck, Commodore, convulsed with paroxysms of pure ecstasy."

"That will do, you sarcastic bastard. I'll see you tomorrow morning."

Kane's image faded.

Later, in *Sister Sue's* control room, Grimes and Williams studied the gnomonic chart. It would be a simple enough operation to shift ship—although something of a nuisance. Luckily the ship possessed a rarely used gyro compass, which had now been started, with a repeater on the bridge. Williams had painted a mark on the inside of one of the big viewports to coincide with the lubber's line. That would be, for the purposes of this short voyage, "forward." The Green Hornet, grumbling that this was a spaceship, not an airship, had not been capable of working out the great circle distance and courses so Grimes had done it himself.

Grimes looked at his watch.

"All right, Mr. Williams, make it lift off stations. I shall want Control fully manned until we're underway, then just one officer besides myself until we're ready to set down."

He took his usual seat, controls at his fingertips, displays before his eyes. He waited until the others—Williams, Connellan, Venner and Stewart—were at their stations before putting the inertial drive on standby. Mr. Venner obtained permission from Aerospace Control to lift ship.

Sister Sue shuddered then rose slowly from the apron. Grimes set course by turning her about her vertical axis, watching the repeater card until the lubber's line was on the correct reading. Then there was the application of lateral thrust and, at an altitude of only two kilometers, the ship was underway on the first leg of the great circle course.

The officers watched interestedly. Save as passengers, during spells of planetary leave, atmospheric flights were outide their experience. Grimes, of course, during his Survey Service career had often handled pinnaces proceeding from point to point inside a world's air envelope. He had done so often enough, too, in *Little Sister*.

Sister Sue swept majestically—and noisily; would there be any complaints from the pampered people in the mansions and chateaux and castles over which she was clattering?—in an east northeasterly direction, the fast westering sun throwing her long shadow over fields and forests. Grimes increased vertical thrust to give her safe clearance over the Golden Alps, a range of snow-capped crags bare of vegetation for most of their towering height, whose sheer yellow rock faces reflected the sunlight as though they were indeed formed from the precious metal.

Beyond the mountains the ship dropped again, into shadow, into deepening dusk, into darkness. There were no cities on the land below her, no towns, no villages even. There were only sparsely scattered points of light, marking the dwelling places of the very rich. It was like, Grimes thought, the night sky of the Rim Worlds, out toward the edge of the galaxy, an almost empty blackness.

He flew on toward the dawn, toward Port Kane.

Chapter 34

Port Kane was a cluster of white domes, dominated by a graceful, latticework control tower, on the western bank of the broad, slow-flowing Rio del Oro. There was something familiar about that tower, thought Grimes. Then he laughed. It was obvious that Michelle must have had some say in its design. It was almost a replica of a far more famous erection in the city of Paris, on faraway Earth. It dwarfed the relatively squat, far more solid in appearance, towers that were the spaceships. All three of them, like *Sister Sue*, had started their working lives as Epsilon Class tramps of the Commission's fleet. They had been altered, however, the one-time symmetry of their hulls broken by added sponsons. A laser cannon turret, another turret for the quick-firing projectile cannon, a third one for the missile launcher. . . . Two of the ships gleamed dull silver in the light of the rising sun. The third one had been painted a green that once had been vivid, that now was dull and flaking. A hundred or so meters clear of this vessel—*Pride of Erin*, she had to be—the triangle of scarlet flashing beacons had been set out.

"Port Kane Control to *Sister Sue*," came the mechanical voice from the NST speaker. "Control to *Sister Sue*. Set down between the beacons."

Mr. Stewart acknowledged. Grimes applied lateral thrust until he had the triangle of beacons centered in the stern view screen. He cut vertical thrust, just enough so that the ship was almost weightless. She fell gently, touched, shuddered and then was still.

"Finished with engines," ordered Grimes.

He looked out through a viewport, saw a group of figures standing on the pale gray concrete of the apron and staring up at him. He took a pair of binoculars from the box, looked down at them. There were two men and a woman. One of the men was short, with a ruddy face and a neat, pointed, white beard. He was wearing a green uniform with four gold bands on each sleeve. The other one, also a captain to judge from his sleeve braid, was tall. His face was almost obscured by a luxuriant, red-gold hirsute growth. His uniform was black with a black-and-gold kilt in lieu of trousers, with a gold trim on his long socks. The woman, too, was tall. What she was wearing could have been a short-skirted business suit in sober gray had it not been for the rather ornate golden epaulets. The lines of her face were harsh, her mouth wide but with thin lips, her nose a prominent beak.

Grimes said to Williams, "Looks like the bold masters of *Pride of Erin, Spaceways Princess* and *Agatha's Ark* down there. I may as well meet them now. You can come with me."

The ramp was just being extended from the after airlock door as they stepped out of the elevator cage. They marched down the gangway, Williams in the lead. Once they were on the ground the mate fell back to let Grimes precede him.

"Captain Grimes?" asked the little man in the green uniform.

"Yes. And you're Captain O'Leary, aren't you? And Captain MacWhirter, and Captain Prinn. A very good morning to you all."

"And the top o' the morn to you, Captain. Or should I be sayin' Commodore? We didn't think that we should like havin' the Survey Service—no disrespect intended to yourself—bossin' us around, but the way things are, you could be the lesser of two evils. We thought we'd be after seein' you, bright an' early, before Drongo tells you his side of it. . . ."

"I'm only ex-Survey Service," said Grimes, not realizing that he had lied until the words were out. "And I'm not your commodore yet. But what seems to be the trouble, Captain?"

"Oh, 'tis these El Doradan Navy liaison officers, or gunnery officers, or observers, or whatever they're supposed to be when they're up an' dressed. Space puppies, all of 'em, but puttin' on the airs an' graces of admirals. I've a still wet behind the ears junior grade lieutenant callin' himself the Honorable Claude Ponsonby. His daddy is Lord Ponsonby—whoever *he* might be. Captain MacWhirter has a Count—not that he counts for much! An' Captain Prinn has a Count too—although he calls himself a Graf. . . ."

"The Graf von Stolzbert," said Grimes.

"Yes. How did you know?"

"His. . . ." He corrected himself. "Commodore Kane told me. And it's Commodore Kane who makes the rules. What can I do about it?"

"You're Survey Service, Captain Grimes. Or ex-Survey Service. You've been a senior officer in a *real* navy, not a glorified yacht club. Drongo Kane says that you're to be in

158

charge of things. We're relyin' on you to call the puppies to heel."

"Do any of you have any naval experience?" asked Grimes.

"No, Captain," O'Leary said. "I was with a small outfit called the Shamrock Line, out of New Erin. You may have heard of the New Erin Sweepstake? I won it. At about the same time the Shamrock Line went broke. Thinkin' that I was well on the way to winnin' an even larger fortune I bought one o' their ships. . . ."

"An owner/master, like myself," said Grimes. "And you, Captain MacWhirter?"

"I was in the Waverley Royal Mail," said the Scot. "My old uncle Hamish died and left me the lot. In whisky, he was. In those days I was a religious man an' a total abstainer. So I sold the distillery an' all the rest of it an' bought me a bonny wee ship." He laughed mirthlessly. "It's driven me to drink, she has."

"I know what it's like," said Grimes sympathetically. He turned to the tall woman, who was regarding him through cold gray eyes that matched the short hair swept severely back from her high, pale forehead. "Captain Prinn?"

"Captain Agatha Prinn," she corrected him, "to distinguish me from Captain Joel Prinn, my late husband. I was a rich woman, an heiress, on Carinthia. You have heard, perhaps, of the Davitz Circus and Menagerie? I was a Davitz, the last Davitz. But circuses bore me and I have no great love for animals. I sold my interests in the family business and went for a cruise in a Cluster Lines ship, where I met my future husband, at that time a Chief Officer. He paid off on our return to Carinthia and we were married. He persuaded me to buy for him the Commission's *Epsilon Puppis*, which was up for sale. He renamed her *Agatha's Ark*. . . ." She smiled frostily. "I can see that you're wondering how I came to be a shipmaster myself. I accompanied my husband on his voyages, signed on as purser. I became interested in navigation and spacemanship and studied. Finally I passed for Master on Libertad." She smiled again. "Libertad qualifications are recognized throughout the galaxy."

But only just, thought Grimes. He wondered just how much that Certificate of Competency had cost. He wondered, too, what had happened to Captain Prinn I. Obviously Captain Prinn II wasn't going to tell him.

"So," he said. "So." He looked at *Pride of Erin* and at the other two vessels in line beyond her. "I see that you've all been armed."

"Aye," said MacWhirter. "An' every day we've been pittin' our skills against electronic enemies in yon gunnery simulator—" he waved a hand toward one of the white domes— "while the El Doradan Navy puppies have been standin' around an' sneerin'. . . ." He went on enviously, "I don't suppose that ye'll be needin' gunnery instruction, Captain Grimes. . . ."

"A session in the simulator never did anybody any harm," said Grimes. "I'll be using it, and so will Mr. Williams here, my chief officer—although both of us have seen action. And my third officer holds a Survey Service Reserve commission but I'll make sure that he brushes up his gunnery."

"It looks, Captain," said O'Leary enviously, "as though *you'll* have no trouble with whatever puppy they foist on you!"

A uniformed port official, a humanoid robot, approached the party. He saluted Grimes smartly.

"Sir, Commodore Kane instructs that you be ready to commence discharge at 0800 hours. The Commodore will call upon you at 0930."

"Our master's voice," said Agatha Prinn sourly.

And then they all drifted back to their ships.

"Sign here, Grimes," said Drongo Kane. "All four copies."

Grimes signed.

He had read the document carefully and found that its provisions were as good as could be expected. He did not think that he had missed anything in the small print. For a quite substantial consideration he agreed to put his ship, his officers and himself at the service of El Dorado Corporation until such time as the contract would be terminated by mutual consent or, with an option for renewal, after the passage of three Standard Years. He, as master of *Sister Sue*, had been given the rank of Company Commodore with authority not only over the other shipmasters but to deal, on behalf of the corporation, with planetary governments. Items of equipment on loan from the El Dorado Corporation were to be returned, in good order and condition, on expiration of the contract; there was a penalty clause covering failure, for any reason, to do so.

Any and all profits accruing from ventures engaged upon were to be divided between the corporation and the chartered vessel—sixty percent to the charterer and forty percent to the ship. The cost of stores, services and the salary of the El Doradan representative aboard would, however, be deducted from the charteree's percentage. The monies remaining were to be divided among the crew according to the provisions of Lloyd's Salvage Agreement, the higher the rank, the bigger the share. All parties agreed to accept the rulings of the Prize Court which would be set up on El Dorado.

And so on, and so on.

"And now, Commodore," said Kane, "I shall take you ashore, to my office, to introduce you to your captains. You've already met them, I know, but you have not done so yet officially."

"As you please, Commodore," said Grimes.

He put one copy of the Charter Party into his safe while Kane picked up the others from the desk. He took his cap from the hook on which it was hanging, looked at it, at the badge, before putting it on. At least, he thought, there was nothing in the charter party that required him to wear El Doradan uniform.

"Oh, one small thing, Grimes," said Kane.

"Yes?"

"That passenger of yours. You can't leave an outworlder here, you know. And if you have a civilian aboard what will be, essentially, a warship you're liable to run into all sorts of complications. Legally speaking he could be classed as a pirate, you know."

"I'll put him on my Articles," said Grimes. "Assistant Purser or something."

"Do that."

Kane led the way out of Grimes' day cabin.

Chapter 35

They were gathered in a lounge in the main dome of the spaceport administration complex, standing in two groups. There were the three tramp captains; there were four young people, three men and a woman, in the purple and gold uniform of the El Doradan Navy. Grimes looked at these latter curiously and, he was obliged to admit, apprehensively. Which of them was the Graf von Stolzberg, his . . . son? He

had half expected to see a mirror image of himself, but. . . .
There had been more genes than his involved.

The young man was blond haired, like his mother, and
blue eyed. He was much taller than Grimes and with more
than the mere suggestion of a paunch. With less fat to
smooth them over his features might have been craggy.
Yes, the likeness was there. Grimes hated himself for remembering the old saying: Our relations are chosen for us, but
thank God we can choose our friends.

"Good morning, gentlebeings," said Kane jovially. "I'd like
to introduce you to your leader, Commodore Grimes, master
of the good ship *Saucy Sue.*"

"*Sister Sue,*" growled Grimes.

"Sorry, Commodore. So *Sister Sue* isn't saucy."

"Get on with it, man," muttered Captain MacWhirter.

Kane shot a nasty look in the Scot's direction, then continued. "You've already met your captains, Commodore Grimes.
But here, with them, are our own liaison officers. The Honorable Claude Ponsonby, attached to *Pride of Erin.* . . ."

"Glad to have you aboard, Commodore," said the tall,
weedy, young man, extending his right hand. Grimes, thinking sourly that he, as the senior officer, should have made the
first move, shook it. It was limp, almost boneless, in his.

"Count Vishinsky, of *Spaceways Princess.* . . ."

The stocky El Doradan lieutenant, as heavily bearded as
MacWhirter, although his whiskers were glossily black, committed the same solecism as Ponsonby although his grip was
much firmer. Obviously, thought Grimes, in the opinion of
these space puppies an El Doradan aristocrat outranked an
outworld commodore.

"The Graf Ferdinand von Stolzberg, of *Agatha's
Ark.* . . ."

The Graf looked down disdainfully on the man whom he
did not know was his father, clicked his heels and bowed
stiffly. Grimes bowed back, repressing the urge to murmur,
"Ah, so. . . ."

"And now, Commodore, your own pet. The Countess of
Walshingham."

The Countess was a tall, slim blonde with, as revealed by
the miniskirt of her uniform, excellent legs. Her jacket bulged
in the right places. Her face was strong, with high
cheekbones, a square, dimpled chin, a wide, full-lipped
mouth, a short, straight nose. Her gray eyes looked at
Grimes, who had extended his hand, disdainfully.

"Go on, Wally," urged Kane. "Shake paws with the commodore!"

"Don't call me Wally!" she snapped. "The correct title, *Baron*, is Countess."

Nonetheless she touched hands briefly with Grimes.

"And now," said Kane, motioning the others toward the round table.

They seated themselves—Grimes on Kane's right, the three tramp captains on the right of him, then the El Doradan officers. A robot steward brought in a tray with a huge coffee-pot, mugs, a bowl of brown sugar crystals, a jug of cream. There was a pause in conversation while the drinking vessels were filled.

"And now," said Kane again. "You have all heard of your commodore. He was quite famous while he was an officer in the Federation Survey Service. Or should I have said 'notorious'? As an owner-master—although only recently of a *real* ship—he has maintained his Survey Service reputation. For a short while he was captain of the spaceyacht owned by my wife, the Baroness Michelle. She speaks highly of him. You may rest assured, ladies and gentlemen, that I would have never trusted command of our enterprise to anybody less capable than Commodore Grimes. . . ."

"When do I get my medal?" Grimes asked sardonically.

"You're in this for money," Kane told him. "Not for honor and glory. But, before we go any further, does anybody not approve of the commodore's appointment?"

MacWhirter muttered, "I'm no historian, Commodore Kane, but didnae the old time pirates, on Earth's seas, elect their commanders?"

"You are not pirates, Captain MacWhirter. At the moment you're not anything. You're just shipmasters whose vessels have been fitted with defensive armament. Once the Letters of Marque have been issued you will be privateers."

"You never used to be so fussy about legalities, Commodore," Grimes could not resist saying.

"In the old days, Commodore," said Kane, "I was not a naval officer. I am now. But didn't you, when you were in the Survey Service, bend the law now and again? But enough of this. Kalla had been blockaded, although so far no large force has been dispatched to deal with the rebels. Our agents on the planet have informed us that the Kallan government will be happy to issue Letters of Marque so as to leave their own navy free for planetary defense. Work will begin on mounting your armament tomorrow, Commodore Grimes. I suggest that you and your officers avail themselves of the battle simulators, and that your Mannschenn Drive chief acquaint himself with the temporal precession synchronizer. . . ."

"I have already raised that point with Mr. Malleson," Grimes said. "He tells me that he was among those involved in the development of the device."

"Good. Well, ladies and gentlemen, I shall want you off planet, on your way to Kalla, as soon as your commodore is ready. Meanwhile—as most of you know already—all the facilities of Port Kane are open to you and your crews." He smiled expansively. "Enjoy, enjoy!"

The meeting was over.

Grimes walked back to his ship in the company of the other tramp captains. He was pleased to see that discharge was well under way, was going fast and smoothly with busy stowbots stacking crates and cases and cartons into trucks that carried them into one of the domes.

"Yon's The Happy Kangaroo," said MacWhirter, pointing. "The liquor was runnin' a mite low. Would there be Scotch in your cargo, Commodore?"

"Yes," said Grimes.

"An' haggis, maybe?"

"I'm afraid not."

"Ah, weel. A man canna have everything. . . ."

"As long as there're willing popsies, Mack," said Captain O'Leary, "why worry?" He turned to Grimes. "But that'll not be worryin' you, Commodore, will it now? I saw your Catering Officer—a bit of all right as long as you like red hair. An' a green-skinned wench—a New Donegalan, would she be? An' now you're gettin' the Countess. . . . Whoever said that rank has its privileges wasn't far off the mark!"

"I consider this conversation quite disgusting, Captain O'Leary," said Captain Prinn. "I am sure that Commodore Grimes would never consider a liaison with one of his female officers."

"One of them might consider a liaison with him, Aggie," said O'Leary.

"I do not think that Commodore Grimes is that sort of man," said Captain Prinn.

Evidently, Grimes thought, she had taken a shine to him. He wondered if she would take a shine to the Graf von Stolzberg.

The others left him at the foot of his ramp. He looked up

at the gantry that was being erected to one side of the ship, presumably for the installation of the armament. He was joined there by Williams.

"How did it go, Skipper?" asked the mate. "Everybody happy in the Service?" He did not wait for an answer. "The boys are happier now. Most of the engineers are already across at The Happy Kangaroo. Their chiefs let them go. Mr. Malleson and old Mr. Stewart are playing with some new-fangled gadgetry in the Mannschenn Drive room—a synchronizer or some such. The Green Hornet's sulking hard because I wouldn't let her go ashore with her boyfriends. I let Vic off, though. He's gone to brush up his gunnery in the battle simulator they have here. I shouldn't mind a bit of a refresher course myself. . . ."

"Off you go, then, Mr. Williams. I shall be staying on board. Ms. Connellan can look after the discharge."

"That's what she's doing now. The stowbots here are so good that she'll not be able to do any damage."

Grimes went up to his quarters, where he was joined by Mayhew.

"I suppose, Captain—or should I say Commodore—that you'll be wanting a rundown on this morning's meeting," said the telepath.

"Yes."

"All right. First, Captain O'Leary. He rather resents having you placed in authority over him; he thought that he'd be able to roar through space on his ownsome, seeking whom he might devour. But he realizes that an experienced naval officer in charge will be to everybody's benefit. He will do what he's told—but more often than not will argue about it first.

"Captain MacWhirter. His general attitude is very similar to O'Leary's, although he's less of a romantic and far more of a real mercenary. And, unlike O'Leary, he has a great respect for titles of nobility. That comes of his being a citizen of the Empire of Waverley. If only *you* had a title, preferably a Scottish one, he'd follow you into a black hole.

"Captain Prinn. For all her appearance and manner another romantic. And she, too, has that absurd respect for titles. She's thrilled to be having a real Graf, the son of a real Princess, as a junior officer aboard her ship. He will be pampered. I wonder what she would think if she knew who the Graf's father is. . . ."

"That will do, Mr. Mayhew."

"Sorry, Commodore. And would you like my analysis of the El Doradans?"

165

"Please."

"First, the Honorable Claude Ponsonby. Don't be fooled by his appearance and manner. He's tough, and could be vicious. His god is money and he's determined that the operation will be a success, no matter who suffers. He, like the other liaison officers, will receive a substantial percentage of the profits.

"Now, Vishinsky. For all the dissimilarity in appearance and manner a man cast in the same mold as Ponsonby. He'll see to it that Captain MacWhirter toes the line.

"The Graf von Stolzberg? He's an El Doradan, of course, despite his ancestry. . . ." Grimes winced. "But, because of his ancestry, he's also something of a romantic. He hides that side of his character beneath his stiff manner. I think that he will get along *very* well with Captain Prinn—she, too, is a repressed romantic. . . ."

"The prince and the pirate queen," sneered Grimes. "I hope that they will be very happy."

"Come, come, sir," chided Mayhew. "You may be commodore—but that doesn't give you *droit du seigneur* over your subordinates, especially those who're captains of their own ships. Do you wish me to continue?"

"Yes. Go on."

"There is little more than I can say about the Graf von Stolzberg. He's young and romantic and an affair with an older woman, such as Captain Agatha Prinn, will do him far more good than harm. Out of uniform and with hardly more than a hint of cosmetics she will be a very attractive woman."

"Stop harping on it, Mr. Mayhew."

"Very good, sir. Now, the Countess of Walshingham. . . . I'll describe her this way. If she and our own Green Hornet could swap bodies and accents you'd never know that there had been an exchange. The other three El Doradans are, in their ways, loyal to their planet. She is loyal only to herself. Furthermore she is a man-hater."

"Another female-chauvinist bitch," said Grimes.

"It was Commodore Kane's idea of a joke to appoint her to your ship," Mayhew said.

"That bastard!"

"Just so, sir. Just so. I, like yourself, am firmly of the opinion that he must have ridden to his parents' wedding ceremony on a bicycle. Anything more, Commodore?"

"That's enough to be going on with, I think. Oh, you might see if Ms. Granadu has any shipboard uniforms, shorts and shirts, in the slop chest your size. She's a fairish needlewoman and should be able to knock up a pair of assistant purser's shoulderboards for you."

"Some get promoted," said Mayhew with a grin, "and others demoted. But as one of your officers I shall be entitled to my share of the spoils."

"If any," said Grimes.

"If any. Aren't you just a little sorry that you accepted that commission in the Reserve?"

"Just a little," admitted Grimes. (It is useless trying to lie to a telepath.) "Oh, and when you see Miss Granadu ask her to come up and see me."

"And I'll tell her to bring the coins and the book," Mayhew said.

Grimes shook the three antique coins in his cupped hands, let them fall to the deck. Two tails and a head. Seven. Two heads and a tail. Eight. Three heads. Nine. Another three heads, another nine. Then eight, and again eight for the final throw.

Kou. Sudden encounters. A bold, strong woman appears on the scene. One should not contract a marriage with such a woman. . . .

Nine in the third place. He proceeds with difficulty, like one who has been flayed. His position is fraught with danger, but despite this he will commit no great error. . . .

"Well," said Grimes, "that, at least, is comforting."

"There's more—and worse—to come, Captain," said Magda.

She continued reading.

Nine is the fourth place. The inferior men have escaped from restraint, like fish from a bag. This will give rise to evil. . . .

"Didn't we have this once before?" asked Grimes.

"Yes. But that time the lines were not so ominous."

"And that time," said Grimes thoughtfully, "there was only one strong woman to worry about. Now there are two."

Chapter 36

The few days at Port Kane were busy ones for Grimes. Personally he oversaw the installation of *Sister Sue's* armament—the laser cannon, the quick-firing projectile gun and the missile projector. There was the fire-control console to be fitted in the control room; instrumentation required for normal, peacetime purposes had to be relocated to make room for it. Malleson, too, was busy. The operation of the precession synchronizer would be his concern. He assured Grimes that he had been one of those involved in the original development of this device and that he was looking forward to seeing it in operation.

When he could spare the time Grimes played around with the battle simulator, pitting his wits and skills against the computer representing an enemy commander unless, as sometimes happened, one of the other captains was on hand to play that part. When he was matched against O'Leary or MacWhirter, maneuvering the blob of light that represented his ship in the tank, every simulated battle was for him a walkover. With his one vessel against both of theirs he invariably won; the tramp masters seemed to be quite incapable of deploying all their armament simultaneously. There was always the time lag when they switched from laser to quickfirer to guided missile. But whoever came up against Captain Agatha Prinn, he conceded, would have to be *good*. She took to naval gunnery like a duck to water.

Now and again his captains would be accompanied by their El Doradan officers who, having affixed their signatures to the privateers' Articles, signing on as fourth mates, were now wearing the uniforms of their putative employers. The Honorable Claude looked faintly absurd in the *Pride of Erin's* green, although his outfit was far better cut and of greatly superior quality to Captain O'Leary's. The *Spaceways Princess* rig of tunic and kilt suited Vishinsky, especially since his robot tailor had succeeded in imparting a cossack quality to the upper garment. In *Agatha's Ark's* severe gray business suit with the touch of gold on the shoulders the Graf von Stolzbert looked more like a diplomat than a spaceman. Perhaps, thought Grimes, watching the young man as he played the attentive squire to his captain, a diplomat was what he should have been. He was rather ruefully amused. He wished that he were able to advise his son. But then, what would he, could he say? Beware of older women? Beware of *all* women? And who was he, Grimes, to dish out such advice? Don't do as I do, my boy, do as I say. . . .

Williams and Venner were frequent visitors to the dome housing the battle simulator, as were the control-room officers from the other ships. Now and again the Green Hornet condescended to try her hand, usually in the company of the Countess of Walshingham. The Countess was still wearing her El Doradan uniform and had yet to sign *Sister Sue's* Articles.

It was not all work and no play for the privateers, however. There was The Happy Kangaroo, the pleasure dome which Grimes and his people had first learned about at the Countess of Wilberforce's prayer meeting. There were refreshments, solid and liquid, all of high quality. There was a gaming room. (Kane, in a jovial mood, told Grimes that the returns from this were almost sufficient to pay for the other entertainments.) Grimes was no gambler but he looked in one evening to watch O'Leary, Vishinsky and other officers, including his own Mr. Venner, playing *vingt et un*. The dealer and banker was the girl who had carried around the collection bag at the finish of that dreary evening in El Dorado City. She seemed to be doing far better for Drongo Kane than she had been doing for the missionaries. She was dressed differently, too, wearing a bunny uniform that showed her long, sleek legs to best advantage.

But Grimes was watching Venner more than he was watching her. Rear Admiral Damien had warned him not to play cards with the man—yet he was losing heavily, as was everybody except the house.

There was music, and there was dancing, and there was a cabaret whose underclad performers made up in enthusiasm for what they lacked in terpsichorean skill. And there was enthusiasm, Grimes knew, off stage. Slumming these girls might be but they were enjoying it. *Sister Sue's* junior engineers were no longer fighting among themselves for Ms. Connellan's favors; they had far better and tastier fish to fry.

Grimes knew what was going on and felt the occasional stab of jealousy. He could have had his share of what was going—but he did not like sharing. He was a snob, and he knew it, but the thought of sampling delights that Denning,

169

Singh or Paulus (his pet dislikes!) had already sampled re-pelled him. He wanted, a captain's lady, not an officers' mess.

Now and again he would call the Schloss Stolzberg to talk with Marlene. She was polite enough but that was all. He suggested that he come to the castle for a brief visit before departure; she told him that as a commodore he had far too many responsibilities. He asked her if she would come to Port Kane; after all, he told her, she would wish to see her son again before the privateers set off on their venture. She smiled rather sadly and said that she knew that Ferdinand was being very well looked after and that the young man might be embarrassed if his mother, a woman some years younger than Captain Prinn, made her appearance. Of course, Ferdinand would be spending his last night on El Dorado in his mother's home and it certainly would not do for Grimes to be there to.

He hoped that the El Dorado Corporation or Drongo Kane or whoever would soon decide that it was high time that the privateer fleet was underway.

Chapter 37

He sat at a table in The Happy Kangaroo, by himself, nursing his drink. He did not, unlike most of the other spacers, consider that free liquor was a valid excuse for get-ting drunk. Malleson and Mayhew had been with him but the Mannschenn Drive chief had wanted to try out a new system in the gaming room, where a roulette table was in operation. Mayhew had gone with the engineer. Was he a telekineticist as well as a telepath, Grimes had wondered idly. A few tables away the Green Hornet and the Countess of Walshingham were sitting. They were not actually hand in hand but con-veyed the impression that they were. Elsewhere in the room were three kilted officers from Spaceways Princess, another trio from Pride of Erin in their green and gold finery and a quartet from Agatha's Ark, their noisy behavior in contrast to the gray sobriety of their uniforms. A dozen of the volunteer bunnies were looking after them. He wondered briefly where most of his own people were. Williams, he knew, was staying on board, with Magda Granadu to keep him com-

170

pany. Neither Mr. Crumley nor Mr. Stewart was much of a shore-goer. And he had heard talk of a picnic and bathing party at a nearby ocean beach—a beer and bunnies orgy, he thought sourly. That would account for the absence of his junior officers.

He watched the stage more with censorious interest than with enthusiasm. Once he would have enjoyed a turn of this nature; now it rather repelled him. He thought that he knew why. Years ago, when he had been a watchkeeping officer aboard the Zodiac Class cruiser *Aries*, one of his shipmates had been a reservist, a lieutenant who, in civil life, was a second mate in Trans-Galactic Clippers. This young man had a fund of good stories about life in big passenger ships. There was one captain, he told his listeners, who was a notorious womanizer. "We even used to pimp for the old bastard," said the storyteller. "If he got fixed up at the beginning of the voyage the ship was Liberty Hall. . . . But if, for some reason, he failed to score it was *hell*. . . . We all had to observe both letter and spirit of company regulations *and* a few extra ones that he thought up himself just to make our lives miserable!"

Grimes had no real desire to emulate the TG captain, but. . . .

He looked morosely at the stage, at the naked girl who was dancing, an old-fashioned waltz, with a gleaming, humanoid robot. Great art it was not. It was not even good pornography. The girl was gawky and her movements were stiffer than those of the automaton. Her feet were too big.

Somebody dropped into the chair that had been vacated by Malleson. He was dimly conscious of a white collar with a black bow tie, of smooth shoulders, of long, gleaming legs. *A bunny*, he thought. *Another rich bitch putting on the Lady Bountiful act. . . .*

She said, "You look as though you'd rather be in The Red Kangaroo, on Botany, John."

He turned his head to look at her properly.

"Michelle," he said.

It was by no means the first time that he had seen her scantily clothed but this bunny rig imparted to her a tartiness. It suited her, he decided.

She raised a slim hand commandingly and a robar glided up to their table on silent wheels. She said, "I can see what you're drinking. I'll have the same." She addressed the frontal panel of the machine, gay with little winking lights, and ordered, "Two pink gins."

171

"Coming up," the thing replied in a mechanical voice. A section of panel dropped down to form a shelf and on to it slid two misted goblets. Grimes reached out for them, put them on the table.

He said, "And some little eats."

A dish of nuts of various kinds appeared on the shelf.

"Still Gutsy Grimes," murmured the Baroness.

"Just blotting paper," said Grimes, between nibbles.

She raised her glass to him and said, "Here's looking at you. . . ."

"And at you," he replied.

She sipped—not as daintily as had been her wont when he first knew her, thought Grimes—and then gestured toward the amateur performer on the stage.

"Ashley," she said scornfully, "thinks that she's the best since Isadora Duncan, but. . . ."

"Who's she?"

"Lady Ashley Mortimer."

"No, not her. Isadora Duncan."

"Really, John, you are a peasant. She was a famous dancer who lived in the twentieth century, old style. But don't you find the entertainment here boring?"

"I do, frankly."

She said, "I'd rather like to see your ship."

He looked at her intently and asked, "Won't Drongo mind?"

"The Baron," she said, with a subtle emphasis on the title, "is in El Dorado City, in conference with Baron Takada and others. It is my understanding that very soon now you will be given orders to lift for Kalla." She tossed the remains of her drink down her throat. "Come on." She rose to her feet.

Grimes finished his drink, snatched up a last handful of the nuts and then extricated himself from his chair. Together they walked to the door, out into the warm night.

The four ships stood there, floodlit towers of metal, three silvery in the glare, one a dull green. On the side of one of the silver ships a flag had been painted, a purple burgee with a gold ball in the upper canton, a commodore's broad pennant.

"That's her," said Grimes. "*Sister Sue.*"

She said, "I wish that somebody would name a ship after me."

"You could always ask Drongo to do that little thing."

"Him!" she snorted with such vehemence that Grimes was

not only embarrassed but felt an upsurge of loyalty to his own sex.

They strolled slowly over the apron to the foot of *Sister Sue's* ramp. There was a sentry on duty there, one of the omnipresent robots, attired in approximation of the uniform of the Federation Survey Service Marines. The thing saluted with mechanical smartness. Grimes acknowledged with deliberate sloppiness.

He and Michelle walked up the gangway to the open airlock door, into the vestibule. The elevator cage, already at this lower level, carried them swiftly and smoothly up to the captain's flat. Grimes ushered his guest into his sitting room. She sprawled with elegant inelegance in one of the armchairs by the coffee table, her long, slender legs stretched out before her. Grimes took the seat facing her. He saw that Magda had laid out his usual supper—a thermopot of coffee, a large dish of napkin-covered sandwiches. Michelle, too, noted this offering. She bent forward and lifted the napkin. The sandwiches were of new bread, with the crust left on, cut thick—as was the pink ham that was the filling.

She smiled. "You have a female catering officer, don't you? It looks as though she spoils you as thoroughly as Big Sister used to. . . ." Her expression clouded slightly. "I hope that I am not . . . trespassing. Or poaching."

"No, Michelle. She's already spoken for."

"Oh. Do you think I could have some coffee?"

"Of course."

There was only one mug on the tray but there were others in a locker. Grimes got one out. He filled both vessels with the steaming, aromatic brew, remembered that she preferred hers unsweetened. He added sugar liberally to his own drink.

She nibbled a sandwich.

She said, "Marriage—or marriage to Baron Kane—seems to have coarsened me. Once I would sneer at this sort of food. Now I enjoy it."

"Mphm," grunted Grimes through a mouthful.

"This cabin," she said, "is more *you* than your quarters aboard *The Far Traveler*. . . . And even if you don't have a golden stewardess you do have a golden girl. . . ." She waved a half-eaten sandwich toward the miniature Una, astride her gleaming bicycle, on the shelf. "Rather pretty. Or even beautiful."

Grimes got up and lifted the figurine and her wheeled steed down to the deck. "Ride," he ordered. "Ride. Round and round and round. . . ."

173

She clapped her hands gleefully. "One of Yosarian's toys, isn't she? But aren't they rather expensive?"

"I didn't buy her," said Grimes stiffly. "She was a gift. From Mr. Yosarian and. . . ."

"And from the lady who was the model?" She laughed. "No doubt one of your ex—or not so ex—girl friends. You know, I've always been sorry that you were so overawed by me when you were my yachtmaster. But now that you're an owner-master, *and* a commodore. . . ."

"But not a baron," said Grimes.

"But still a privateer," she told him, "as the first Baron d'Estang was. . . ."

There was something more than a little sluttish about her posture. Her bodice had become unbuttoned. The pink nipple of one firm breast seemed to be winking at him. The invitation was unmistakable.

Yet when he got up from his chair and moved toward her she put up a hand to fend him away.

"Wait," she said. "I have to use your bathroom first. Through there, isn't it?"

"Yes."

She rose sinuously from her seat, walked, with swaying buttocks, to the bedroom, through which were the toilet facilities. Grimes poured himself the last of the coffee from the thermopot. He was still sipping it when she came back, standing in the doorway between day and sleeping cabins.

The glossy white Eton collar and the black bow accentuated her nakedness. A highborn lady she might be—and, at this moment, a tart she most certainly was.

But a high-class tart, thought Grimes, as he got up and went to join her in the bedroom.

In the day cabin the miniature Una Freeman continued her tireless rounds while the solidograph of Maggie Lazenby looked down disapprovingly.

"And now," he whispered, "what was all this about, darling?"

She murmured, "The laborer is worthy of his hire."

He said, "But this was a bonus."

"And for me, John. And for me. Besides. . . ."

"Yes?"

"I don't pretend to possess the faculty of prevision. . . . But. . . . But I don't think that you'll be coming back here, ever. I just had to take this chance to do with you what we should have done a long time ago."

"Thank you," he said.

She kissed him a last time, her lips moist and warm on his, then gently disengaged herself from his embrace. She swung her long, long legs down to the deck, swayed gracefully into the bathroom. When she came out she was dressed again in her bunny costume.

"Don't get up," she told him. "I can see myself ashore."

"But...."

"Don't get up, John." She blew him a kiss. "Good night. Good-bye, and the very best of luck."

She vanished through the doorway.

She screamed briefly. Grimes flung himself off the bed and ran to the door. She straightened up from rubbing her right foot and glared at him.

"That bloody golden popsy of yours," she snarled. "It was *intentional!*"

"She's only a toy," said Grimes.

"And a dangerous one." She grinned. "I'd better go before I kick her off her bicycle and then jump on her!"

She waved and then was gone.

Grimes told the tiny cyclist to stop, picked her up and put her back on her shelf. The integument of the metal body in his hands seemed almost as real as the human skin that, only minutes ago, he had been caressing.

Chapter 38

Sister Sue's control room was fully manned.

Grimes was in the command chair, and Williams seated at the stand-by controls. Old Mr. Stewart was looking after the NST transceiver and Ms. Connellan and the new fourth officer, the Countess of Walshingham, were at their stations by the radar equipment. Venner was attending the recently installed battle organ. It was SOP in the Survey Service to have all armament ready for instant use during lift-off and, thought Grimes, what was good enough for a regular warship was good enough for a privateer.

He looked around him at his officers. Williams was his usual cheerful self and old Mr. Stewart looked like an elderly priest performing a ritual of worship to some electronic deity.

175

Venner, with violent death at his fingertips, was grinning mirthlessly. He would welcome the excuse, Grimes knew, to push a few buttons. The Green Hornet seemed to have a smaller chip on her shoulder than usual. The Countess was conveying the impression that she was holding herself icily aloof from everybody except the second mate.

Grimes didn't like her. He did not think that anybody, save Ms. Connellan, would or could like her. She had made a scene—only a minor one, but still a scene—when, at long last, she had deigned to affix her signature to *Sister Sue's* Articles of Agreement. She had scrawled, in a large, rather childish hand, *Walshingham.* "What are your given names?" Grimes had asked her. "That's no concern of yours, Captain," she had replied. "How do we address you?" he had persisted. "As Your Ladyship, of course." "You are a junior officer aboard this vessel," he had told her. "Here you are not a Ladyship." "I am a Ladyship anywhere in the galaxy. But you may address me as Countess."

(The Green Hornet, Grimes knew, called her new friend Wally. He said, "You will be addressed as Miss Walshingham. Or, if you prefer it, Ms.")

"Port Kane Control to flagship," came a voice, Kane's voice, from the NST radio speaker. "Lift when you are ready. *Pride of Erin, Spaceways Princess* and *Agatha's Ark* are under your orders."

Grimes turned to face the transceiver with its sensitive microphone. "Commodore Grimes to Commodore Kane and to masters of *Pride of Erin, Spaceways Princess* and *Agatha's Ark*. The squadron will proceed in echelon—first *Sister Sue*, then the *Pride*, then the *Princess*, then the *Ark*, as rear commodore. . . ."

The Green Hornet muttered something about Survey Service bullshit.

"Ships will lift at twenty-second intervals and will maintain station. Acknowledge in order named."

The acknowledgments came in.

"Stand by!" At Grimes' touch on his controls the mutter of his hitherto idling inertial drive deepened to a rumble. "Execute!"

Sister Sue shook herself, then clambered slowly into the calm morning air toward the blue sky with its gleaming, feathery streaks of high-altitude cloud. Grimes looked out and down through a viewport, saw that there was a small crowd of women outside the dome that housed The Happy Kangaroo. The volunteer hostesses, he thought. Most of them

176

were still in their bunny costumes. Several of them were waving. Michelle was not among them and he felt a little stab of disappointment. Probably she would be with Kane, watching the privateer fleet's departure from the control room at the top of the lattice-work tower. He transferred his attention to the glassed-in cage but could see nobody; the sunlight reflected from the windows was too dazzling. And was Kane, he asked himself wryly, playing King David to his Uriah the Hittite? But it was a far-fetched analogy. Apart from anything else it was the ill-fated Uriah who had been the cuckolded husband.

He wished, too, that the Princess had come to the spaceport to watch the ships, carrying both her son and the man who was his father, set out.

Grimes, he admonished himself, *you're a sentimental slob*.

The Countess announced in a high, clear voice, "*Pride of Erin* is lifting, Commodore."

"Thank you, Miss Walshingham."

He stepped up the thrust of his inertial drive.

"*Spaceways Princess* is lifting. . . ."

"Thank you."

In the stern vision screen the spaceport buildings were dwindling fast.

"*Agatha's Ark* is lifting."

"Good."

Up drove the four ships, and up. The flickering altimeter numerals in the screen told their story of ever and rapidly increasing distance from the ground. Soon, thought Grimes, it would be time for the first test of his captains—and of himself. Never before had he been called upon to assume responsibility for the movements of more than a single ship. He had discussed the maneuver that he was about to attempt with the three other tramp masters, had told them that it was one frequently carried out by Survey Service squadrons shortly after lift-off. He had instructed them in signals procedure. It was a quite spectacular evolution, especially during the hours of darkness, but as long as everything was working properly there was no risk.

"Stand by inertial and reaction drive controls," he ordered. "Acknowledge."

In the screen he saw paired brilliant lights, one red and one blue, blossom into life on the gun turrets of the other ships, so sited as to be visible to all concerned. *Sister Sue* was now displaying similar illuminations.

His hand poised over his inertial drive controls, he looked

to Williams, whose fingers were on the light switches. The mate nodded.

"Execute!"

The clangor of the inertial drive ceased suddenly. In the screen Grimes saw the blue lights on the other ships wink out as one. He felt the inevitable weightlessness as *Sister Sue* began to drop.

"Execute!"

As the red lights were switched off blue incandescence and white vapor burst from the sterns of the ships. Acceleration slammed Grimes down into his chair.

Not bad, he thought, *not bad at all. . . .*

"*Pride of Erin* is out of station," said the Countess coldly. "She is lifting relative to us."

"She's not going to come sniffing up our arse, is she?" asked Grimes coarsely.

"No, sir."

He had seen worse, he remembered. There had been one quite spectacular balls-up many years ago when he had been a junior officer aboard *Aries*. The cruiser, with four escorting destroyers, had lifted from Atlantia. One of the destroyers had not only accelerated violently but had deviated from trajectory, missing the flagship of the squadron by the thickness of the proverbial coat of paint, searing her plating with the fiery backblast.

Anyhow, there was no point in wasting reaction mass. He ordered the required signals to be flashed, cut the reaction drive and restarted inertial drive simultaneously.

The fleet lifted steadily.

Once clear of the Van Allens, trajectory was set for the Kalla sun. Grimes wondered what prevision, if any, he would experience during the moments while the temporal precession field of the Mannschenn Drive built up. What visions of battle and carnage would he see?

But there was only a voice—his voice—singing, not very tunefully.

I murdered William Moore as I sailed, as I sailed,
I murdered William Moore as I sailed,
I knocked him on the head till he bled the scuppers red
And I heaved him with the lead
As I sailed . . . .

Then inside the control room the warped perspective

snapped back to normality and colors resumed their proper places in the spectrum. Outside, the stars were no longer points of brilliance but resembled writhing nebulae.

Grimes looked at Williams.

The mate, obviously, was unaware that his captain was destined to kill him. *But*, thought Grimes, *there is an infinitude of possible futures. There are probabilities and improbabilities—but there are no impossibilities.*

He unbuckled himself from his chair, went to look into the screen of the mass proximity indicator. All the ships were there, as they should have been. Soon, thought Grimes, he would carry out trials of the synchonizers with which the privateers were fitted, and then there would be a few practice shots. There was no urgency, however. Until those Letters of Marque were issued *Sister Sue* and the others were just innocent merchantmen proceeding on their lawful occasions.

"Deep Space routine, Mr. Williams," he ordered. "You know where to find me if you want me."

He went down to his day cabin, where he was joined after a few minutes by Mayhew.

Chapter 39

"I have that damned prevision again," he told the telepath. "The Ballad of Captain Kidd. I murdered William Moore, and all the rest of it."

"I know," said Mayhew.

"You would. But I don't like it. There're a few people aboard this ship who tempt me to commit murder—but Williams isn't one of them."

"But it's not a certainty, Commodore. It's no more than one of the many possibilities."

"A probability, Mr. Mayhew."

"But still not a certainty."

"Then I'll just have to hope for the best. Now, you've got your fingers on the pulse of the ship. Is everybody happy in the service?"

"At the moment, sir, yes. Even Her Highness the Countess of Walshingham."

"She's not a 'highness.' She's only a Countess."

Mayhew grinned. "Of course, sir, you are more familiar with aristocratic ranks and ratings than we low, common spacemen are. Oh, have you seen dear Wally's pet yet?"

"No."

"I have. The thing gives me the creeps. Outwardly it's no more than a cat—a big one, black, with a white bib and socks. But the fur's synthetic and the claws are razor-sharp steel and the skeleton is steel too. And the battery that powers its motors will deliver at maximum capacity for all of twelve standard months. The brain's organic, though. A feline brain, modified, with absolute loyalty to the Countess. And it's programed to kill—anybody or anything—to protect her or if she so orders it. And it's programed to self-destruct if its mistress dies."

"So there's a bomb of some kind inside it," said Grimes.

"That I don't know, sir. I don't possess X-ray vision."

"Presumably dear Wally knows."

"But unless she's actually thinking about it there's no way that I can tell."

"What is she thinking about now?"

Mayhew looked pained.

"First you tell me that you do not approve of . . . snooping. Now you tell me to snoop." He creased his brow in concentration. Suddenly and surprisingly he blushed. "Oh, no," he muttered. "No. . . ."

"What is it, Mr. Mayhew?"

"It's embarrassing, that's what. Ms. Connellan and the Countess are both off watch. How would *you* like to experience the sensation of that green, greasy skin against yours? Those fat, floppy breasts. . . ."

"That will do, Mr. Mayhew."

The telepath grinned. "Well, you asked for it, sir, and you got it. The trouble is that I did too."

Chapter 40

Sister Sue and her consorts fell steadily through the warped continuum toward the Kalla sun. Now and again the Mann-schenn Drive would be shut down aboard all vessels so that a practice shoot could be held; this was necessary as the targets

180

used would be outside the temporal precession fields and therefore visually invisible. At fairly close range, of course, they would show up in the screens of the mass proximity indicators—but MPIs are essentially indicators only and do not fix the position of an object, large or small, with the accuracy of radar. This latter, naturally enough, can be employed only in Normal Space Time. Too, as Grimes never ceased to impress upon his own officers and the other shipmasters, to change a vessel's mass while the interstellar drive is in operation is to court disaster.

"You'll warp the field," he would say. "You'll finish up lost in time as well as in space. You won't know if it's last Christmas or next Thursday. Of course, when there are two ships in close proximity, with temporal precession fields synchronized and overlapping, it will be possible to use missiles or projectile weapons *as long as what you throw does not leave the effective limits of the combined field.* But laser, of course, you can use in any circumstances."

For the first practice shoot Grimes had released from his ship a large balloon with a skin of metallic foil. He ordered his fleet into line astern formation and drove out and away from the target until it was no more than a tiny spark on the screens. He then steered a circular trajectory about the target. Much to the annoyance of Williams and Venner, who wanted to demonstrate their skill, he let *Pride of Erin* be the first to engage the make-believe enemy, using the quick-firing cannon. The target was unscathed. Then it was the turn of *Spaceways Princess.* The flashes of the bursting shells could just be seen through the control-room binoculars but the speck of light in the radar screen still shone, indicating that the balloon was still intact. Finally *Agatha's Ark* had her turn. The spark vanished as the balloon was torn to shreds.

"Well done, *Agatha's Ark,*" said Grimes into the microphone of the NST transceiver.

"She must have been using the gunnery computer," came O'Leary's aggrieved voice.

"I was *not,* Captain O'Leary," said Agatha Prinn tartly.

"An' why should we not use the computer?" demanded O'Leary. "It's supposed to be used, isn't it, Commodore? In an actual battle we'd all be usin' our computers. . . ."

"In an actual battle," said Grimes, "you could have suffered one or more direct hits, playing merry hell with your electronics. But as long as your seat-of-the-pants gunnery is up to scratch you stand a chance of surviving."

Another balloon was launched and this time laser was used

181

against it. *Agatha's Ark* opened the action but without success. *Spaceway Princess* did no better; neither did *Pride of Erin*. Then Venner sulked while Williams took over the fire control. The Green Hornet and the Countess looked on disdainfully, as did the big black cat with its white markings that had accompanied its mistress to the control room.

The mate stared into the repeater screen. "Range . . ." he muttered. "Acceleration. . . . With laser there's no deflection to worry about. . . ." He manipulated the controls with sure fingers. Then with his left forefinger he stabbed down—once, again and again, loosing off one-second pulses.

"Got it, Billy!" said Venner, who was watching the main display.

From the transceiver came Agatha Prinn's voice. "Nice shooting, *Sister Sue*."

And then there was O'Leary complaining again. "I'd have got that damn' balloon if ye'd let me use my laser like a sword. Just one good slash, an'. . . ."

Again Grimes had to explain. He said patiently, "As I told you before, you've suffered direct hits. Your jennies have packed up. All you have to give you juice is your power cells. When they're dead, you're dead. You *must* conserve energy."

"Ye're a mon after me own heart, Commodore," broke in Captain MacWhirter.

So it went on. It became obvious that somebody aboard *Agatha's Ark*, probably Captain Prinn herself, was a very good gunner. The *Princess* would never be better than fair and those aboard *Pride of Erin* would not be able, as Williams put it, to shoot their way out of a paper bag. Grimes had three good gunnery officers aboard his own ship—himself and Williams and Venner.

The privateers graduated from balloons to moving targets—practice missiles fired from *Sister Sue* and programed to steer a random trajectory. Reluctantly Grimes conceded that against these it was necessary to make use of the battle computers.

There were other drills—these in the use of the field synchronizers and, just as important, the techniques to be employed in breaking free from synchronization. It was extremely unlikely that any merchantmen would be fitted with the synchronizing device but all too probable that Hallicheki warships would be so equipped. As with the gunnery, *Agatha's Ark* put up the best show, with *Spaceways Princess* a runner-up. *Pride of Erin's* performance left much to be desired.

182

"They couldn't *wriggle* out of a paper bag," said Williams disgustedly. "I hope that Captain O'Leary never tangles with a real warship."

"I hope that none of us do," said Grimes. "Come to that, I hope that the Hallicheki haven't gotten around yet to defensively arming their merchantmen. We're in this business, Mr. Williams, to make money, not to take lives."

"Rather strange words to be coming from you, Skipper," said the mate. "If only half the stories one hears about you are true you've done more than your fair share of killing."

"When I was pushed into it," Grimes told him. "Only when I was pushed into it."

And would this William Moore Williams push him into it? he asked himself. He hoped that he would not. Yet, twice, there had been the warning, the prevision.

I murdered William Moore as I sailed. . . .

The voyage continued.

Daily there was Carlotti radio communication with Port Kane, coded messages back and forth. These messages were not only to and from Grimes; the Countess of Walshingham was also keeping old Mr. Stewart busy. The radio officer should not, legally, have informed his captain of this traffic but he did so. Her signals, out and in, were coded. Grimes ran them through the coding machine with which he had been supplied by Kane—and it was at once obvious that the El Doradan was using a code of her own.

So Grimes called in Mayhew.

"More snooping, Captain?" asked the telepath. "This privateering is having a bad effect on your ethical standards."

"We haven't started privateering yet," said Grimes. "Well, as you almost certainly know, dear Wally is in daily communication with her happy home world. All messages out and in are in a code to which I don't have the key. I'd like to know what's cooking."

"At this moment," said Mayhew, "dear Wally, as you call her, is engaged in romantic dalliance with our other non-favorite lady. I have no desire again to intrude upon their sweaty privacy. But this is what I can do. The purser's office is on the same deck as the radio office. When I see Wally making a call on Stewart I'll snoop. She's bound to be thinking about the message that she's getting off."

Grimes did not have long to wait.

"What she is sending," Mayhew told him, "is daily reports on the conduct of the voyage, and her estimation of the capa-

183

bilities of yourself, your officers and of the other captains. *You* are 'a typical Survey Service officer, a slave to routine and lacking in imagination. . . .' "

"I don't think that her boss, Commodore Kane, shares that opinion," said Grimes.

"He does not, Captain. I took the liberty of eavesdropping now and again during your conferences back on El Dorado. His evaluation of your good self was, 'cunning as a shit-house rat.' "

"Now you tell me. But, more important, what is Kane telling Wally?"

"Mainly routine acknowledgments of her signals. But he is impressing upon her that she must accompany you when you call on the High Cock of Kalla."

"What a title!" laughed Grimes.

"It gains absurdity in the translation," said Mayhew.

"And suppose that I don't wish to have my fourth mate with me when I do my dickerings with His Avian Majesty?"

"Probably you'll be getting orders on that subject from the El Dorado Corporation, through Kane. Even commodores, service or company, have to do as they're told by their superiors."

"And well I know it, Mr. Mayhew. What makes it complicated in my case is that there are two parties giving me orders."

"And you were never very good at taking orders, were you?" said Mayhew.

Chapter 41

The privateer fleet came to Kalla.

Grimes was relieved to discover that the Hegemony had not yet established a blockade of the rebel planet. Without doubt they would be attempting to do so eventually—but the Hallicheki, he knew from past experience of the avian race, were apt to run around in circles squawking like wet hens before they actually got around to Doing Something. When they did take action, however, it would be with a cold-blooded viciousness.

Kalla is an Earth-type world, although with a somewhat

denser atmosphere. It has the usual seas, continents, islands, rivers, mountain ranges, deserts, fertile plains, forests, polar ice caps and all the rest of it. There is agriculture and there are industries, although there is little automation. The main means of freight transport is by towed balloon, the more or less streamlined gas bags being dragged through the atmosphere by teams of winged workers. Before the revolution these were caponized males. After the revolution it was the hens who had to do the heavy work.

Sister Sue established first contact with Kalla Aerospace Control, by Carlotti radio, while still seven standard days out. Four days out she was challenged by a vessel of the Insurrectionary Navy. This warship made a close approach and attempted to synchronize precession rates with the privateers' flagship. Had she attempted to do so with *Pride of Erin* she would almost certainly have been successful. Grimes' Mannschenn Drive engineer, Malleson, knew all about the synchronizer, its uses and abuses. Although the blob of light representing the guard ship was bright enough in the screen of the mass proximity indicator not so much as the faintest ghost of her was ever seen through the viewports.

Then she did what she should have done at first, calling *Sister Sue* on the Carlotti radio.

A squawking voice issued from the speaker. "*Karkoran* to leader of squadron. *Karkoran* to leader of squadron. Come in. Come in."

The screen came alive and from it looked out the face of a great, gaudy bird—hooked beak, fierce yellow eyes, a golden crest over green and scarlet plumage.

"*Sister Sue* here," said Grimes. "Company Commodore Grimes commanding. Identify yourself, please."

"Flight Leader Kaskonta, Commander of the Inner Starways. I am to escort you and your squadron to Kalla."

"I am obliged to you, Flight Leader."

"I shall be obliged to you, Commodore, if you will allow me to synchronize."

Grimes hesitated briefly. He told Williams and Venner, both of whom were in the control room, to stand by the ship's fire control. He did not expect any trouble—there were never any male avians aboard the warships of the Hegemony—but it would cost nothing to be prepared. He called Malleson, who was in the Mannschenn Drive room.

"All right, Chief. She's one of ours. I hope. Let her synchronize. But stay handy."

There was a brief, very brief period of disorientation. Outside the viewports the stars were still pulsating nebulosities—but against their backdrop, big and solid, was the Kalla ship. It was strange, Grimes thought not for the first time, how spaceship design varied from race to race. The insectoid Shaara, for example, with their vessels that could have been modeled on old-fashioned beehives. . . . The Hallicheki, whose ships looked like metal eggs sitting in lattice-work eggcups. . . .

This was one such.

Probably she had started life as a merchantman but she was far more heavily armed than any of the privateers, a real cruiser rather than an auxiliary cruiser. Her fighting capabilities, however, would depend as much upon the quality of her crew as upon that of her armament. Grimes, who tended at times to be a male chauvinist, thought that she would be able to take on a comparable warship of the Hegemony with a fair chance of success. He did wonder, though, how and where these fighting cocks had received the necessary training. Probably this had been financed, for some promised consideration, by the El Dorado Corporation.

All officers were now in the control room.

"Put out a call to *Pride of Erin*, *Spaceways Princess* and *Agatha's Ark*, Mr. Stewart," ordered Grimes. "Tell them that we are proceeding to Kalla under escort. Tell them, too, that the authority still rests with myself."

The squadron, with *Karkoran* still in watchful attendance, established itself in synchronous orbit about Kalla. Grimes had been told that none of the ships would be allowed to land but that he could make the descent in one of his boats for an audience with the Lord of the Roost. He talked with Captain Prinn by NST radio, told her that until his return she would be in charge of the little fleet. This did not go down at all well with Captain O'Leary. And Williams, left in command of *Sister Sue* during Grimes' absense, was not pleased either. "You mean that she's the commodore now, Skipper?"

"I appointed her vice-commodore at the beginning of the trip, Mr. Williams."

"I thought that it was rear commodore, sir. And rear is junior to vice. Of course, I'm only a Dog Star Line man, not used to all these naval titles. . . ."

"Don't try to be a space lawyer too, Billy. Captain Prinn, in my opinion, is the person most suitable to be my deputy. I called her the rear commodore because hers is the sternmost ship of the squadron."

"But I thought, sir, that during the commodore's absence his second-in-command would be in charge."

"You're in temporary command of *Sister Sue*, and that's all. And that's plenty. Should you want to get in touch with me, my wrist transceiver will be within effective range of the ship."

He went down to his cabin to pick up his best uniform cap, the one with the scrambled egg on the peak still untarnished, with the especially large horse-and-rider badge. Apart from that he was making no attempt at ceremonial dress. He was not in the Survey Service any longer—apart from that Reserve Commission which was a secret to all save Mayhew and Venner—and did not have in his wardrobe such finery as an epauleted frock coat, with sword belt and sword, or a gold-trimmed fore-and-aft hat. His shipboard shorts and shirt would have to do. He had made inquiries and learned that Port Kwakaar, near which the Lord of the Roost had his palace, was well within Kalla's tropics.

Williams accompanied him to the boat bay. Mayhew, wearing a uniform that looked as though he had slept in it, was awaiting him there. So was the Countess of Walshingham. Her shirt and shorts could have been tailored by one of the big Paris houses. Her cat—that evil beast!—was with her.

Grimes said, "We are not taking *that* down with us, Ms. Walshingham."

"Why not, Commodore?"

"Because I say so. In case you don't know, the Hallicheki are an avian people. There's a strong possibility that they may not like your pet, and an equally strong one that your pet will not like them. It is vitally important that we do not annoy the planetary ruler. I have to get the Letters of Marque from him for a start. And I want to get permission for the ships to land to take aboard such stores as are necessary."

"Birdseed?" she sneered. "Or nice, fat worms?"

He said, "If Commodore Kane had not requested that I take you with me you would be staying aboard. Commodore Kane said nothing about the cat."

"Go to my cabin," she told the . . . animal? "Go to my cabin and wait for me."

It made a noise that was more growl than mew, stalked out of the boat bay. Sulkily the Countess clambered into the fat torpedo hull of the boat. Mayhew followed her. Grimes, after saying, "She's all yours, Mr. Williams. Don't start any wars in my absence!" went in last. He found that the fourth officer

187

was already seated forward, at the controls. He resisted the urge to tell her to get aft, with the telepath. After all, she was a qualified spaceperson. And he was a captain—no, a commodore—and as such should not be doing his own chauffeuring.

The Countess seemed to be capable enough.

She sealed the little spacecraft and made the necessary checks. She reported readiness to depart to the control room.

"Shove off when ready," came Venner's voice from the transceiver. The little inertial drive unit grumbled, then snarled. Ahead of the boat the door in the shell plating opened, exposing the chamber, from which the air had already been evacuated, to space, to a view of black, starry sky and the curved, luminous limb of the planet, glowing greenly.

The inertial drive almost screamed as the Countess made a needlessly abrupt departure from *Sister Sue*, the sudden acceleration forcing Grimes and Mayhew back in their seats.

"We are not a guided missile, Ms. Walshingham," said Grimes sternly when he had recovered his breath.

"Time, Commodore, is money," she said. "As soon as we get those Letters of Marque we shall be able to start making a profit."

Probably, thought Grimes, she was a shareholder in the El Dorado Corporation—and as money hungry as the rest of them.

Chapter 42

Port Kwakaar was, in some ways, just another spaceport. In other ways it was exotic. The administration buildings, for example, were domes that looked as though they had been woven from straw, and the control tower was a huge tree on top of which another such nest was perched. There were ships on the apron—not only Hallicheki vessels but a couple of the Commission's Epsilon Class star tramps. There were mooring masts to which were tethered sausage-shaped balloons below which were slung flimsy-looking baskets. There were Kallans in the air, male birds to judge from their gaudy plumage. These gave the descending boat a wide berth.

"*Sister Sue's* small craft," squawked a voice from the transceiver speaker, "land by the beacon. Land by the beacon."

The Countess acknowledged, then slammed the boat down alongside the tripod atop which a bright, scarlet light was flashing. Grimes winced. On the return trip to the mother ship, he decided, he would take the controls himself—and if dear Wally didn't like it she could go and cry on the Green Hornet's shoulder.

"Open up, Ms. Walshingham," he ordered.

He was first out of the boat and saw two figures walking toward him, one human, one Hallicheki, both male. The man was dressed in an expensive looking gray coverall suit, the bird only in his brilliant plumage. Grimes recalled a dictum of his academy days: *If it moves, salute it; if it doesn't move, polish it.*

So he saluted.

The man inclined his head in reply. The bird lifted his right wing, on the end of which was a claw-like hand.

"Commodore Grimes?" asked the human, the faint disdain in his voice and on his fine-featured face conveying the impression that, as far as he was concerned, commodores were six a penny.

"Yes," said Grimes.

"I am Lord Francis Delamere, Ambassador for El Dorado on Kalla."

"Delamere?" asked Grimes. "I know two Delameres. Cousins. One is a Commander—probably a Captain by now— in the Federation Survey Service. The other is a Dog Star Line Company Commodore."

"Indeed? Younger sons of younger sons of younger sons, possibly. But let us not waste time talking about obscure members of my family—if, indeed, they are members."

"There is a strong facial resemblance, Lord Francis."

"Indeed? You will leave your boat here, Commodore Grimes, and you and your officers will be taken to the palace of the Lord of the Roost by airship. . . ."

"In one of *those* things, Franky?" demanded the Countess, who had just disembarked. "You must be out of your tiny mind!"

"In one of those things, Wally," said Lord Delamere coldly. "When in Rome, do as Rome does."

"And when in Baghdad," added Grimes, "do as the Baghdaddies do."

Not only did Delamere and the Countess and the Kallan look at him coldly; so did Mayhew.

189

"Come!" ordered the avian and set off toward the mooring masts with an odd scuttling motion, the tips of his claws/hands just brushing the ground. The humans followed him toward the mooring masts, to a flimsy-looking ladder that was propped against the basket of one of the balloons. Delamere was first up this and as soon as his weight was in the car the aerostat started to fall. He threw out a bag of some sort of ballast—sand or earth to judge by the sound that it made when it hit the concrete—and restored buoyancy. Grimes was next, and did his own ballast dumping. Mayhew followed him, then the Countess. It was obvious that she had no intention of doing any manual work so Grimes had to oblige.

Five dejected-looking hens, their drab plumage dusty, appeared. The cock bird picked up lines that were made fast to the car at one end, trailing on the ground at the other, and attached them with cliphooks to collars about the scrawny necks of four of the females. The fifth one climbed clumsily up the lattice-work mooring mast and, using her beak, cast loose the line securing the nose of the balloon to the skeletal tower. Delamere threw out another bag of ballast, a small one. The male took to the air, his wings beating strongly, squawking orders in his own language. The females flapped their pinions and lifted, straining against the towlines. The untethered bird lifted too, flying abeam of and a few meters distant from the basket. She turned her head to glare at the occupants. If looks could kill they would all have died at once.

It was not a comfortable ride. There was no seating inside the car and its last use, to judge by a lingering, acrid odor, must have been for the carriage of organic fertilizer. There was a swaying motion and, now and again, jouncing as minor turbulence was encountered. The treetops beneath them, viciously spiked coronals with leaves like bayonets, looked far too close. The air through which they passed was heavy, hot and humid.

And then, ahead of them, on the summit of a low hill was the palace of the Lord of the Roost, a towering structure that could have been made of wickerwork but which gleamed metallically, pierced at intervals with circular ports. The hapless hens fought to gain altitude. Grimes suggested to Delamere that more ballast might be dumped. Delamere told Grimes that he was a spaceman, not an airman, and that, in any case, any attempt to make the work of the towing team easier would be frowned upon by the male Kallans.

190

"You have to remember," he said, "that these hens are being punished for the crimes that they committed when they were the rulers."

The male bird, well in the lead by now, flew into a port at the very summit of the tower. The free female followed him but did not enter the building and perched on a protruding spar. The balloon labored ahead and upward. When it was close enough the hen dropped from her perch, swooped down and caught the dangling mooring line in her beak, flew with it to the pole on which she had been sitting, made it fast. Grimes watched proceedings with great interest mingled with apprehension. He could foresee what he categorized as one helluva tangle. But he need not have worried. Delamere, who knew the drill, unsnapped the towlines from the forward end of the car as they slackened, threw them out and clear. The hens flapped wearily groundward. The breeze, such as it was, was just enough to push the balloon in toward the building, although there was no actual contact.

"Do they expect us to *jump*?" demanded the Countess.

Grimes had been just about to ask the same question.

He could see movement inside the circular opening. From it a gangway was pushed out, an affair of woven slats that did not look as though it would support a healthy cat. But it was rigid enough and did not sag sufficiently to make contact with the basket rim.

"You first, Commodore," said Delamere. "I have to stay to valve gas."

Carefully Grimes clambered out of the car until he was kneeling on the flimsy gangway. He was tempted to make the short passage to the safety of the tower on his hands and knees. There was no handrail of any kind. But to crawl to an audience with the Lord of the Roost would not, he knew, enhance his image. He pushed up and did a little jump forward. He was standing. He did not look down. He knew that as long as he walked toward a light that gleamed in the very center of the port he would be safe. (He knew it—but he did not quite believe it.) He walked, fighting down the temptation to break into a near run, to get it over with as quickly as possible. He proceeded with befitting dignity until a sidewise glance told him that he was in safety.

Then he turned to watch the others cross the perilous bridge.

He hoped that he had not looked so unhappy as the Countess and Mayhew were looking. Lord Delamere, after valving a last dribble of gas, sauntered across exuding insouciance.

Chapter 43

Grimes supposed that the dimly lit apartment into which they were led could be called a throne room. There was no throne, however. There was a horizontal bar at human eye level on which the Kallan leader was roosting, gripping the perch with his huge, clawed feet. There were other bars at lower levels on which lesser dignitaries stood (sat?). All the avians were males, brightly plumaged. Among the feathers of some of them precious metals and jewels reflected what little light there was, seemed to concentrate it before throwing it back. In one corner of the big room sophisticated recording equipment was humming almost inaudibly, panel lights gleaming. There was a rather unpleasant acridity in the air. Grimes managed to restrain himself from sneezing. The Countess did not even make an effort.

"Your Winged Mightiness," said Lord Delamere, "I present to you the privateer commodore and his officers."

The Lord of the Roost squawked derisively, "He is a cock, and he has a hen officer!"

"She is only a very junior officer, Mightiness."

"She may remain, but she will keep silent." The glaring, yellow eyes turned to Grimes. "I am told that you have an offer to make to me, Commodore. Speak."

"Your Winged Mightiness," Grimes began. He tried to think of what to say next. He had assumed that Lord Delamere would be doing the haggling, would already have done the haggling. "I have come," he went on, "to offer my services, the services of myself and my ships. I have learned that Kalla is threatened by the Hegemony. Your own fleet, gallant though it is, will be fully employed protecting your world." He paused for thought. "Warfare is more than actions between opposing fleets of warships. There is economic warfare. . . ."

"Are you a spaceman or a banker?" demanded the great bird.

"I am a spaceman, Mightiness. Perhaps my words were ill chosen. By economic warfare I mean the destruction of the enemy's commerce. . . ."

"Which you will do for your profit." The Lord of the Roost emitted a discordant sound that could have been a laugh. "But do not bother me any more with your talk, Commodore. You are a spaceman, not a salesman. I have seen you now, as well as having heard many reports about you. The Lord Delamere has already made the deal on your behalf. You will harry Hallicheki shipping, for the benefit of the El Dorado Corporation and, of course, for your own benefit. The Letters of Marque have been drawn up. You will be fighting for money, whereas our ships will be fighting for Kalla's freedom from the harsh rule of the Hegemony. Korndah will give you your precious papers, then you may go."

One of the lesser birds hopped down from his perch, scuttled to a very prosaic looking filing cabinet that was standing beside the recording apparatus, opened a drawer, used his beak to withdraw a bundle of documents. He hopped/shuffled to Grimes, dropped the papers into the commodore's hands. Grimes removed the elastic band securing them. He tried to read what was on the top one but in the dim light it was impossible.

"Do not worry, Commodore," squawked the Lord of the Roost. "All is in order. You can read the authority that I have given you at your leisure. Now you may go, back to your ships, and commence operations as soon as possible."

"Your Mightiness," said Grimes, "there is one favor that I wish to ask of you."

"Speak."

"I request permission for the fleet to land and to replenish certain items of consumable stores."

"The permission is not granted. You can replenish your storerooms from those of your victims."

"But I also want to top up the water tanks. On leaving El Dorado I ordered an exercise in the use of reaction drive. As a result of that our stocks of reaction mass have been reduced."

"I am not a spacebeing, Commodore." The Lord of the Roost gabbled briefly in his own language to one of his aides, received a raucous reply. Then, "Very well. I am told that in warfare the rocket drive, the reaction drive, might be employed. Your fleet may come in to the spaceport at first light tomorrow morning, and will depart as soon as the tanks have been topped up."

"Thank you, Mightiness," said Grimes.

"Oh, one more thing, Commodore. Do not trust hens."

The audience was over."

193

At the end of the corridor they found that the towing team had again been harnessed to the balloon car, were hanging on to projections on the tower, the lines slack. Delamere was first into the basket and began to dump ballast. During the time that they had spent with the Lord of the Roost, Grimes realized, more bags of sand had been loaded and gas replenished. The Countess was next aboard. She and her compatriot obviously did not love each other and were avoiding physical contact. Mayhew was next, and then Grimes, the precious Letters of Marque tucked into his shirt, made the short but perilous passage.

The balloon was cast off from the mooring spar and the towing team beat their wings clatteringly, then pulled the clumsy aircraft out and away from the tower. The flying escort took up their stations. On the return trip Grimes did not admire the scenery but looked through the documents. There was one set of papers for each ship. That issued to *Sister Sue* authorized her to make war upon all enemies of the Independent Nest of Kalla, wherever found. It stated, too, that one Commodore Grimes, while master of this vessel, was fully responsible for the conduct of *Pride of Erin*, *Spaceways Princess* and *Agatha's Ark*. The signature was a jagged scrawl written with some brownish medium. *Blood?* wondered Grimes. There was an ornate gold seal, bearing the likeness of a rapacious bird with outstretched wings, its taloned feet gripping a planetary orb. The other Letters of Marque were in duplicate—one copy for each captain, the other for the commodore. In each of them it was stated that overall responsibility for the operation rested with Grimes.

So, he thought wryly, *whoever carries the can back it's going to be me. He who sups with Drongo Kane needs a long spoon. So does he who sups with Commodore—correction!—Rear Admiral Damien. . . .*

The balloon sagged down toward the spaceport mooring masts. Lord Delamere valved gas. He miscalculated and had to compensate by dumping a small bag of ballast.

Grimes was amused and thought, *He's no more perfect than his cousins umpteen times removed. . . .*

Mooring procedure was carried out quite efficiently. The humans clambered down the light ladder to the ground.

Delamere said, dismissively, "I'll see you tomorrow morning, Commodore."

Grimes led the way to the waiting boat. Inboard, he took the pilot's seat. The Countess glared at him but went aft to sit with Mayhew. Grimes, starting the inertial drive, lifted with deliberately exaggerated caution. He heard the girl mutter something about Survey Service throw-outs with only two speeds, Dead Slow and Stop. His prominent ears reddened but he maintained his sedate ascent.

Chapter 44

"Well, Mr. Mayhew?" asked Grimes.

"To begin with, sir, the Lord of the Roost is not human. . . ."

"A blinding glimpse of the obvious. I'm not a telepath but even I could see that."

Mayhew flushed. "Let me finish, sir. I meant that his thought processes are not human. He would be incapable of being devious. He despises you for fighting for profit but realizes that you will be useful to him in the struggle for Kallan freedom."

"The free rooster in the free barnyard," said Grimes. "I don't think that our two liberated ladies would approve of such freedom."

"With the Hallicheki," said Mayhew, "it's a clear choice. Either the cocks or the hens must rule and roost. The cocks are the more intelligent, the more honest. The hens have mean, petty minds. And didn't the ones who were towing us *hate* us! All the time they were thinking of tearing the flesh from our bones with their sharp beaks. Oh, we're on the right side, sir. No doubt of that."

"And Delamere?"

"I think that what you were thinking about him was quite correct."

"Talking of Delamere, I suppose that his distant relative is still in the Survey Service."

"Very much so. He's a four-ring captain now, and loved by everybody."

The telephone buzzed.

"Commodore here," said Grimes.

Williams' face formed in the little screen and he said, "The boat's back and inboard, sir. Wally's finished her mail run. The way she's carrying on it must be beneath her dignity to act as postwoman."

"My nose fair bleeds for her. Tell Mr. Stewart to arrange NST hook-up between all ships. I'll give the captains time to read their Letters of Marque, then I'll be up to control to give them a pep talk."

Chapter 45

One by one, at thirty-minute intervals, the four ships dropped down to the spaceport. By the time that *Agatha's Ark* was landed the hoses connected to *Sister Sue's* intake valves were already throbbing as tons of reaction mass—water—were being pumped into her tanks and teams of dingy, sullen hens, bullied into activity by strutting male birds, were connecting the pipes to *Pride of Erin* and *Spaceways Princess*.

There was, of course, no planet leave for the privateer crews. Those officers who had come ashore to supervise the work about their ships would not stray from the spaceport. They were all too conscious of the smoldering hate with which the work-hens regarded them, of the haughty disdain for mere mammals evinced by the arrogant cocks.

Grimes stood at the foot of *Sister Sue's* ramp to await Lord Delamere. Mayhew was with him. They were approached by a stocky, dark-featured man wearing master's uniform with the badge of the Interstellar Transport Commission on his cap.

This person made a sketchy salute. Grimes replied.

"Good morning, Captain," said the ITC master.

"Good morning, Captain," replied Grimes.

"Jones is the name, Captain. Of *Cross Eppie*." He waved his hand toward one of the two Epsilon Class tramps. "Or *Epsilon Crucis*, if you want to be formal."

"Grimes," said Grimes, introducing himself.

"Of *Sister Sue*," said Jones unnecessarily. Then, "What is this? An invasion? Four ex-Epsilon Class tramps, all armed to the teeth. . . . We've been half expecting a couple or three Hegemony cruisers to come roaring in, but. . . . And you must be on *their* side. . . . The Kallan rebels, I mean."

"Mphm," grunted Grimes, filling his pipe.

"Why all the lethal ironmongery, Captain?" persisted Jones.

"Defensive armament," muttered Grimes through a cloud of acrid smoke.

"Are you blockade runners, then? And have you any idea of the sort of punch packed by one of the Hegemony's cruisers? Those vicious hens'd chew you up and shit you out in five seconds flat."

"Thank you for the information," said Grimes coldly.

"I'm just trying to be helpful, Captain. I *know* these people. I've been running to the various Hallicheki planets for the last twenty years. I think that the commission's very foolish to be maintaining trading relations with Kalla."

"So you're a blockade runner too, Captain Jones. And, like me, you just go where you're sent."

Jones would have made a reply, a heated one possibly, but there was a clattering noise from overhead. The men looked up. Dropping down from the murky sky was a helicopter, a small one, little more than a basket dangling beneath rotors. It landed. Delamere stepped out of the flimsy-looking cab. Grimes saluted him—not the sort of salute that he would have given to an admiral or to a pretty girl but a curt greeting to an equal. The El Doradan nodded in reply.

"Excuse me, Captain Jones," said Grimes. "I have matters to discuss with my agent."

Followed by Mayhew he walked toward the little aircraft.

"I have arranged for you to see the ex-Minister of Star Shipping," said Delamere. "She will be able to give you information about the Hallicheki trade routes."

"That will be useful," said Grimes. "Do you have transport laid on?"

"Not necessary, Commodore. The . . . prison is only a short walk from here."

The prison—or that part of it in which the ex-Minister was confined—was no more than a hovel, a dingy *kraal*. In it a filthy, more-dead-then-alive hen was chained by one leg to the central pole, was squatting in her own filth. Her skin was scabbed where feathers had been plucked out and the dun plumage around these patches was darkly matted. Where one eye had been was a still oozing wound.

There were two cockbirds in the malodorous hut. Guards? Interrogators? Delamere—who must have been an accomplished linguist—addressed one of the gaudy beings in the Hallicheki language. It sounded like a comedian imitating a parrot. There was a squawking reply from one of the avians.

197

"She will not talk," said Delamere to Grimes. "But do not worry. There are . . . methods."

There was a cacophony of squawks from the larger and gaudier Kallan, answered only by the female's sullen silence. There was a tearing out of a beakful of feathers from the hen's breast—which elicited an agonized screech. There was a vicious beak poised menacingly over the remaining eye—and a low, gobbling sound from the prisoner which Grimes did not need to be told was supplication.

The ex-Minister talked. When she faltered she lost yet more plumage. That of newly shed blood was added to the other stinks in the hut. But she talked and Delamere translated. Mayhew recorded the interrogation.

At last, to Grimes' great relief, it was over. He, with Delamere and Mayhew, left the hut. The air outside was warm, humid, heavy and, compared to the atmosphere inside a well managed starship, almost unbearably stuffy. Compared to that inside the hut it was like champagne after pond water.

"Happy now, Commodore Grimes?" asked Delamere.

"I'm not, My Lord. I thought that I should be fighting on the right side; now I'm not so sure. Was that cruelty necessary? There are other ways—drugs and the like—to get beings to talk."

"The Hallicheki, male or female, are a cruel race, Grimes."

"I still don't have to like them."

"As long as you do what your Letters of Marque entitle you to do, likes and dislikes don't come into it."

"I suppose not."

As they approached *Sister Sue* Grimes saw that the water hoses had been withdrawn and were being reeled in. They were still connected to the other three ships. He saw, too, that officers from the two ITC tramps were talking with people from the privateers, looking up at the armament as they did so. It didn't matter. Only one person knew what trajectory the fleet would follow once it was clear of the Kallan atmosphere—and that one person was Grimes. (And, he realized, Mayhew—but he and the telepath were working for the same boss.)

"Good luck, Commodore, and good hunting," said Delamere.

The two shook hands briefly, without much enthusiasm on either side. The El Doradan clambered into his helicopter and clattered skyward.

"Well, Mr. Mayhew?" asked Grimes when they were back on board and sitting in the commodore's day cabin.

"She spoke the truth, sir," said Mayhew. "And Lord Delamere's translation was a faithful one. The trade route between Kookadahl and New Maine seems the most promising. Much of the freight is carried in the ships of the Hegemony. From Kookadahl to New Maine there are tree pearls, mainly for transshipment to other human worlds. Quite precious, as you know. Attempts have been made to grow the pearl tree, from smuggled seeds, on other planets but they have never been successful."

"Spare me the botany lesson, Mr. Mayhew."

"Sorry, sir. Tree pearls, and *ferancha* skins and ingots of gold and platinum. . . . The other way the pickings wouldn't be so good. A horrid sort of fish meal that they make on New Maine for the Hallicheki market. Things like eels, pickled in brine. Too—and this is what suits *our* purpose— one of the Terran ships, the Commission's *Epsilon Draconis*, selected to be a possible victim of piracy, is on that trade. Her assistant purser is really, like myself, a PCO from the Survey Service."

"But will the Hallicheki institute a convoy system?" wondered Grimes aloud. "Will they arm their merchantmen?"

"I don't think so," Mayhew told him. "Or, at least, not at first. Even if there are spies for the Hegemony among the crews of the ITC tramps—which is extremely unlikely—it will take some time to organize convoys, to fit defensive armament and all the rest of it. The Hallicheki Admiralty will be at least as slow as ours when it comes to dedigitating."

"You could be right," conceded Grimes. "You probably are right."

He dismissed Mayhew and sent for Magda Granadu.

She brought the coins and the book.

Grimes shook the ancient discs of silvery alloy in his cupped hands, feeling—as he had before—that he was standing at the focus of supernatural lines of force. *It's no more than superstition,* he told himself. *But. . . .*

The coins clinked between the concavities of his palms. He let them drop to the deck.

Two tails and and head. . . . Yin. . . .
Two heads and a tail. . . . Yang. . . .
Three tails. . . . Yin. . . .
Three heads. . . . Yang. . . .
Two tails and a head. . . . Yin. . . .

Three tails. . . . Yin. . . .

The trigrams: Chén, thunder, arousing. K'an, water, dangerous. . . .

The hexagram: Hsieh. Escape. . . .

"It all looks rather ominous," said Grimes to the woman.

"It is," she murmured as she consulted the book.

Escape. Advantage will be found to the south and west. If no further expeditions are called for, good fortune will come from returning home. . . .

"That doesn't sound too bad," he said. "But the south and west? Austral and Port Woomera?"

"There's more," she told him. "There's the commentary, and the lines. . . ."

Here the trigram depicting danger is confronted by that depicting powerful arousal. By movement there is an escape from peril. . . .

"A blinding glimpse of the obvious," he said.

The lines. . . .

Sixth in the third place. He travels in a carriage, with a porter to handle his baggage. Such behavior will tempt robbers to attack him. However firm and correct he may try to be, there will be cause for regret. . . .

"But *I'm* supposed to be the robber," he said.

Nine in the fourth place. Remove your toes. Friends in whom you can trust will then approach.

"Remove my *toes*, Magda?"

"The interpretation, Commodore," she told him, "is that you remove hangers-on from your immediate circle, thus allowing true friends to approach."

"Hangers-on?"

"I could name a few. Her Highness Wally, for one. And for all the use the Green Hornet is, she's another. And. . . ."

"That'll do."

Six in the sixth place. The prince looses an arrow from his bow and hits a falcon sitting on top of a high wall. The effect of this action will be in every way advantageous. . . .

"A falcon," said Grimes. "So I shall be taking some Hallicheki ships."

"You should not take it literally, Commodore. According to the interpretation—he removes the most powerful of his enemies and escapes from their domination."

"It could be worse," he said. "Much worse."

"But there's still danger," she told him.

Chapter 46

Through the warped continuum fell the four ships, their temporal precession rates unsynchronized, using their mass proximity indicators to maintain a rather ragged line astern formation.

Grimes ordered frequent drills. He had been able to stock up on missiles and ammunition for the quick-firing cannon on Kalla. (He had, too, been appalled at the price charged for these martial necessities by the Kallans.) He decided to let Captain O'Leary make the first capture. The sooner that *Pride of Erin* was on her way to El Dorado with her prize and out of the commodore's hair the better. Captain MacWhirter would be the next to go. *Spaceways Princess* came in the barely competent category. *Agatha's Ark* he would keep with him as long as possible. Then, when *Sister Sue* was a ship alone, it would be time to instigate the incident that would give the Survey Service the excuse to crack down on the privateers. He would be rather sorry, he admitted to himself, when the time came. He was enjoying being a commodore, with a small fleet under his command. He was looking forward to deploying his squadron, even though it would be against only unarmed merchantmen.

The ships maintained a Carlotti listening watch but broke radio silence rarely, and then transmitted only on very low power. Aboard the flagship was a plotting tank and in it Grimes was able to record the positions of merchant shipping traversing a sphere light-years in diameter. It was a fascinating exercise, requiring considerable navigational skill. Vessels outbound from New Maine to Kookadahl would not be worth bothering with. What value would a cargo of stinking fish paste be? But, at last, there was a ship, one of the Hegemony's freighters, bound from Kookadahl to the Terran colony.

The squadron steered an intercepting trajectory.

Presumably the Hallicheki captain would have a mass proximity indicator in her control room. Possibly she would become perturbed to see an obvious formation heading toward her. She might assume that it was a squadron of Kallan warships, commerce raiders, and squawk for help.

In *Sister Sue's* Main Carlotti Room old Mr. Stewart was standing by, watching his rotating Mobius Strip antennae, his dials and oscilloscopes. He had his orders. As soon as *Krorkor*—that was the name of the Hallicheki ship, learned from her transmissions in English to the Carlotti station at New Maine—began to send, a characteristic squiggle would appear in one of the screens. Immediately Stewart's especially designed computer would match crests with troughs, troughs with crests. In the oscilloscope the wavy line of green luminosity would be replaced by one almost straight. From the speakers of any transceivers tuned to the Hallicheki ship would issue . . . nothing.

Grimes, now, rarely strayed from the control room, taking catnaps in his command chair, nibbling snacks and drinking coffee brought up to him by Magda, fouling the atmosphere with the acrid fumes from his vile pipe. He was reasonably happy when Williams or Venner had the watch, distinctly uneasy when Ms. Connellan was in charge. As fourth officer the Countess of Walshingham should have been sharing the chief officer's watchkeeping duties but Grimes had told his mate, "Find some sort of job for that snooty bitch, Billy, that doesn't bring her anywhere near Control!"

Mr. Stewart was undergoing a far less wearing time than his captain. The responsibility for jamming the victim's transmissions, should she attempt to make any, was divided between *Sister Sue*, *Spaceways Princess* and *Agatha's Ark*. Captain O'Leary had been ordered to instruct his radio officer to monitor all Carlotti signals originating from anywhere at all. *Pride of Erin* was the squadron clown, one of those ships incapable of doing anything right, inevitably slow off the mark. It would be good to be rid of her.

Slowly, steadily, the range closed, could be measured in light-minutes and, at last, in kilometers. The Hallicheki captain finally squawked—or tried to squawk. Stewart, who had the Carlotti watch, jammed her before she could do more than clear her scrawny throat prior to speaking. Grimes, no longer in his chair, stood over the main MPI screen, staring into the sphere of velvety blackness in which were the four bright sparks—the potential victim, the other three privateers and, in the exact center, *Sister Sue's* reference marker. He saw that relative bearings were no longer changing as they had been. He realized what had happened, was happening. The Hallicheki had shut down her drives—Mannschenn and

202

inertial—as the preliminary to a major alteration of trajectory. This, inevitably, was a time-consuming process. And when the gyroscopes had swung the ship, turning her hull about its axes, which way would she be heading? Grimes guessed—and, as it turned out, correctly—that the panic-stricken hen would put the raiders right astern and then increase not only the thrust of the inertial drive but the intensity of the temporal precession field.

"Stop Mannschenn!" he ordered Williams, who was in the 2 I/C seat. "Stop inertial drive. Pass the order to all ships. Make it Action Stations!"

"I've only one pair of hands, Skipper," the mate grumbled—but it was a good-humored whinge. The subdued clangor of the inertial drive slowed and ceased while Grimes was still making his way back to his own chair. He managed to pull himself into the seat despite the cessation of acceleration and the consequent free fall. The thin, high note of the Mannschenn drive deepened to a hum, then died away. As the temporal precession field faded the stridulation of the alarms shrilled to near inaudibility. Colors sagged down the spectrum and perspective was a meaningless concept.

And there was that song again.

I murdered William Moore as I sailed, as I sailed. . . .

Then everything snapped back to normal—colors, sounds, perspective. Grimes stared into the two miniature repeater screens before him—mass proximity indicator and radar. The Hallicheki ship was a radar target now, just inside the extreme range of two thousand kilometers. So she had not yet restarted her interstellar drive, was still in normal space-time. Obedient to the touch of the captain's fingers the powerful directional gyroscopes deep in *Sister Sue's* bowels rumbled and Grimes felt himself pressed into the padding—under his buttocks, along his spine and his right side—of his chair by centrifugal forces. He brought the tiny spark that was the merchantman directly ahead, held it there and then reactivated the inertial drive, on maximum thrust.

"General chase!" he ordered and heard Venner repeat the words, heard acknowledgments from the other ships. He hoped that all that he had ever heard about Hallicheki spacemanship—not held in very high regard by the Survey Service's officer instructors—was true. By the time that the fumbling hens had gotten their vessel onto the new trajectory, with inertial and interstellar drives restarted, the privateers would be almost within range. (Of course, if the avian captain had any sense she would steer toward the pursuit, not away from it. Grimes remembered a ride that he had taken in a ground car, years ago, through the Australian countryside, and a witless hen that had run ahead of the vehicle, swerving neither to left nor right. He *knew*, somehow, that his quarry would be equally witless.)

He glanced up and out through the viewports. The stars were hard, bright—and there were those other, unnatural constellations, the recognition lights of the vessels of the fleet, ahead of *Sister Sue* now after the alteration of trajectory. Closest was the vividly green display of *Pride of Erin*. Grimes did not need to look into his radar screen to see that the range was closing, that *Sister Sue* would soon sweep past her. O'Leary's spacemanship must almost be down to Hallicheki standards. And there was *Spaceways Princess*, scarlet, and *Agatha's Ark*, blue. Grimes thought of perpetrating a pun about arclamps but thought better of it.

In the radar screen the tiny, distant spark that was the merchantman vanished but still showed in the MPI. So she was underway again.

"Stop her!" ordered Grimes, suiting the action to the words as far as his own ship was concerned. "Pass the order."

"To all ships. Stop inertial drive," he heard the Countess's voice.

So Venner must now be at his battle console, thought Grimes.

"Mr. Williams," he said, "set up the graticules and graduations in the main MPI. Let me know how much, if at all, I must come around to keep the target ahead. . . ."

"Aye, aye, Skipper!"

"Ms. Connellan, stand by the NST transceiver. . . ."

"But we'll not be needing it for a long while yet. Sir."

"Stand by the NST!"

That would keep her from getting underfoot.

"We're lucky, Skipper!" he heard Williams say. "Just bring her right ahead, and keep her there, and we've got her!"

"Good. To all ships, Ms. Walshingham. Put target ahead. Restart all drives. General chase!"

There was again the brief period of complete disorientation as the temporal precession field built up, as the tumbling, precessing gyroscopes of the drive dragged the ship with them into her own warped continuum.

And again Grimes heard the ballad of Captain Kidd.

And what can I do about it? he asked himself. *What can I*

204

*do about it? Captains, even privateer captains, don't go
around murdering their senior officers. . . .*

But Captain Kidd had done so.

Chapter 47

It is axiomatic that a stern chase is a long chase.

The chase would have been a very long one, and quite possibly unsuccessful, had not Survey Service pattern gover-
nors—obtained from whom, and at what expense?—been
fitted to the Mannschenn Drive units of the four ships when,
at Port Kane, the other modifications had been made. With
this hyperdrive in operation things were uncomfortable.
There was always the feeling of walking a thin, swaying wire
over an abyss that was the Past, maintaining balance with extreme difficulty. There was the frightening knowledge—in
Grimes' mind at least—that he and all aboard *Sister Sue*, as
was the ship herself, were at the mercy of a swirling field of
force and of the man controlling—trying to control!—it. But
Malleson was better than highly competent. He was designer
as well as engineer. He knew—Grimes hoped—what he was
doing. He would allow not the slightest fluctuation of field
strength.

Obviously Captain O'Leary's Mannschenn Drive chief was
neither so confident nor so competent. *Pride of Erin* straggled
badly. She was well astern when the flagship and *Spaceways
Princess* and *Agatha's Ark* finally overhauled their fleeing
quarry and stationed themselves about her, the three points of
an equilateral triangle.

"Make to *Princess* and *Ark*," ordered Grimes, "synchronize
at will!"

He heard the Countess repeat the order into the Carlotti
transceiver microphone as he pressed the button that had
been installed among the other controls of the wide arms of
his chair.

The thin, high keening of the Mannschenn Drive wavered,
took on an odd, warbling quality. Inside the control room
things . . . flickered. It was like watching one of the very
earliest movies in some museum of the cinematic arts. It was
like being inside such a movie.

Abruptly the flickering ceased and the whine of the drive resumed its normal quality. Looking through his viewports Grimes could see the hard, bright, colored sparks that were the recognition lights of the *Ark* and the *Princess* against the backdrop of blackness and stars that still had the semblance of vague nebulae. Of the Hallicheki ship there was, as yet, no visual sign although she was showing up on the radar screen as well as in the MPI. To all practical intents and purposes the four wheels were sharing their own tiny universe; relative to them the rest of the continuum was warped.

"Let us see the target, please, Mr. Venner," said Grimes.

The laser cannon could be used as a searchlight. It came on now. Yes, there she was—a distant, silver egg sitting in a silver skeleton eggcup. She could not escape by throwing herself out of synchronization. She could not even stop her Mannschenn Drive so as to emerge into normal space-time. To all intents and purposes her interstellar drive was a mere slave to the more powerful units aboard the privateers and would be so for as long as the synchronizers were in operation. But the Hallicheki captain still exercised full control over her inertial drive. Suddenly she reduced thrust and began to fall astern, out of the trap. Almost immediately, almost as one, the three raiders fell back with her, regained their stations. She applied a lateral component—but before she was dangerously close to *Agatha's Ark* Captain Prinn was doing likewise and Grimes and MacWhirter were maintaining their distances off with contemptuous ease.

"Ms. Connellan, Ms. Walshingham," ordered Grimes, "try to raise her on NST and Carlotti."

The two women obeyed. It was the Green Hornet who got through on the normal space-time radio. In the screen appeared a bird's face—yellow beak, dun plumage, mad yellow eyes.

"Who are you? Who are you? What are you doing?"

Ms. Connellan passed a microphone to Grimes.

He said, "You are under arrest. You will complete your voyage to such port as we shall decide under escort. Do not attempt to escape."

"But you are . . . human." (She made it sound like a dirty word; in her language it most probably was.) "The Hegemony is not at war with Earth!"

"At the moment, no," admitted Grimes smugly.

"You are pirates!"

"We are not," Grimes told her. "We hold Letters of Marque issued by the Lord of the Roost on Kalla."

"Rebel worm! We will pluck the feathers from his skin, the skin from his flesh and the flesh from his bones! We. . . ."

"You'll have to catch him first, Captain. Meanwhile, are you coming quietly?"

"No!" came the screeched reply. "No! No!"

And somebody must be playing with the Hellicheki ship's inertial drive controls like a demented pianist; ahead and astern she darted, to one side and the other. It was all quite useless.

"This," said Grimes, "is getting to be rather boring. Mr. Venner, tickle the lady, will you. Use the quickfirer. Reduced charges, of course, and solid shot. And for the love of all the Odd Gods of the Galaxy, don't miss!"

This admonition was necessary. To diminish the mass of a ship running under interstellar drive is to ask for trouble and, almost certainly, to get it. But *Sister Sue* was now part of a four-ship system enclosed by a common precession field. As long as those projectiles hit and adhered to their target the overall mass of the system would not be changed.

The merchantman's last application of lateral thrust had brought her almost dangerously close to *Sister Sue*. This suited Grimes. At this range not the most incompetent gunnery officer could miss his target—and Venner was highly competent. From the muzzle of the quickfirer issued a stream of bright tracer that, with apparent laziness, drifted across the black gulf between the two ships like a swarm of luminous bees, striking her in a ragged line from stem to stern.

The noise inside that ovoid hull, thought Grimes, must be deafening—but, at the very worst, there would be no more than a very minor puncture or two that would be automatically sealed.

"Piracy!" the Hallicheki captain was screeching, her words almost drowned by the drumbeat of the striking shot.

"That was just a sample," Grimes told her.

"Terry pirate! I demand. . . ."

"You are in no position to do any demanding, Captain. You are a prize of war. Do you want another taste of gunfire? After all, it is your cargo that I want, not you and your crew. Your bodies, alive or dead, are of no importance."

"Pirate! Filthy pirate! All right. I . . . surrender. But as soon as I can I will scream to the Hegemony!"

"And much good may it do you, Captain."

Meanwhile, where the hell was *Pride of Erin?* Captain O'Leary had been told that he would be taking the first prize in. Captain O'Leary, Grimes saw, was no more than a dim

207

spark right astern, just within range of the mass proximity indicator.

"Ms. Walshingham," he said, "call *Pride of Erin*. Tell her to shake the lead out of her pants. Gods! She'd be late for her own fucking funeral!"

The Countess spoke into the microphone of the control-room Carlotti transceiver. Her voice was cold and arrogant. It was that of the lady of the manor tearing a strip off a delinquent under gamekeeper, using what she would consider to be lower-class vocabulary for effect but retaining her upper-class diction.

"*Sister Sue* to *Pride of Erin*. . . ."

"*Pride of Erin*. I've been after havin' me troubles. . . ."

"*Sister Sue* to *Pride of Erin*. Shake the lead out of your pants. Gods! You'd be late for your own fucking funeral!"

"*What did you say?*" shouted Grimes to the fourth officer. "That was no way to make a signal to another ship!"

"I said what *you* said, sir."

Insolent bitch! he thought. *I'll deal with your later.*

Captain O'Leary's voice came from the speaker of the Carlotti set. It was obvious that the man was holding himself in with an effort. He, he was implying, could be correct even when his alleged superior could not.

"I'm doin' me best, Commodore, but I'm not a miracle worker. I'll be with you as soon as me time-twister can get me there. I'll. . . ."

There was a confused gabbling. There were yells.

There was nothing.

Grimes stared into the repeater screen. The Hallicheki ship and the *Ark* and the *Princess* were still there. *Pride of Erin* was not.

"Mr. Williams," he said, "check the main MPI. See if you can find *Pride of Erin*."

But he knew that O'Leary, his ship and his people were gone, tumbling down the temporal gulfs like a dead leaf whirled to oblivion by an autumnal gale.

If the Walshingham bitch had not spoken as she had, the thin-skinned master of *Pride of Erin* would have taken no risks with his malfunctioning interstellar drive.

But why blame her?

I'm a fine commodore, he thought. *My first action, with nothing fired but a few practice shells, and one of my ships lost. . . .*

He hoped that in the remote past or the distant future

208

O'Leary and his crew would find a world do their liking.
   If they survived.

Chapter 48

So it was *Spaceways Princess* that took in the first prize
while *Sister Sue* and *Agatha's Ark* continued their cruise.
   Shortly after Captain MacWhirter's ship had been detached
from the squadron Captain Prinn made a personal call to
Grimes. He was glad that it was during Williams' watch. It
was bad enough that he should overhear what was said; it
would have been far worse had it been any of the other officers.
   She looked out at him from the screen of the control-room
Carlotti transceiver, her normally harsh face even harsher
than usual. Behind her Grimes could see others of the *Ark's*
crew, among them the young Graf von Stolzberg. All of them
were regarding him with condemnation.
   "Commodore Grimes," she said, "I am serving notice that
after this cruise I shall refuse to put out again under your
command. It is my opinion, and that of my officers, that you
deliberately goaded Captain O'Leary into taking unjustifiable
risks. Why could you not have done as you did eventually,
ordering Captain MacWhirter to take charge of the prize?
That would have given Captain O'Leary time to make the
necessary adjustments or repairs to his Mannschenn Drive.
But you were foolishly inflexible and insisted that he close the
main body of the fleet without delay. Furthermore you
couched your message in words of a kind that should never
be used by a commanding officer to those serving under him.
That brutal message was contributory to the disaster."
   She moved to one side. Marlene's son (Grimes' son) came
forward.
   "Commodore Grimes, speaking as the El Doradan representative aboard this vessel, I put myself as being in complete
agreement with what has been said by Captain Prinn. I shall
report to Commodore Kane and to the El Dorado Corporation upon your unfitness to command any further privateering expeditions."

And what about your fellow El Doradan? Grimes thought but did not say. *What about the El Doradan representative aboard* my *vessel? She's one of* your *lot, Ferdinand my boy. She made O'Leary blow his top. . . .*

He asked coldly, ignoring the young officer, "Is that all, Captain Prinn?"

"That is all, Commodore Grimes. Over and out."

"She's got it in for you, Skipper," said Williams sympathetically.

"And rightly so, Billy. Rightly so."

"It was that bloody Wally's fault!"

"Everything that happens aboard a ship," said Grimes tiredly, "is the captain's fault. And everything that happens in a squadron is the commodore's fault." He laughed without much humor. "It's a pity that O'Leary's given names were Patrick Joseph, not William Moore. That would have taken one weight off my mind . . ."

"But *I'm* William Moore, Skipper," said the mate. "William Moore Williams."

"I know," said Grimes.

He went down to his day cabin, sent for the Countess of Walshingham.

When she came her cat was with her. The animal(?) sat down on the deck and stared, in an oddly hungry manner, at the golden figurine of Una mounted on her golden bicycle. It ignored Grimes—which was just as well. Did it, he wondered, recognize a fellow robot? Did the mini-Una possess some sort of organic brain, just as the evil black and white beast did?

"Must you bring that creature with you?" Grimes demanded irritably.

The tall girl stood there, superb in her tailored uniform, looking down at him disdainfully as he sat behind his desk.

"I thought you knew, sir," she said, "that all El Doradans have their guardians, their watch animals. Felix is my protector. Should anybody attempt to do me harm he will attack."

"And you think that I might attempt to do you harm?"

"You would like to, sir, wouldn't you? You wish that you possessed the punitive powers of the old-time captains on Earth's seas."

"Frankly, Ms. Walshingham, I do wish just that. What you did merits a flogging, if nothing worse. How are you people trained—if at all!—in the El Doradan Navy? Don't you know that an officer passing on a message from his captain to an-

210

other captain is supposed, if necessary, to . . . to *edit* the message, to put it into the proper Service terminology?"

"Since when, sir, was this armed rabble a Service?"

Grimes kept his temper. He said slowly, "It may interest you to know, Ms. Walshingham, that Captain Prinn, blaming me for what happened to Captain O'Leary. . . ."

"That bog-Irish slob!"

"Quiet, damn you! Captain Prinn put through a personal call to me. She holds me responsible for what happened to *Pride of Erin* and condemns me for it. So do all her officers—including *your* compatriot the Graf von Stolzberg."

"That mother's boy!"

"I have not yet written my report on your conduct and capabilities. When I do so I shall see that you read it. I do not think that Commodore Kane will continue to think highly of you when *he* has done so."

"I could hardly care less, sir. The Commodore is not a true El Doradan."

"He is your commanding officer. So, come to that, am I as long as you are on my books."

She flushed. "As the representative, aboard this ship, of both the El Doradan Navy and the El Dorado Corporation. . . ."

"You are still my fourth mate. That will do, Ms. Walshingham. Get out, and take that animal with you!"

"With pleasure, sir."

When they were gone Grimes sent for Mayhew.

"That *bitch*," he said. "That arrogant *bitch*! Did she realize what she was doing, what the results were likely to be, when she passed that message?"

"I don't think so, sir. She is, as you say, arrogant. Captain O'Leary was a member of the lower orders. She feels no more sorry for him and his crew than she would for a dog or a cat belonging to somebody else and not to her."

"But there was an El Doradan officer aboard *Pride of Erin*."

"A *man*, Captain. She despises all men, aristocratic or otherwise. Even so, she has her needs."

"I thought that the other bitch, the green-skinned one, was satisfying them."

"So did I. I have been refraining from prying into their sweaty amours. I'm not a prude, sir, but I am fastidious. And, I suppose, something of a snob. I could not bring myself to make love to a woman who was not, like me, a tele-

211

path. And, very unfortunately, such women are usually either very plain or very unintelligent. Or both."

Grimes poured more gin for both of them.

He said, "It's dear Wally's love life that I'm concerned about, not yours. As long as she's getting her odd form of satisfaction she's a little less of a bitch than she would be normally. That goes for the Green Hornet, too."

"That's the odd thing, Captain. The pair of them are passing through a heterosexual phase. Not all the time, but for a lot of the time. Bestowing their favors upon the junior engineers. I don't suppose you want to know the details. . . ."

"I don't."

"That's just as well, Captain. I'd hate to have to find them out for you."

"Ours is a nice ship, ours is," said Grimes glumly.

Chapter 49

The next capture was effected without incident and Captain Prinn was ordered to escort the merchantman to port. Her farewell was a cold one. She did not even wish Grimes the usual good luck and good hunting when she and the prize were detached. Alone in the warped immensities *Sister Sue* cruised the space lanes, maintaining her listening watch, waiting for the Terran ship that was to be the next victim, that was to be the excuse the Survey Service needed to put a stop to the El Doradan privateering operations.

Grimes' officers sensed that something was wrong.

Vessels, within easy range, were picked up by the mass proximity indicator. Some of those ships, identifiable by their routine Carlotti radio transmissions, were of Hallicheki registry, bound for New Maine with their rich cargoes. Yet Grimes ignored them. There were mutterings. Soon, everybody knew, *Spaceways Princess* and *Agatha's Ark* would be allocated their shares of prize money—and *Sister Sue* had yet to earn a more or less honest cent.

There was one ship, passing quite close, that, like *Sister Sue* herself, was maintaining radio silence. Grimes knew who she was—after Mayhew had told him. She was the FSS destroyer *Denebola*. She had among her people a Psionic

Communications Officer. Through the telepaths her captain sent a message to Grimes. It was: "Continue cruising until you fall in with *Epsilon Draconis*, New Maine to Carinthia with valuable transshipment cargo. Her master has been instructed to surrender without a real struggle. Her PCO, on articles as assistant purser, is a Survey Service officer. All other officers hold Reserve Commissions and know what is expected of them."

"Long-winded bastard," commented Grimes. "Commander Cummings, isn't it? Never uses one word when three will do."

"It shouldn't be much longer now," said Mayhew. "That's just as well, sir. The natives are getting restless. I quote, 'When is the old bastard going to take his finger out and find us a prize?' According to Sparks he's missed at least four good chances since Aggie left us . . . And, 'He's scared, that's why. He needs at least one other ship to hold his hand when he makes like a bold, bad pirate. . . .'"

"Mphm!" grunted Grimes indignantly around the stem of his pipe.

At last a spark of light that could only be the Epsilon Class tramp appeared on the MPI screen. Mr. Stewart monitored her routine transmissions. Mayhew established telepathic contact with her PCO. Trajectories converged.

"But, sir," expostulated Williams, "she's a Terran ship!"

"Carrying the Hegemony's cargo," said Grimes. "That makes her a legal prize, a blockade runner."

"Are you *sure*, Skipper?"

"Of course I'm sure. Our Letters of Marque empower us to seize Hallicheki cargoes, no matter by whom carried."

"Even transshipment cargoes?" asked Williams.

"Yes," said Grimes firmly.

(He would have to check that point later, he thought. Probably what he was about to do was piracy—and that was what Damien wanted, anyhow.)

The interception and the capture went as planned.

Epsilon Draconis went through the motions of attempting to escape from the precession synchronization field. Captain Mulligan, his fat, florid face filling the screen of the NST transceiver, raved and ranted convincingly, shouting, "You'll swing for this, you bloody pirate!" Mr. Venner went into his act with the quickfirer, raking the struggling prey from stem to stern. "Accidentally," there was one round in the drum that did not have a reduced charge and that did carry a high explosive warhead. This blew a large hole in one of the stern vanes.

"Was that necessary?" roared Mulligan.

This time he was not play-acting.

"Are you coming quietly?" asked Grimes.

"Yes, damn you. But somebody is going to get the bill for repairs—and I hope it's you!"

"He's very annoyed with you, sir," said Mayhew when, after the setting of a new trajectory for privateer and prize, he and Grimes were discussing matters in the commodore's day cabin.

"That's his privilege," said Grimes. "I just wanted my act of piracy to look realistic."

"You did just that. Well, sir, I've been in touch with *Denebola*. She's making all speed to intercept. She has one of the new Mark XX Mannschenns so she'll be showing up in the MPI screen at any time now. And now, if you'll excuse me, I'll go down to the wardroom to mingle with the peasantry. Venner, Malleson and Magda want me to make up a four at bridge."

"Do you play for money?" asked Grimes.

"Of course, sir. It discourages wild bidding."

"Isn't it cheating, as far as you're concerned?"

"It would be, if I used my talent. But I don't. When I sit down at the card table I . . . switch off. If—*if!*—I win it's just due to luck and skill, nothing more."

"Mphm." Grimes grunted, then laughed. "I remember that Rear Admiral Damien warned me against playing cards with Venner, but he didn't mention you."

"In ships where I am known for what I am," said Mayhew, "I don't play cards. For obvious reasons. And I do enjoy a game now and again. . . ."

He got to his feet and drifted out of the cabin.

Chapter 50

From: Kenneth Mayhew, Lieutenant Commander (PC) FSS
To: Rear Admiral Damien FSS, OIC Operation Jolly Roger

Sir,

I have to report as follows on the circumstances of the death, in the line of duty, of Lieutenant Commander Victor Venner FSS.

As planned by yourself and others the Interstellar Transport Commission's ship *Epsilon Draconis*, Captain Mulligan FSSR, was intercepted and seized by *Sister Sue*, Captain Grimes FSSR. After the capture normal deep-space routine —or deep-space routine as normal as possible in the circumstances—was resumed. After discussing various matters with Captain Grimes I went down to the wardroom for a game of bridge with Mr. Malleson, the Mannschenn Drive chief engineer, Ms. Magda Granadu, the ship's purser and Lieutenant Commander Venner. Rather unusually no other off-duty personnel were in the compartment.

I freely admit that I should have used my telepathic powers to make a check. I did not do so for two reasons. Firstly, when I play cards with non-telepaths I deliberately "close down" the portion of my brain that acts as psionic transceiver. Secondly, I had become increasingly disgusted by the glimpses I had caught of the off-duty activities of various officers, these being Ms. Kath Connellan, second mate, Ms. Walshingham (the Countess of Walshingham), fourth mate and El Doradan liaison officer, Messrs. Denning, Paulus and Singh, junior inertial drive engineers, and Messrs. Trantor and Giddings, Mannschenn Drive juniors.

I did not foresee that my prudishness would have such disastrous consequences and accept, without reservation, whatever punishment you may consider called for.

We were, as I have said, playing bridge. I was partnered with Ms. Granadu; Lieutenant Commander Venner with Mr. Malleson. I had opened the bidding with one no trump. Mr. Malleson bid two hearts. Ms. Granadu bid two no trumps. We were waiting, it seemed a long time, for Lieutenant Commander Venner to make his bid. I realized that he was staring at the door into the alleyway. I turned to look at what had attracted his attention. It was Ms. Connellan. She was holding a heavy pistol—later identified as a Bendon-Smith scattergun, El Doradan Navy issue—and pointing it straight at us. Behind her were Denning and Paulus, both of them armed with wrenches, and Trantor, with a big screwdriver.

She said, "Freeze, all of you! We're taking the ship. Grimesy isn't the only bastard around here who can play at pirates!"

I "switched on" then. What I received was garbled, the outpourings of minds that were vicious, greedy and—insofar

215

as the men were concerned—not a little scared. The women —the Green Hornet (as she was nicknamed) and the Countess—were the ringleaders. Later I was to learn that the intention had been to seize *Sister Sue* and to take her and the prize to one of the planets of the Duchy of Waldegren. The immediate attention, however, was to capture and restrain the captain and all loyal officers.

"Get away from the table," ordered Ms. Connellan. "Get down onto the deck, on your faces, with your hands behind you!" She made a jerking motion with her gun as she said this. For a second, for less than a second, we were no longer in the field of its fire.

The first card that Lieutenant Commander Venner flipped from his hand caught Ms. Connellan in the throat. The sharp plastic sliced through skin and flesh, severed a major blood vessel. I remember being surprised to see that her blood was red and not green. She fired her pistol before she dropped it to put her hand up to the spurting wound. The pellets tore a wide, ragged gash in the carpet but did no other damage.

Before she had fallen, before she had even started to fall, Lieutenant Commander Venner's second card caught Mr. Denning just above the eyes. He screamed and threw his arms out violently, letting go of the heavy wrench that he had been holding. I think that if Lieutenant Commander Venner had not been concentrating on his third shot, the one that sliced off Mr. Trantor's right ear, he would have seen the clumsy missile coming and dodged it. As it was, it struck him on the left forehead, killing him instantly.

Ms. Granadu picked up the pistol and covered Mr. Trantor and Mr. Denning, both of whom were bleeding profusely, and Mr. Paulus. They were cowed and allowed themselves to be driven into one of her storerooms, which she locked. Mr. Malleson and I tried to do something for Lieutenant Commander Venner but he was beyond aid. As a telepath I knew that the spark of life had been extinguished. Ms. Connellan expired while we were kneeling by our dead shipmate. . . .

Scrawled comment, signed Damien.
Vivid writing. The man's wasted in the Survey Service; he should be a novelist. If we weren't so short of trained telepaths I would encourage him to forsake space to enter the literary profession.

Chapter 51

The Countess entered Grimes' day cabin without knocking. The big, evil cat stalked behind her.

He looked up from the papers on his desk.

"Yes?" he demanded sharply. Then he saw that she was holding a pistol, a stungun, and that it was pointing at him. She pressed the trigger. Grimes was paralyzed but not unconscious. Perhaps she had used the weapon on lower power only or, possibly, the metal desk had acted as a partial shield.

He heard, from somewhere on a lower deck, the sound of an explosion.

She smiled viciously and remarked, "I let Katy have the heavy artillery. It sounds as though she's used it."

He said nothing. He could not. But he thought, *Billy will have heard the shot. He'll investigate.*

She said, "Don't expect the mate to come to hold your hand. I've already dealt with him. I hope that Katy soon finishes what she's doing. There should be somebody more or less conscious in the control room. . . ."

She strolled around the day cabin, the cat at her heels.

"Not bad, not bad. . . . This accommodation will do for me as soon as I've had you . . . removed. I might even keep your . . . ornaments. Old girl friends, are they? As you may have guessed, my tastes run more to the female form divine than to the hairy-arsed male version. . . . That one on the bicycle . . . she's rather butch, isn't she?"

With an effort Grimes was able to turn his head. (The paralysis was wearing off.) He saw the Countess lift the tiny golden woman on her little gleaming steed down from the shelf, set the models down on the deck.

"How do you make this thing work?" she asked. "I'd like to see it in action."

As though in obedience to her words the slim, golden legs, with feet on the pedals, began to move. The bicycle and rider made one circuit of the cabin and then, as though demonstrating her skill as a cyclist, the miniature Una released her grip of the handlebars—which turned so that the handles were pointing forward. From each of them projected a blade.

217

Grimes remembered having seen this sort of thing once before. That time he had been the subject of attack by a murderous bicycle.

The Countess aimed her pistol and fired, again and again. Against the tiny robot it was quite useless. The cat pounced, but it was too slow. One of the blades caught the girl on her vulnerable right heel. It came away red. She screamed and fell to the deck. The bicycle dashed in for the kill. The blades drove into her right temple, piercing the skull, penetrating the brain.

And now, thought Grimes dully, *for the Big Bang*. Its mistress dead, the cat would self-destruct. How powerful was the bomb hidden in its body? Powerful enough to devastate the day cabin and all its occupants, living and dead. Powerful enough, probably, to blow the nose off the ship.

But the Countess was still living—after a fashion. Her long legs were twitching. The fingers of her outstretched hands were opening and closing, scrabbling at the deck. She was moaning softly and wordlessly.

The cat was chasing the deadly, glittering toy which, twisting and turning, was trying to get itself into a position to deliver an attack. A heavy paw went out, batted the tiny rider off her saddle, knocking the bicycle off balance. It fell to its side and lay there briefly, its wheels still spinning. The front one turned at right angles to the frame as it tried to right itself. But the animal was too fast for it. Jaws opened wide and closed, metal on metal, and . . . crunched. There was a brief sputter of blue sparks, the acridity of ozone.

The rider, the tiny golden woman, was running now. The cat dropped the twisted remains of the bicycle, started after her. The beast was fast, agile, but its prey was even—although barely—more so. How long could the chase go on? How long would the Countess go on living? How long would it be before the watch beast realized that its mistress was dead and detonated the explosive device built into it?

"Captain!" somebody was saying. "Captain!"

Grimes withdrew his horrified attention from the macabre chase, saw that Mayhew had come into the cabin. There was blood on the telepath's hands and clothing (not his own, Grimes was to learn later).

"We must get it out of the ship," Mayhew said urgently. "We must get it out before it detonates!"

Grimes found that he could speak.

"We . . . can't. Not while the drive is running. We must not . . . discharge mass."

218

"You were firing off guns."

"That was . . . different. All the mass stayed within the combined fields."

"Then shut down the drive. Come up to control. I can handle both Una and the cat."

Handle Una? wondered Grimes. Surely that figurine did not run to a brain, either electronic or organic.

He felt strength seeping into him. From Mayhew? He managed to get up from the chair in which he had been slumped. The cat, still chasing the little golden woman, brushed against his leg but ignored him. The Countess was beyond noticing anything. Mayhew went to him, supported him, led him to the door. As soon as they were through, the figurine scampered out into the alleyway, followed by the animal.

He ignored them. Painfully, he pulled himself up the ladder and through the hatch into Control. Williams was there, slumped in his seat, unconscious. He staggered to the command chair, sank into it. His fingers went to the controls set in the armrests.

"The overall monitor," urged Mayhew.

He activated the rarely used Big Brother Is Watching system. In the stern vision screen he could see, at will, into every compartment of the ship. He was able to follow the sternward progress of the little golden girl, the vicious black-and-white predator, the flight and pursuit down the spiral staircase surrounding the axial shaft.

"Mr. Malleson is in the Mannschenn Drive room," said Mayhew.

Don't nag me, he thought.

He said, "Tell *Epsilon Draconis* that I'm shutting off the synchronizer and shutting down the drive. . . ."

He heard, from the NST transceiver, "What am I supposed to do? Make a break for it, or what?"

Tell him to get stuffed, he thought.

He said, "Ask him to stand by, please. We have problems."

He looked out through the port. *Epsilon Draconis* was there, hard and distinct against the background of vaguely swirling darkness, the nebulosities that were the stars. As the whine of *Sister Sue's* drive deepened to a rumble and then died she faded, vanished, and abruptly the stars became hard points of light.

And. . . .

And, *I murdered William Moore as I sailed, as I sailed. . . .*

But William Moore Williams was there, sprawled in his seat and snoring.

Grimes returned his attention to the screen.

Deck after deck after deck, the tiny golden woman, the big black-and-white cat, hunted and hunter, while in the commodore's day cabin the ham-strung Countess breathed her last. Deck after deck after deck. . . .

He took a sideways look. *Epsilon Draconis* was still with him. She, too, had shut down her Mannschenn Drive, was standing by to render assistance should it be required.

Deck after deck after deck. . . .

"Open inner airlock door," he said to Mayhew.

"Door opening, Captain."

The miniature Una was in the chamber, the cat hard upon her heels.

"Close inner door. Open outer."

He switched to an exterior view of the hull. He saw the door open, saw the sudden flurry of ice crystals. The cat now had the golden figurine in its mouth, was tumbling over and over as it fell into the nothingness.

There was an eye-searing flash and then the screen was dead.

"What *are* you doing?" came Captain Mulligan's petulant voice from the NST transceiver.

"Tell him," said Grimes to Mayhew, "just dumping garbage."

He regretted the words as soon as he had uttered them. The Countess's cat had been no more than garbage, dangerous garbage at that, but the figurine of Una had been not only a gift, a thoughtful gift evocative of old memories, but it had saved his life and the lives of all those aboard *Sister Sue*, all of those, that is, who still had lives to save.

Chapter 52

"I suppose," said Grimes, "that we shall have to return her effects and papers to her next of kin on El Dorado. . . ."

As Billy Williams and Magda Granadu watched, he looked through the listing of personal possessions and then, finally, picked up the dead woman's passport.

A waste, he thought, as he stared at the three-dimensional photograph. *A waste. But she was a vicious bitch, after all. A female-chauvinist bitch. . . .*

And then he started to laugh.

"What's the joke, Skipper?" asked the mate.

"Her name, Billy. Wilhelmina Moore, Countess of Walshingham. . . ."

"But what's so funny about that?" asked Williams.

Chapter 53

The three ships hung there, in the warped continuum, the destroyer's synchronizer making slaves of the Mannschenn Drive units of the other two vessels.

From the NST transceiver came the voice of the destroyer's captain.

"*Denebola* to *Sister Sue*. You are under arrest."

"Acknowledge," said Grimes to Williams.

"*Sister Sue,* stand by to receive boarders."

"Acknowledge, Mr. Williams. Then carry on down to the after airlock to do the courtesies."

The mate was all concern.

"Sir, can't we fight? What will they do to you?"

"Not as much as they'd like to," said Grimes. "Don't worry, Mr. Williams. It will all come right in the end."

"I said, sir, that we should never have taken a Terran ship. . . ."

"But we did. Never mind, it was by *my* orders. You're in the clear. Off with you, now. Be polite, but not servile. I shall be in my cabin."

He got up from the command chair, turned to Mayhew.

"You're in charge, Ken, until Billy comes back. You know where to find me if you want me."

He went down to his day cabin, lowered himself into his armchair. *Let the Survey Service take over now,* he thought. *I've done their dirty work for them. It was rather dirtier than I thought that it would be—but isn't it always that way?*

He filled and lit his pipe, looked up through the blue smoke that it emitted at the empty shelf upon which the figurine of Una Freeman had stood. He found that he regretted the loss of that gift very deeply. If—*if!*—he ever saw Una again he would tell her of the circumstances. Meanwhile he could expect a quiet voyage back to Earth, under escort and with a prize crew on board, an official rapping of the knuckles, an unofficial pecuniary reward and then a resumption of his tramping life. He hoped that Williams would stay with him, and Magda Granadu. Old Mr. Stewart probably would. Malleson and Crumley probably would not. As for the others—he would not wish to be in their shoes. But their defense, almost certainly, would be that they had mutinied against a captain who had turned pirate.

There was a knock at his door.

"Yes?" he called.

"Sir," said Williams, "the officer in charge of the boarding party to see you."

"Send him in."

"You are under arrest," she said.

Grimes stared up at her. On the shoulders of her silvery spacesuit were the scarlet tabs that showed that she was a member of the Corps of Sky Marshals. She had removed her helmet and was holding it under her left arm. Her face, given a coat of gold paint, would have been the face of the figurine destroyed by the killer cat.

"Aren't you pleased to see me?" she asked.

"Yes. Of course. But aren't you . . . ? Shouldn't you, I mean, be on Austral?"

"I was recalled to the Corps for a refresher course. And piracy, as you know, is the concern of the Sky Marshals as well as of the Survey Service."

"Mphm. Well. Glad to have you aboard, Una."

"I'm glad to be aboard, John. This is far more capacious than that bloody lifeboat."

"Yes. I'll tell my purser to organize a cabin for you."

She said, "Don't bother. This will do very nicely." She grinned. "I have to have some place to interrogate my prisoner. Somewhere well away from the other accommodation so that the screams won't be heard."

"Oh."

"Don't just sit there grinning. Put that vile pipe out for a start—and then you can help me out of my spacesuit. And the rest . . ."

"But I have to get up to Control, Una. To give some orders."

222

"Don't worry," she told him. "I'll be giving the orders from now on."

More than once during the voyage back to Earth Grimes would think, *Where is that bloody cat now that I need him?*